BLOOD'S
ECHO

For my husband, Michael, who showed me I could fly.

BLOOD'S ECHO

AN OBSESSION WITH THE CARTEL
COULD COST DET. VERANDA CRUZ
HER BADGE. AND HER LIFE.

ISABELLA MALDONADO

MIDNIGHT INK
WOODBURY, MINNESOTA

FIRST EDITION
First Printing, 2017

Book format by Bob Gaul
Cover design by Ellen Lawson
Editing by Nicole Nugent

Midnight Ink, an imprint of Llewellyn Worldwide Ltd.

This is a work of fiction. Names, characters, places, and incidents are either the product of the author's imagination or are used fictitiously, and any resemblance to actual persons, living or dead, business establishments, events, or locales is entirely coincidental.

Library of Congress Cataloging-in-Publication Data
Names: Maldonado, Isabella, author.
Title: Blood's echo / Isabella Maldonado.
Description: Woodbury, Minnesota: Midnight Ink, 2017. | Series: A Veranda
  Cruz mystery; # 1
Identifiers: LCCN 2016033193 (print) | LCCN 2016039303 (ebook) | ISBN
  9780738750804 | ISBN 9780738751337
Subjects: LCSH: Policewomen—Fiction. | Women detectives—Fiction. | Drug
  traffic—Fiction. | GSAFD: Suspense fiction.
Classification: LCC PS3613.A434 B58 2017 (print) | LCC PS3613.A434 (ebook) |
  DDC 813/.6—dc23
LC record available at https://lccn.loc.gov/2016033193

Midnight Ink
Llewellyn Worldwide Ltd.
2143 Wooddale Drive
Woodbury, MN 55125-2989
www.midnightinkbooks.com

Printed in the United States of America

Acknowledgments

Going from police work to writing is a big leap, and there are many people who made the journey possible. Before I mention all of those wonderful souls who helped bring this story to light, I would like to thank the men and women of the Phoenix Police Department who walk the thin blue line every day. Their tireless commitment to the community they serve is summarized by their motto: Protection, Respect, Integrity, Dedication, and Excellence (PRIDE).

Every story has a beginning. This one began as a small seed. The first person I discussed it with was Deborah J Ledford, one of those bright, shiny lights in the world. She also happens to be an extremely gifted author, screenwriter, producer, editor, mentor, and friend. She assured me the seed, if properly nurtured, could grow into something wonderful. Then she rolled up her sleeves and got to work. She was my beta reader, editor, and sounding board as I navigated through the drafts until this tale was ready.

So many aspiring authors toil alone at their computers. Their only desire, to get their story into the hands of readers. To make that happen, someone has to believe in a new writer enough to convince a publishing house to gamble on a long shot. Terri Bischoff, acquiring editor for Midnight Ink, is a true visionary who understands alchemy. I am forever grateful that she gave this story the chance to find its audience.

Nothing is like a fresh set of eyes, especially when they're attached to a first-rate mind. Nicole Nugent, editor with Midnight Ink, spent countless hours to make the words sparkle. Her dedication and commitment make her a pleasure to work with.

In this economy, many publishing houses are hesitant to commit resources to an unknown writer. Midnight Ink, an amazing publisher with a talented team of professionals dedicated to the art and craft of writing, was willing and able to make a leap of faith. Thank you for taking a chance on this debut author.

Every day, brave first responders and support personnel from the Phoenix Fire Department put their lives on the line to keep the community safe. This includes the efforts of their team of investigators who work to find the cause and origin of fires. I am very grateful for the technical expertise of Ret. Captain Steve Franklin, Arson Investigator, Phoenix Fire Department. The information he provided about fire investigations was invaluable to this story. Any inaccuracies about the manner in which these cases are solved are solely mine.

Fresh from my retirement after over two decades on the force, I moved to Arizona and joined the Sisters in Crime Desert Sleuths Chapter in Phoenix. They are an amazing and talented organization that truly celebrates every member's success along the way. Their encouragement, support, and wisdom made all the difference in making my writing more professional.

I am blessed with a wonderful family, whether blood-related or bound by love. Their acceptance of me, with my many foibles, warms my heart as nothing else can. First and foremost are my husband, Michael, who encourages my dreams, and my son, Max, who inspires me every day. In addition to relatives and in-laws, I consider some of my closest friends to be family. Words cannot express my gratitude for your love and support over the years.

Finally, I would like to thank readers of crime fiction. They are smart, funny, loyal, smart, interesting, shrewd, smart, curious, and did I say smart? I love engaging with readers. After all, they are the reason I write.

FIVE HUNDRED KILOS OF white death snaked through downtown Phoenix. As the tractor-trailer lumbered toward the warehouse district, Det. Veranda Cruz of the Phoenix Police Drug Enforcement Bureau crouched beside a cinder block wall with her team. She squinted against the midday glare and peered down the alley. Sweat trickled along her spine under her ballistic vest. She glanced at her watch. The delivery was six minutes overdue.

Sergeant Fromm's voice carried through her earpiece. "Air support confirms target vehicle is approaching."

Finally. Veranda inched back to be sure she wasn't seen from the street. Her pulse quickened as she prepared for the takedown. Her hand rested on the grip of her holstered Glock. The plan was for the tactical team to stop the truck when it reached the loading dock, then make entry into the warehouse and detain everyone inside. Veranda and her team would then move in to take charge of the investigation.

More than thirty Phoenix Police Department officers and detectives lay in wait over a three-block grid in a sector known as the Duce. The nickname originated in the twenties, when the area was filled with produce warehouses, some of which remained. From her informant, Flaco, Veranda had learned the Villalobos cartel used one of the buildings as a distribution center. Flaco had revealed that Bartolo Villalobos, *comandante* in charge of narcotics trafficking, would personally take delivery of today's heroin shipment. Two years of painstaking investigation were about to pay off. The other detectives had accused her of an obsession with the cartel. If they knew the truth, they would have her thrown out of the Drug Enforcement Bureau. None of that mattered now. She would put cuffs on Bartolo at last.

Black-clad tactical personnel hunkered in rapid-deployment formation in the alley opposite hers, their armored vehicle hidden several blocks away. Veranda tilted her head up and spotted a countersniper on the roof across from her. She knew two more peered through rifle scopes perched atop surrounding buildings. She flicked a glance at the detectives from her team lined against the wall behind her.

The streets were abandoned. Municipal offices were empty on Sundays, and the scorching summer heat drove most pedestrians inside. In the distance, she heard the rumble of a semi grind through its gears as the driver downshifted to turn a corner.

Her cell phone vibrated in a nylon pocket on her vest. She tugged it out, scanned the text message, then pressed the transmit button on her radio. "All units, target vehicle is rerouting. Repeat. Target is changing course. We need to reposition."

A moment later, Sergeant Fromm spoke in her ear again. "I have verification from air support. Target has just turned southbound onto Jackson. We've been compromised. Abort the operation."

She cursed and mashed the transmit button. "All units stand by." Her mind raced. If Fromm would agree to deviate from the ops plan and move the tactical team, they could still seize the truck. She might not catch the king rat in the trap, but she could prevent the drugs from poisoning her city.

There was no time for finesse. She pushed the button again. "SAU can redeploy to intercept at Dawkins and Eighteenth." SAU, the Special Assignment Unit, was the name for the Phoenix Police tactical team. Her heart pounded as she waited for Fromm's response. The countermand of her supervisor's orders was a breach of protocol. Borderline insubordinate.

Everyone assigned to the operation shared the radio channel. The silence stretched as police personnel spread throughout the net of their perimeter waited to hear how Fromm would react.

The SAU sergeant would have heard her transmission, but he had to follow procedure. Her muscles tensed as she heard the SAU leader seek direction from the supervisor officially in charge of the operation. "Sergeant Fromm?" he prompted.

Fromm sounded irritated as he responded. "Do it."

SAU members and Drug Enforcement Bureau detectives ran in every direction. Patrol cars screeched down alleys. The stench of hot tires hung in the air.

Dante Washington, one of her fellow DEB detectives, touched her elbow as the others raced across the street. "What happened, Veranda?"

"No idea, I just got a text from my informant. All he said was they were changing routes." She pushed away from the wall. "They've still got their load, though."

Blades whirred in the background as the helicopter pilot broadcast through her earpiece. "Target vehicle turned again. Now headed eastbound on Main."

"That's two blocks west of here." She sprinted down the alley.

"Wait for backup, Veranda." Dante chased after her. "The rest of our team followed the SAU guys."

She ignored him. Racing around a corner, she spotted a tractor-trailer grinding to a halt. The driver's door swung open and a figure jumped out, legs pumping as he hit the ground.

Veranda slid her Glock from its holster. "Police, don't move!" she yelled to his retreating back as he darted into another alley. "Shit!" She ran after him into the narrow side street and skidded to a stop. The driver pushed an elderly bystander over the iron railing of a short flight of cement stairs that led to the rear door of a produce warehouse. She flung her body under the falling man just before he hit the pavement. As she fought to get air back into her lungs, a metal warehouse door slammed shut.

"You okay?" She holstered her gun and looked the old man over carefully. He groaned but nodded.

She vaulted up the stairs and yanked the door open. She could barely make out a figure on the far side of the vast space. He disappeared through a side exit. She dodged crates of corn, onions, and watermelon overturned in her path, then spun and darted back onto the cement steps. She ran to the side of the warehouse to intercept him there. As she rounded the corner of the building at full speed, she slammed headlong into Dante.

Dante recovered first. "Which way did he go?"

She pointed. "I've lost sight of him, but he ran out of this side door. Did you see him?"

Dante shook his head. "He's gone."

"The hell he is." She bolted ahead, eyes searching for any sign of the suspect.

Dante pounded up behind her. "We've got the semi with the shipment. We don't need the driver."

She narrowed her eyes and turned to face him. "My intel, my bust, my rules. Nobody walks."

"Fine. Let's start with this side street then."

She scanned the area. A rustling noise caught her attention. She spotted a dumpster halfway down the alley. "If I was trying to get away, I'd lie low. Find a place to hide."

Following her gaze, Dante snorted. "No way is the dude gonna hide in that. It's already a hundred and fifteen out. The inside of that dumpster's an oven. He'd be extra crispy in minutes."

"He's not a rocket scientist and he doesn't have a lot of choices." She pulled her Glock back out of its holster and motioned to Dante.

Leather creaked as he slipped out his gun and followed her. They approached the dumpster at right angles, weapons trained on the heavy lid.

She slowed her breaths, and then nodded. Dante jerked the lid open.

"Police, drop your weapon!" Her vision constricted to the small space inside the reeking trash container. Sound muted. Time slowed. The metallic ring of a gun barrel pointed directly at her. Her gaze took in the whitened skin at the first knuckle of an index finger on the trigger.

She fired.

Blood bloomed on the man's white undershirt. He clutched his chest with his free hand and slumped into the garbage.

She jumped inside the dumpster, taking care to land on the pistol in the driver's slackened right hand.

Dante landed beside her and placed two fingers to the man's neck. "Nothing."

———

An hour later, Veranda sat in a cramped booth in the rear section of the police mobile command center as the engine rumbled under her seat. She figured the brass had to call the behemoth, filled with the latest electronics and equipment, out to a scene at least once a month to justify its existence.

Two men stared at her across a laminated table that jutted from the wall. The athletic one wore a gold shield clipped to his belt and had introduced himself as Sergeant Diaz. The older one said he was Detective Stark. She swallowed a lump in her throat. Every police shooting was investigated. Procedure. Protocol. It didn't matter what they said. She was guilty until proven innocent.

It was her first fatal shooting, but she knew that everything depended on how she handled this interview. She had killed a man, something the Department did not take lightly. Because she could be prosecuted criminally, they had Mirandized her, offered her a union representative and a lawyer. It was a trap. If you asked for a lawyer, you looked guilty. If you didn't, you looked stupid.

A digital voice recorder rested on the table next to a circular coffee stain. Diaz switched the device on.

She drew in a breath and hid her sweating hands under the table. "Let the games begin," she muttered.

Diaz narrowed his eyes and turned the recorder off. "This isn't a game." He leaned forward. "I don't know if you understand that you're on the wrong end of an interrogation, Detective Cruz, and you'd better take it seriously."

She held up her hands, fingers spread. "I'm an open book. Fire away." This was not getting off to a good start.

Diaz switched on the recorder again. "The date is Sunday, July seventeenth. The time is fourteen hundred hours. Present for this interview are Sergeant Richard Diaz of the Professional Standards Bureau,

Detective Samuel Stark of the Violent Crimes Bureau Homicide Squad, and Detective Veranda Cruz of the Drug Enforcement Bureau."

She recognized Stark. The legendary detective had the highest closure rate in Homicide. He'd been there since she joined the department thirteen years ago and showed no sign of retiring. His thick silvery hair and mustache were contrasted by black eyebrows. His gray eyes bored into her.

Diaz leaned forward. "We are conducting a joint initial interview of Detective Cruz regarding the use of deadly force during the arrest of an individual suspected of transporting heroin." Diaz glanced at the man next to him. "Detective Stark is leading the criminal investigation, and I am conducting the departmental investigation into this matter."

She faced quadruple jeopardy. An officer could be terminated, sued, and jailed for any use of force deemed unjustified. Finally, a federal case could be brought for violating a suspect's civil rights. The departmental and criminal interrogations usually occurred separately, but they'd informed her they would conduct the initial interview jointly and then split the investigations. She clenched her fingers, unsure if the deviation from protocol was good or bad for her.

Stark's rumbling baritone cut through the silence. "Detective Cruz, you've been advised of your rights and you've also signed an official Notice of Investigation. You have elected not have an attorney or a union representative present for this interview. Is that correct?"

She nodded.

"Detective Cruz, you have to speak. The voice recorder will not reflect that you nodded your head in agreement."

"Yes, I was read my rights, received my NOI, and waived counsel."

Stark shook open a pair of reading glasses, put a notepad on his lap, and pulled out a pen.

He's a dinosaur. She wondered if he used a typewriter for his reports. She glanced at Diaz, who propped an iPad on the table and unfolded a keyboard.

"Detective Cruz." Stark slid the glasses onto a crease halfway down his long nose. "How did you develop intelligence about the shipment?"

"I have a confidential informant who's a member of the Villalobos cartel. I can't provide his name outside my direct chain of command, but he's officially registered as my CI at the Drug Enforcement Bureau."

This would be her strategy, she decided. Answer all of their background questions in detail. Appear forthcoming. "He's been feeding me info about shipments and other Villalobos family business for the past two years. After a couple of months, I had the first major bust from his intel. I asked my sergeant for a task force exclusively to run interdictions on the cartel."

Diaz adjusted his screen. "For the record, an interdiction is what DEB detectives call it when you intercept a delivery in transit?"

"Yes. We've seized tons of drugs, thousands of weapons, and millions in cash, vehicles, and other property."

"How is your task force set up?" Stark asked.

"My supervisor, Sergeant Fromm, coordinates it. We have agents from the FBI, DEA, US Marshal's Office, National Guard, the state police, and several local departments. We operate out of the fusion center at DEB headquarters."

Stark appeared to contemplate her response. "So the Phoenix Police Department has oversight of the task force?"

"We do. The Villalobos cartel uses Phoenix as its US distribution hub. Since we're a large department with a lot of resources, the Feds are happy to support us as long as they get a piece of the action when we make a big seizure."

Diaz leaned forward. "What about jurisdiction?"

8

"All Phoenix officers on the task force are deputized as federal marshals. It gives us a lot more arrest and prosecution power and we don't have to worry about jurisdiction if we leave the city. We've had to do that sometimes when my CI gives me something outside Phoenix."

Diaz narrowed his eyes. "What you're saying is that Sergeant Fromm is technically in charge of the task force, but you set the agenda because they're working from your intel?"

She needed to be careful here. "The Feds on our task force have access to international databases and the latest equipment. They also come in handy when diplomatic issues are involved, but Fromm put me on point. Since it's my CI, I'm in charge of picking the target shipments so I don't burn him."

Diaz considered her for a long moment. "How do you choose the shipments?"

"Interdictions take a lot of advance work and planning. I couldn't stop every single shipment. I targeted the ones that would cause the most damage to the cartel. The operations I set up were some of the largest in the history of our department."

"What's your end game with the cartel?" Diaz asked.

"I've been building a racketeering case against Bartolo Villalobos. He's the family member who runs their entire trafficking division. If I don't catch him in possession, it will probably take me another year to compile enough evidence to hold up against the best lawyers drug money can buy."

Diaz quirked a brow. "In possession?"

Veranda nodded. "My CI told me we've seized so much of the cartel's product that Bartolo would personally oversee today's shipment. My goal was to catch him with the tractor-trailer at his warehouse. Then I could use evidence from the previous interdictions to tie him in to all of it. Unfortunately, he was one step ahead of us. The warehouse was empty."

Stark glared at Diaz. "We're getting off track. Your CI texted you to advise that the truck changed routes?"

She turned to Stark. This was the minefield. Time to shorten her answers. "He did. I have no idea why they would reroute. All of our other interdictions have gone like clockwork."

Diaz straightened. "When the semi altered course, you ran through back streets to intercept it on foot?"

"I knew I could get there faster than our vehicles." She shrugged. "And the truck was too big to maneuver well in side streets."

"What happened when you approached the semi?" Diaz asked.

She knew the trick. Ask an open-ended question, hoping the interviewee would ramble and reveal something.

She gave the minimum response. "I saw the truck's cab door open. The driver jumped out. I ordered him to stop, but he took off."

"Did you see a weapon?" Diaz looked like a bird dog on point. Eyes locked on hers, he sat motionless, waiting for her response.

"Not at that time. I lost him when he ran through a produce warehouse. Then I met up with Detective Dante Washington from my task force." She hesitated. "I mean *our* task force."

Stark scribbled on his notepad. "What did you say to Detective Washington?"

"I told him we should clear the dumpster in the alley. I thought the suspect might have tried to hide."

Diaz raised his eyebrows. "You didn't wait for more backup to search the alley?"

"No. It seemed like two detectives were enough to clear one dumpster."

Stark stifled a chuckle.

Diaz reddened. "Once the lid was up, what happened?"

Another open-ended question. "I recognized the driver crouched inside. He had a gun pointed straight at me. I could see him start to squeeze the trigger."

"You say you saw him squeezing the trigger?" Diaz glanced at Stark as if he wanted confirmation that this was ludicrous.

She sensed the need to explain. "Time seemed to slow down so that I could see his finger barely move a fraction, then everything sped up and it was over in a split second."

Stark waved his hand in a dismissive motion. "You're describing time distortion. Common in these situations."

Diaz didn't look convinced. "What was Detective Washington doing?"

"I don't know. All I could see was the gun pointed at me."

"Tunnel vision," Stark said under his breath.

Diaz seemed determined to latch on to an issue. "Did you identify yourself prior to discharging your weapon?"

"Yes, but his finger remained on the trigger."

He dug for more. "Did you hear Detective Washington radio for backup, or the dispatcher ask for your location?"

"No. I couldn't hear anything."

Stark waved again. "Auditory exclusion. Also common."

Diaz glared at Stark before returning his attention to Veranda. "Did you attempt to render assistance after the subject was no longer representing a threat?"

"Yes, Dante and I jumped into the dumpster and gave him first aid while we waited for rescue. Fat lot of good first aid will do when you have a forty-five caliber gunshot to the heart."

Stark's mustache twitched.

Diaz let the silence stretch out. Finally, he gave her an appraising look. "Is there anything you want to add to your statement at this time?"

"No."

He glanced at his watch. "This concludes the initial interview with Detective Veranda Cruz. The time is fourteen twelve hours. Detective Cruz, please ensure that you are available for further interviews as the investigation into this matter continues." He leaned forward and switched off the recorder.

Veranda was spent. Bartolo had slipped through her fingers again. In the back of her mind, she worried about her CI. Flaco had not contacted her since his last text. She stood and turned to leave.

"Detective," Diaz said as he came up behind her. She glanced over her shoulder but did not answer. "Here's my card. I want you to call me anytime, day or night, before you conduct any operations involving the Villalobos cartel."

At this, she turned to face him and gripped the card in his outstretched hand. "I'll certainly call you if there's anything you need to know."

He closed his hand over hers, holding the card firmly in place.

"That's not what I said, Detective. I don't want you to run interdictions while I conduct my investigation. There may be repercussions from your actions today."

He took a step closer so they were only inches apart and locked eyes with her. "You're playing a dangerous game with stone-cold killers, Detective. I don't like it." He released her hand, the business card still in her grasp.

She spun on her heel and smoothly pulled open the door with a concerted effort to portray a sense of calm she did not feel.

2

BARTOLO VILLALOBOS LOWERED THE branding iron and contemplated his captive. Primal instincts told him his prey was growing weak. He looked around the dusty warehouse at thirty-seven of his men. Like wolves, they waited for their alpha to deliver the death blow to the thrashing quarry. Bartolo knew he must prevail or, filled with bloodlust, his pack would turn to another leader.

"Put the iron back in the fire, Pablo," he said, holding the metal rod out to his second-in-command. Pablo stepped forward to take the branding iron. Bartolo scrutinized the man in front of him. *He is almost ready.*

Flaco sat quivering in the hard metal chair. Chains bit into his arms. Smoke curled up from his heaving bare chest, filling the air with the acrid scent of charred flesh. Urine soaked through his pants, puddled on the seat in front of his crotch, and dripped onto the cement floor.

"You know how to make the pain stop, Flaco." Bartolo bent at the waist to look directly into watery eyes that gazed back in terror. "Just give me a name, that's all. I already know the rest."

Flaco drew a shuddering breath. "It's a—a narc." His slight Mexican accent grew thicker. "On the Phoenix Police force." He slumped and hung his head down.

Bartolo's eyes sought Adolfo's in the crowd of onlookers. Adolfo, his older brother, had a gift for reading people. The questioning look on his brother's face reflected Bartolo's own surprise at the information.

He turned back to Flaco and whispered. "Your death could take hours, *amigo*." He pulled a jewel-encrusted dagger from a sheath at his hip and slid the tip of the blade under Flaco's chin, forcing his head back up. "If you want mercy, don't lie to me. Phoenix narcs don't investigate international crime. Feds do."

Flaco panted. "N-no. Let me explain. There's a task force. It's run by the Phoenix PD out of their narcotics bureau."

"A task force?"

"Yeah, DEA, FBI." Sweat ran down from his scalp in rivulets. "And a bunch of other Feds. That's who's been after you."

"But you told me earlier it was one person targeting our—"

"And I was telling the truth. One of the detectives . . . " He coughed, foam spewing from his lips. "Leads the task force. That's who put them on to you."

"With information from you!" He spat in Flaco's face. "Do you know how I found you?" He dragged the point of the knife gently along Flaco's cheek. "I had everyone's cell phone cloned at our last meeting. I read every text message. Tracked every call."

The men shifted in the shadows around him. *Good*. He was glad they knew they were being watched. "I ordered the route change to see if the traitor would send a text." The knife tip bit into Flaco's face. "I can trace the number you sent it to. But that will take time. I don't like to wait."

Blood trickled down Flaco's jaw.

Bartolo withdrew the point of the blade. "I'm running out of patience, *cabrón*. Give me the name." Bartolo leveled the tip of the dagger directly in front of Flaco's left eye. His hand perfectly steady. The implication clear.

"Her name is V-Veranda." Flaco seemed to hesitate, then straightened and squared his shoulders. "Veranda Cruz."

"A woman detective? Bullshit."

Flaco's voice steadied and he returned Bartolo's stare. "I am already a dead man. I speak the truth with my last breath." His features contorted with anger. "She's been watching you. She knows everything about your family. And she's going to take you down."

Bartolo slapped him hard across the face. Flaco screwed his eyes shut as his captor moved to stand behind him. Bartolo grasped a hank of hair and yanked his head back, exposing his throat to the ornate knife. With expert swiftness, Bartolo sank the blade deeply into Flaco's flesh just beneath his left ear and jerked his arm hard to the right. A crimson plume burst into the air in a rhythmic stream of spurts as Flaco jerked and gurgled. Finally, he slumped, motionless.

Bartolo turned to the man standing a few paces to his left. "Pablo, clean up that mess. Put the body in a bag and wait for my instructions." Pablo nodded and pulled rubber gloves from his back pocket. "Everyone else, get back to work."

Bartolo pondered his next move. During the hours before his death while being tortured, Flaco had described an ongoing campaign by someone in law enforcement to target his family. Flaco had held out as long as he could to avoid revealing her identity. Why?

Adolfo's approach interrupted his thoughts. Bartolo's lip curled as his tall, elegantly dressed brother walked toward him, carefully skirting the blood spatter. His older sibling had no stomach for violence.

"What do we do about the task force?" Adolfo asked.

"You heard Flaco," Bartolo said. "It's not so much the task force, it's *her*. She leads them and she's on a crusade." He eyed the other man thoughtfully, "We take care of her, and our problem goes away."

Adolfo shifted. "You'll run this by *Papá*—"

"It's my decision!"

Adolfo pursed his lips. "We don't take out cops in the States. It brings too much heat. Our losses are the price of doing business. We have to—"

"I didn't say we were going to kill her," Bartolo interrupted. "You misunderstand." He snatched a paper towel from Adolfo's outstretched hand and wiped the dagger. "We will make an example out of her."

"What do you mean?"

Bartolo despised the anxiety in his brother's voice. Adolfo's hesitance to act was one of many reasons Bartolo had risen to the top of the family cartel instead of the firstborn. "I have a plan. It involves this *pendejo*'s body"—he nodded toward the spot where Pablo grunted as he pulled Flaco's limp form into a large bag—"and our Phoenix mole."

"Our mole is only for emergencies."

Bartolo gritted his teeth. "We've lost millions over the past two years because one *puta* detective has a hard-on for us. She must be stopped. If you had any *cojones*, you'd understand that."

Adolfo reddened. "This is the impulsive crap you pull, Bartolo. You're not in charge of this family. You need to clear this with *Papá*. Especially when it could compromise years of—"

"Enough!" Bartolo lowered his voice and glared at his older brother. "We do not argue in front of the men." He took a step closer. "You worry about keeping the books. Let me handle my business. When I am finished tonight, Detective Cruz will lose her task force." He set his jaw. "And her badge."

3

THE SUN BROKE OVER the horizon as Veranda burst through the front door of her mother's family restaurant. *Casa Cruz Cocina* had started as a tiny stucco building with a terra-cotta tile roof. It had been expanded so many times over the decades that it looked like a series of duplexes huddled together in the heart of South Phoenix. *"Mamá, where are you?"*

"Coming, *mi'ja*." Lorena's voice carried from the office in the back.

Veranda wrinkled her nose at the stench of melted plastic and scorched grease.

"Gracias a Dios that you are here." Lorena trotted into the dining area and clutched her daughter's arm. "It's pretty bad this time."

"What happened? Is anyone hurt?"

"No one is hurt. I think your tío Rico left a burner on when he closed last night." She smoothed her apron. "You know it is not the first time. Maybe we should talk to him when—"

"Mamá, tell me about the fire."

17

"Yes, yes, *mi'ja*." Lorena's fingers fiddled with her heavy silver choker etched with an ornate cross. Years of constant wear had bestowed a patina to the piece. "The alarm company called us early this morning. When we got here, they had already put the fire out."

"How bad was it? I can't see any damage here in the dining area." She looked around at the worn floral carpet, booths covered in faux leather and lacquered wooden tabletops.

"We can still keep our doors open. We cannot use the stove and oven. The vent is destroyed." She glanced over Veranda's shoulder in the direction of the kitchen. "But the fryer and the grill still work. We will manage."

"*Mamá*, why were you so frantic when you called me this morning? You told me to get here as fast as I could." After her mother's call, Veranda had thrown on jeans and a fitted top before jamming on tactical boots. She had pulled her long hair into a ponytail and rushed out the door without makeup. "It looks like you have everything under control."

Lorena jabbed a calloused finger toward the kitchen and lowered her voice to a tense whisper, "Listen *mi'ja*, a man is back there poking around. It was just a stupid kitchen fire, and he's making out like our family is a bunch of criminals."

"What man?"

"The firemen called him before they left. He works for the fire department, but he carries a gun. Who ever heard of a fireman who carries a gun?"

Understanding dawned on Veranda. "He's an arson investigator, *Mamá*." She put a hand on her hip. "It's not the case everywhere, but in Phoenix, the fire department sends their investigators to the police academy. After they graduate, they're sworn in as law enforcement officers because they investigate arson-related crimes, arrest people, and testify in court. That's also why they carry guns."

Her mother didn't look satisfied. "He is taking pictures of everything and asking questions. Looking for trouble."

She rolled her eyes. "He's not looking for trouble. He's doing his job. It's standard procedure for a fire."

Lorena's fingers traced the pattern of the cross on her necklace. Concern wrinkled her brow. "He can throw us in jail—or worse, shut the restaurant down—if he thinks we are guilty of something."

Veranda sighed. "Oh, all right. I'll go talk to him, but you have to understand that the police department has nothing to do with the fire department."

Lorena smiled and stood aside to let her daughter pass.

Shaking her head, Veranda strolled into the kitchen. Her mother thought she could simply vouch for her family and the arson investigator would close his notebook and leave. Veranda knew better. He had forms to complete. Reports to file. Just like her.

"Excuse me." Veranda approached a tall, powerfully built blond man wearing khaki cargo pants and a black polo shirt with a Phoenix Fire Department logo embroidered on the chest. His bright blue eyes assessed her.

She proffered a hand. "We haven't met. I'm Veranda Cruz, Lorena's daughter. I'm a detective with the Phoenix Police Department."

His large hand enveloped hers briefly. "Captain Cole Anderson with the Fire Investigations Unit." Then he fell silent. He seemed to be waiting for her to tell him why she had interrupted his examination of the scene.

Veranda shifted her feet. "I was wondering if I could answer any questions you might have."

His eyes narrowed, and she silently cursed herself for acting like a guilty suspect. How many times had she been on the scene of an investigation when someone approached her with an offer to help? Always a huge red flag. She might as well have shouted, *Hi, my family set this fire for insurance purposes and I'm here to throw you off by waving my badge under your nose!* She clasped her hands to prevent herself from smacking her forehead.

He tilted his chin toward the blackened stove. Eyes still on her, he asked, "Were you here when the fire started?"

"No."

"Were you the one who closed up the restaurant?"

"No."

"Do you work here at all?"

"Only in emergencies."

He smiled in a way that seemed almost condescending to her. "Then how could you possibly answer any questions I might have?"

Great. He had already come to some sort of conclusion about her family and their restaurant.

Lifting her chin, she put her hands on her hips. "Captain Anderson, let me explain about this restaurant. It's called *Casa Cruz Cocina*, which roughly translates to 'Cruz Home Kitchen,' because it's our family business. My mother, Lorena Cruz, came here from Mexico with nothing but the clothes on her back and five younger siblings to feed. She couldn't speak the language, but knew how to cook. She and her brothers and sisters started by selling burritos out of an old pickup truck and built the business over more than thirty years into what you see." She swept a hand out in a gesture that encompassed the building.

Anderson put his palms up. "I haven't—"

"The restaurant is our life's blood. It puts clothes on our backs, food on our table, and binds our family together. Our whole community depends on us to provide jobs and donate food. We would never, under any circumstances, deliberately set fire to this place."

"Detective Cruz, may I speak?"

Veranda's cheeks grew warm. "I get passionate where family is concerned." She glanced away.

He nodded and lowered his hands to pick up a notebook from the counter. "I need to complete my investigation before I can comment on my findings. Given your job, I'm sure you understand."

She opened her mouth to launch into a response when her cell phone sounded the special ring tone for her lieutenant. She snatched it from its clip at her waist and turned away. "Yes, boss?"

"Cruz, you need to get in here. Now."

"Sure. I'll wrap this up and be there in twenty."

"I'll give you five. Meet me in the commander's office." He disconnected.

Veranda stared at her phone, wondering what caused the strain in Lieutenant Cornell's voice. Not prone to fits of temper, he sounded angry. Her pulse quickened. Thoughts tumbled over each other as she recalled yesterday's fatal shooting. Had they found a violation?

She turned back to face Captain Anderson. Sandy brows knit, he peered into her eyes. "You okay? You look upset."

"I'm fine. Have to go."

"Perhaps you could answer a question for me before you leave."

"Make it fast. That was my lieutenant."

"Have there been other fires here at the restaurant?"

Her anger rekindled. "What? Do you think we regularly practice insurance fraud or something?" She stepped in close. "We're an honest, hardworking family. This business does very well. We don't need—"

"Slow down, Detective. I was just wondering if there could be a buildup of grease in the vents. Pull your claws in."

Veranda snatched the elastic band from her hair and dragged a hand through her thick locks. She could not sound more like a cornered suspect if she read from the basic interrogation manual. She had been defensive, nervous, even rude. Of course, he could be playing her. Trying to keep her off balance. She had used that tactic.

"Captain Anderson, I apologize if I misunderstood." She clipped the phone back to her waist. "I don't have time to discuss this any further." She turned to go back to her mother.

"Tell your family to replace the ductwork immediately. If they don't keep the vents cleaned out, the next fire could burn down the whole restaurant."

"I will." She retraced her steps to the dining area where Lorena waited.

Her mother rushed to her as she came out of the kitchen. "Is he going to shut us down, *mi'ja?*"

"No, *Mamá*, he's still investigating. He thinks it might have been a grease fire. You'll have to put in new ducts." She leveled a stare at her mother. "When is the last time tío Rico cleaned out the vents?"

Her mother's face clouded. "I will call him and check."

A tone emanated from her phone. She pulled it from its clip and tapped the screen. She recognized the number as one of the Drug Enforcement Bureau task force cell phones.

Dante's voice sounded tense. "Veranda, where are you?"

"On my way. Are you at DEB?"

"Hell no, but you'd better get your ass over there."

"Dante, what's going on?"

"I can't talk on this phone. But I can tell you I've never seen anything like the shit storm that hit DEB today." Her stomach lurched as she heard his final words. "Veranda, you're fucked."

4

VERANDA'S MIND REELED AT the sight of media vans as she turned a corner and drove up to the Drug Enforcement Bureau building. News crews jostled against yellow police tape cordoning off the perimeter of the parking lot. She corrected course and veered into an adjacent parking area in front of a self-storage facility. Heart racing, she scrambled out of the car, lowered her head, and jogged down the sidewalk toward the main entrance of the industrial building.

How was DEB's location compromised? Veranda wondered.

The address of the Drug Enforcement Bureau was a closely guarded secret, even in law enforcement circles. Detectives undertook risky undercover operations, seizing tons of narcotics, cash, and weapons. The criminal organizations involved were so dangerous that every precaution had to be taken to protect the identities of the detectives and their families.

Veranda vaulted the front steps and yanked open the glass door. She darted across the vestibule, flicked her proximity card in front of the reader until she heard a loud electronic buzz and a *click*, then pulled the interior door open.

An eerie silence greeted her. The reception area with its over-stuffed brown leather sofa and coffee table stood empty. It was normally a hive of activity. She frowned as she surveyed the abandoned cubicle with space for two administrative assistants. A gathering sense of foreboding came over her as she took in the stillness around her.

She turned to the supervisor offices that lined the walls of the building, each designated with a name plate outside the door. She recognized Commander Montoya's voice and approached the third office down.

Lieutenant Cornell sat in one of four chairs around a circular gray laminate table with a laptop propped open in front of him. Modular government-issue furniture outfitted each office. Commander Montoya was in the chair next to Assistant Chief Delcore, the only person in uniform, who occupied the third seat. As part of protocol to maintain its secrecy, no one ever came to DEB in uniform. *No longer an issue.*

She knocked on the frame of the open door. All eyes turned to her.

Commander Montoya indicated the empty fourth chair, "Detective Cruz, please close the door and take a seat."

She complied and addressed her lieutenant. "What's going on? Why is the parking lot crawling with reporters?"

Cornell cleared his throat. "Cruz, I'm going to get right to the point. We don't have time to be delicate." He exchanged a brief glance with her commander before continuing. "Our location has been compromised. A body was dumped in our parking lot overnight."

Veranda's pulse pounded in her ears. "What are you talking about?"

Cornell pushed the computer in front of her and tapped a key. The image of a bloody corpse lying facedown in the parking lot appeared. "If you swipe the screen, you'll see a series of pictures taken by Crime Scene in the DEB lot this morning."

Still unsure what this had to do with her, she dragged her finger across the screen. Another image slid in front of her. The body had been turned over. It took all of her training not to gasp. "I know who that is." She looked up at the faces watching her. It was Flaco, but she never mentioned him by name to anyone.

Montoya seemed to sense her hesitance. "It's okay, Detective. We are all in your chain of command. I've already pulled your confidential informant's file and briefed Assistant Chief Delcore. I made other copies too. You'll know why in a minute."

Delcore pointed at the laptop. "Was your CI in contact with other informants?"

She shook her head. "No. He was imbedded in the Villalobos cartel." Then everything clicked into place. Bartolo had somehow flushed out Flaco, butchered him, and dumped his body in her back yard as a warning.

She swiped the screen again. This time the shot captured a close-up of Flaco's bare torso. Amid the bruises, a fresh brand of a wolf's head had been seared on the left side of his chest. "That's the Villalobos family symbol."

Cornell nodded. "They're claiming responsibility, or someone wants it to look that way."

Her gut clenched. "What happened?"

This time Montoya responded. "From our initial visual on the body, it looks like whoever did this tortured him, then slit his throat."

Bile rose from her churning stomach. "I can't believe it. I just met with him yesterday morning." She squeezed her hands into fists. *Did somebody spot us?* She scanned the men around the table. Three pairs of eyes looked back in silence. *They think I screwed up*.

Montoya took off his glasses and placed them on the table. "Public Affairs called me earlier. Reporters are saying their newsrooms all received an anonymous email about a body in the parking lot with

DEB's address. It included your name and photo and said the corpse was your snitch. We're trying to source the original email."

"This can't be happening," she muttered.

"There's more." Assistant Chief Delcore spoke again. "This situation has put us in a predicament. Since our DEB fusion center is no longer secure, we have to relocate immediately." Delcore folded his hands on the table as his eyes locked on hers. "We've had to disperse our personnel and suspend all investigations while we get a handle on this."

Montoya looked at her with a sympathetic expression. "Cruz, we need to get in touch with all of your informants and alert them immediately. They could be in danger. Turn over your casework to Lieutenant Cornell. He will triage your files."

"Triage?" She asked.

Montoya drew a deep breath. "Your routine cases can be reassigned, but we can't follow up on your Villalobos cartel leads while Homicide is working the murder."

"But the task force—" Veranda began.

"Is being disbanded." Delcore interjected with a note of finality.

Warning bells clanged in her ears and she imagined the giant light of a train barreling straight at her. She had to change tracks. "I can't just stop everything. I've got two years of work into the cartel, and twelve other ongoing investigations."

"Cruz, it's over," Cornell said. "Your cover is blown. You can't work in DEB anymore."

A hot mix of fury and despair settled inside her. She had set out to dismantle the Villalobos cartel. Not only had she failed, but Flaco had been brutally murdered and her career as a detective was over. She cast an imploring look at Montoya.

He shook his head. "You can't stay here. You are hereby ordered to report to the Professional Standards Bureau for an interview, and then to the Property Room for the duration of the investigation."

Her jaw tightened. "Why PSB?"

"Your CI was murdered," Cornell said. "For your own protection, we have to document that you followed proper procedure and that you bear no culpability in his death."

"You mean the Department is covering itself in case of a lawsuit."

Delcore bristled. "That's enough, Detective."

She drew on years of undercover work to hide her emotions. She composed herself and launched an offensive from a fresh direction. It was her only chance to go after Bartolo. "I know more about the suspects in this murder than anyone on the Homicide squad. Why not detail me over there on a temporary assignment?" Her heart thudded. She could still put Bartolo behind bars if she pinned Flaco's murder on him.

The men looked at each other. Finally, Montoya spoke. "I'll discuss it with Commander Webster of the Violent Crimes Bureau while you have your PSB interview. If he agrees, and if Assistant Chief Delcore authorizes it, I'll detail you over there on a temp." He held out a hand. "I need the keys to your city vehicle. It went with your assignment here in DEB."

She dug the keys out of her pocket and placed them in his palm. "What about my phone?"

"Keep it until we determine where you're going. Lieutenant Cornell will send you a text with our decision."

She turned her eyes to Delcore.

The decision came down to him.

His face was expressionless. "You're dismissed, Detective. Wait in the reception area for Lieutenant Cornell. He'll drive you to PSB."

Veranda stood and strode out of the office. She could feel their eyes on her back, sense their judgment. She tipped her chin up as she came to a conclusion. She would turn in her badge before she went to the Property Room.

5

VERANDA SCOWLED IN THE front passenger seat of the blue Chrysler 300 two hours later. She turned baleful eyes on Sergeant Diaz's chiseled profile. After a rocky interview, Diaz had looked as if it pained him to let her keep her gun and badge. He kept taking her back through her case files. Asking the same questions in different ways. She could tell he didn't trust her.

Now he was driving her to the Property Room. Giving up her beloved Dodge Charger had added to the loss of her coveted position in DEB. She checked her cell phone for the zillionth time. Still no message about working with Homicide.

She crossed her arms. "This is a complete waste. I could do a lot more good to everyone by helping the Homicide squad."

Diaz kept his eyes on the road. "I would have supported an assignment there, but not when you're holding back."

"I told you the truth." *Just not all of it.* She needed to know what part of the dam needed shoring up. "What makes you think I didn't?"

"You never got specific about how you recruited Flaco."

He had zeroed in on the most critical point. She had no intention of telling him how she had met the young street dealer two years ago. Her main problem was that she had no idea how much Diaz already knew or what he might find out later. She had stayed as close to the truth as possible, omitting a few pertinent details.

She arranged her features into an ingenuous expression. "I caught him dealing near a high school, so I squeezed him to go up his distribution circuit. He knew he was up for enhanced penalties because of the school zone, so I had good leverage. I went through proper channels and registered him as a CI so he could work off his charges."

He gave her a sardonic look. "Yes, Detective, that was the sanitized version you told me in the interview room. But you never explained how Flaco … came to your attention."

Sweat beaded on her forehead. *Damn. It's like he knows something.* She uncrossed her arms and picked at a loose thread on the seam of her jeans while she racked her brains.

A strategy came to her. "Now I remember." She slapped her knee to give the impression of a sudden recollection. "I got a call from Sonny Dever about suspicious vehicles near South Phoenix High School."

"Sonny Dever, the school resource officer?"

"Yes. He asked me to take an unofficial look into the vehicles since he suspected increased drug trafficking in the school. He wanted me to keep my investigation low-key because the principal didn't want to alarm parents."

Diaz tightened his grip on the steering wheel. His knuckles whitened. "I attended Officer Dever's funeral last year after he lost his battle with cancer." He flicked a glance at her before looking ahead. "Such a shame there's no way to check up on your story, and that phone call isn't in your case file, Detective."

She pretended to be hurt by his insinuation. "Dever asked me to look unofficially. I snatched up Flaco driving around the area and took it from there."

"That's strange, because your case files are meticulous and quite detailed. I find it curious that you would leave that out."

If he determined she had lied to him, he could take her gun and badge and suspend her on the spot. Better confess to a lesser sin. "Look, Sergeant, I was new in DEB at the time and wanted to impress people. I had to show that I could develop my own sources and cultivate informants. Women work twice as hard to prove themselves." That last part was actually true. She waited for his reaction.

His hands eased up on the steering wheel. She released a breath. He might gig her for an oversight in her initial report, but that wouldn't result in more than a reprimand.

Diaz cut his eyes to her. "I'll make a note of your ... recollection of how you met Flaco in my report."

Her cell phone vibrated. She pulled it out and read the text message from Lieutenant Cornell. REPORT TO SGT JACKSON IN VCB. YOU ARE DETAILED TO HOMICIDE ON A TEMP PER DELCORE.

She had finally gotten a break.

"What are you smiling about?" Diaz asked.

She tapped in a quick response to acknowledge the message. "Turn this bus around. I've got orders to report to the Violent Crimes Bureau."

"Who authorized that?"

"Assistant Chief Delcore."

Diaz spun the wheel to make a U-turn. "It's a bad idea. You'd be safer in Property."

"I didn't become a cop because personal safety is my top priority. I add value to this investigation. If you can't see that, at least there are others who do."

"Watch it, Detective. I'm still working your case. Understand that you are far from finished with your interviews. You will need to make yourself available to me."

"At your beck and call, I know the drill."

"Your attitude is going to land you in more trouble."

If he knew anything about her, he would understand her sarcasm was a technique to divert attention when she felt threatened. She also used it to distract herself.

After traveling the remaining distance in silence, she got out of the car at the curb and walked across the courtyard to the unassuming squat building that housed police headquarters on Washington Street in downtown Phoenix. A hot breeze blew through the canyon of taller nearby office buildings lining the wide thoroughfare.

She pushed open the glass doors that led to the vestibule and continued through the second set of doors into the lobby. She approached the tall front desk and held up her police ID. The uniformed sergeant waved her through as he spoke on the phone.

She nodded and strode past him on the multicolored tile. She glanced up, as she always did when visiting headquarters, at a video screen with a revolving display of fallen officers. She paused a moment, waiting for her old squad mate, and touched two fingers to her forehead in silent tribute when his smiling face appeared. So young, forever in his sharply pressed navy blue uniform, ready for duty. They had gone through the academy together. He'd been run over by a long haul trucker high on cocaine. She shook her head to clear away thoughts of the past. Time to focus on the present.

Moving to the stairs, she climbed to the second floor and entered the Violent Crimes Bureau's sprawling maze of cubicles. Supervisors inhabited private offices along the windowed outer walls. Senior detectives were assigned desirable corner cubicles, and the rest occupied tiny center compartments that crosshatched the vast space. She kept to the perimeter and headed for the sergeant's office.

"Sergeant Jackson?" she asked, knocking on the doorframe.

A bald man with dark skin and rimless glasses looked up. His large frame seemed to unfold from behind his desk as he stood and crossed the room. He was so tall that Veranda had to tilt her head back to look him in the eye.

"Pleased to meet you, Detective Cruz." He shook her hand and indicated one of two worn chairs facing his desk. "I need to explain a few things before you meet the squad. It's important that you understand the big picture."

Veranda clasped her hands in her lap and looked expectantly at her new supervisor. She had no idea what he'd been told about her. Would he resent her coming to his squad?

Sergeant Jackson considered her before continuing. "Detective Cruz, your CI was murdered while informing for you. Due to the, well … unusual circumstances, Commander Webster agreed that you should assist us in the investigation into his death."

Veranda watched his face. Inscrutable.

The sergeant plowed on. "This is a bit awkward because the lead detective assigned to your CI's murder is also on the nine-nine-eight squad."

The 9-9-8 squad was a specialized detail of senior Homicide detectives that investigated police-involved fatalities. Their job was to determine whether the officer had committed any criminal offense as part of their use of deadly force. They worked these high profile cases in addition to their regular homicide duties.

Veranda ventured a guess. "Stark?" Her throat tightened when he nodded in response. She had to work with the detective who was actively investigating her for shooting the semi driver? Not possible.

Jackson appeared to sense her unease. "Commander Webster reassigned the deadly force investigation to prevent a conflict of interest for Detective Stark."

She let out a breath. "So I can still come to Homicide and work the case with Stark?"

"Yes, but it's strictly a temporary assignment. Some people feel you should be in the Property Room while this is sorted out."

She wondered where Jackson thought she should be.

He rubbed his jaw. "I can use your expertise on this case, but you have to leave once the investigation is over. Is that clear, Detective?"

"Perfectly."

"You'll work with Detective Stark on his squad, but you report to me." He leaned forward in his chair. "Detective Johnson is wrapping up the criminal investigation into your shooting of the truck driver. Stark informed Commander Webster that he found no illegal action on your part in that case, or you wouldn't be here."

She heaved a sigh.

The corners of Jackson's eyes tightened. "There's still the PSB investigation. You're not cleared on that yet. I understand you met with Sergeant Diaz prior to coming here?"

She nodded.

"He will continue to investigate both your shooting and the death of your CI, since they appear to be related. You will be available to Sergeant Diaz at all times."

"He emphasized that point to me." How long would Diaz dig through her files looking for discrepancies? She already felt responsible for Flaco's death, now the Department might make it official.

"There's a reason we need to handle it this way." Jackson got up and closed the office door before resuming his seat. "We need to document that you did everything properly. Lieutenant Cornell tells me you're good at case management. He's confident you handled things right. It may not be your fault the cartel made your CI."

"After killing him, they targeted me. That means it had something to do with my investigation. They didn't just silence my CI; they took me out of the equation."

"Well, I just put you back in," Jackson said. "While PSB looks into your informant's death, you can help us catch his killer. Make a murder charge that sticks and you could salvage the situation."

The knot in Veranda's throat eased. She was getting a chance to go after Bartolo again.

Jackson continued, "I've assigned you to work directly with Detective Stark."

"I'll help in any way I can."

"In case you're not familiar with our setup in VCB, here's a quick overview. Homicide is one of five units in the bureau. The Homicide Unit contains the Cold Case squad and five Homicide squads, each with a sergeant and five to ten detectives."

She gave him a brief nod.

"The Homicide Unit lieutenant assigned this investigation to my squad and Stark's got the lead. It works out because one of our detectives just retired unexpectedly on medical and there's a vacancy. You can use his old desk."

"I understand." She wanted to make it clear she wasn't jockeying for a permanent position. "I'm only on the squad until we close out this homicide investigation."

"I'm glad you recognize that." He cleared his throat. "One more thing, Detective Cruz."

"Yes?"

He looked her up and down. "You'll need to wear something a bit more professional. Faded blue jeans, T-shirts, and boots are fine for narcs, but our detectives wear business attire."

Her cheeks burned. "I'll dress appropriately tomorrow."

Sergeant Jackson stood. "I'll take you to Stark's desk. Follow me."

She trailed behind as the sergeant threaded his way around morbidly festooned cubicles. In an effort to gain privacy, some detectives had strung makeshift curtains across the open partitions behind their chairs. Veranda chuckled as she walked by the dancing skeletons that decorated one length of material, while another featured a military theme.

"Sometimes I think I'm really the chief prairie dog wrangler," Jackson said over his shoulder. Sure enough, one of the prairie dogs popped its head up from a curtained compartment as they passed. Veranda exchanged glances with a pale, thin, dark-haired detective before he sank back down out of sight.

A full-sized plastic skull with glowing red eyes leered at her from atop a divider as they rounded a corner to arrive at a spacious, unadorned corner cubicle. Detective Stark sat in an ergonomic office chair, tilted back as far as it would go. He studied several papers in his left hand as his right thumb and forefinger absently stroked his silver mustache.

"Detective Stark," Jackson said. "I believe you've met Detective Cruz?"

Stark swiveled to face them as he peered over half-lens reading glasses. He laid the papers on his desk and pushed himself up from the seat. Dressed completely in black, including a black silk tie knotted at his throat, he extended a hand. "We're working together now—call me Sam."

She shook it. "Veranda."

"I'll leave her in your capable hands," the sergeant said as he turned to leave.

Sam glanced back at his desk and grabbed the papers. He jammed them into a folder, which he stuffed into a tattered black leather satchel. "We need to talk, but not here." He folded his glasses and slipped them into his shirt pocket. He reached for a black suit jacket draped on the back of his chair, then shook his head. "Too damned hot for this. Let's go."

"Where are we headed?" Veranda fell into step beside Sam as they left the building. Hot air blasted her in the face like a blow dryer when they reached the sidewalk.

"I don't want to walk far in this heat," he said. "Let's grab a coffee at Crazy Jim's down the street."

The scent of Greek food wafted to her when they entered the restaurant. They were promptly seated away from the other cops and city employees at a table in the corner. Sam sat with his back to the wall and ordered black coffee.

"I'll have mine with cream and sugar," Veranda said, anxious to get down to business.

"I don't believe in wasting time with pleasantries," Sam began, "so I'll dive right in."

"Please."

"Your CI was dumped in the DEB lot, and it caused a shit storm on the fourth floor."

She grimaced, knowing he was referring to the Department's executive offices two floors above Homicide in the headquarters building.

Sam met her eyes. "This case has political involvement at local and federal levels. Reporters are sniffing around. I need more info from you than that tap dance you did in the mobile command vehicle yesterday."

She blew out a sigh. She would have to open up a bit wider, but how much could she trust him? "My CI was Guillermo Valencia. Went by Flaco. Just before he died, he told me Bartolo was promoting him from a street-level dealer to a distributor. It was our first chance to catch Bartolo in one of the main distribution centers for the Villalobos cartel. Before that, he always steered clear of his warehouses."

She thought back on the improvised takedown of the tractor-trailer. "That's why I didn't want to abort the mission. He was supposed to be there in person." She spoke the words almost to herself.

Sam made no comment. Veranda was disconcerted by the intensity of his gaze, but years of experience working undercover had taught her to wait out the silence. At times criminals had tried to penetrate her façade. The ability to remain calm under scrutiny had saved her life.

When Sam spoke again, he switched topics. "I understand you had a rectal exam from PSB before you came here. If we're going to work together, I need to know as much as Diaz ... and more."

Veranda recognized the tactic. She had used it herself to keep a suspect unsettled. *He's testing me. Wants to see if I'll open up.* Veranda chose her words carefully.

"Diaz won't find any discrepancies in my files. I documented everything and played by the rules. Had to make certain my cases held up in court because I intended to take down the entire narcotics branch of the cartel."

Well aware the Villalobos family had a phalanx of attorneys, she had meticulously set up one bust after another, gathering intelligence along the way and employing the skills of the entire task force at times. It took patience to build a racketeering case, but she sustained herself with dreams of slapping cuffs on Bartolo. And all of his men.

The waitress delivered their coffee. Sam appeared to come to a conclusion. "You really thought you could bring down a drug lord?"

"That's the short version."

Sam smiled. "Ballsy. Possibly insane." He took a sip. "I like it."

Veranda understood that she had passed some sort of initial test. "I might pay for it with my career before it's all over. Who knows what PSB will do?"

"We can't worry about that now. Those ferrets will be doing everything but rooting through your underwear drawer for weeks. We'll have to work around it when they schedule your interviews. In the meantime, bring me up to speed on Flaco."

"To do that, I need to go back further. This all starts with the Villalobos cartel. The head of the family, *El Lobo*—The Wolf—is Hector Villalobos. He built an empire in Mexico and expanded into the US and South America." Veranda tried to summarize years of research. "He made sure all of his four children were born in America so they would have dual citizenship and could travel over the border. Now that they are adults, each one controls a sector of the cartel. Bartolo is in charge of narcotics trafficking."

Sam raised his bushy eyebrows. "That's keeping it all in the family."

"I'm just giving you a basic overview; it gets a lot more complicated. They have lieutenants, sergeants, and foot soldiers, just like us. Hector lives at the massive Villalobos family compound in Mexico, but his children all have residences in Phoenix. They spend most of their time here in order to protect their investments."

"So, how does this end up on your doorstep?"

Veranda drew a breath and pulled her coffee mug closer. She had to tread carefully. Sam's gray eyes followed her like a poker player watching for a tell. "Not long after I got to DEB, I busted Flaco for dealing. He wanted to work it off. Gave me enough to get two levels up on his distribution circuit, which turned out to be the cartel. I kept working him, went through all the right channels and set things up properly. Within six months, we ran an interdiction on two tractor-trailers full of heroin."

"Your interdictions on the Villalobos cartel began about two years ago?"

She nodded. "The street value was well into the millions. One shipment had five hundred weapons and over forty thousand in cash, along with hundreds of kilos of cocaine."

Sam gave a low whistle.

Veranda had planned to end there, but Sam kept staring at her, so she continued. "I made a project out of the Villalobos narcotics trade. I learned more about their shipment schedules and routes so we could keep up a steady flow of interdictions that has put a serious hurt on them."

"But how does this get to Flaco and to you? I've never heard of a cartel reaching out directly to a narc. Not here in Phoenix anyway."

"Somehow they must've made Flaco. From the condition of his body, they tortured him for information." She dropped her gaze to her coffee mug. Her stomach felt queasy as she recalled the gruesome images. Flaco had been her responsibility. *His death is on me.*

She stirred cream into her coffee to compose her thoughts. "Flaco probably told them I was behind all the interdictions, which is true enough. I pushed everyone I arrested for info on the next shipment. I did research with the DEA agents on our task force to gather more background information and became the subject matter expert on the Villalobos cartel."

"So they wanted to stop you without having to kill you." It was a statement rather than a question.

"Yes, they found a very effective way of getting me out of DEB for good, as well as making an example out of Flaco. Two birds."

"They aren't worried this murder will get too much attention?"

"A drug dealer killed by the criminals he's working for? Please." She waved a dismissive hand. "The press is way more interested in the fact that our undercover facility is exposed, and now detectives are scrambling to protect their own CIs. Command Staff is forced to look for a new location for DEB, and we've got several outside agencies involved in the discussion. Their little stunt totally disrupted regular operations."

"Interesting," Sam said. "The way they set this up shows that the cartel has a deep level of understanding of our procedures. Like they knew exactly what our response would be."

"I'm sure Bartolo is behind this. He's the most dangerous kind of criminal … smart and deadly when cornered." Veranda sipped her coffee. "I believe my interdictions have embarrassed him and that's one of the reasons he's coming after me. He needs to demonstrate that he's ready to take on the responsibility of running the whole cartel. He's in danger of losing the respect of his family and his men."

"Is Bartolo hotheaded enough to personally kill Flaco in front of his men to prove he's still got his, uh, what's the Spanish word for it … *cojones?*"

"He's got a nasty temper, and he can be reckless, but Bartolo doesn't usually bloody his own hands." She paused. "Flaco told me there were rumors that Bartolo had started sampling his product. Narcotics could make him erratic."

"Doesn't matter. If he ordered the killing, he goes down for it too."

Veranda's eyes met Sam's. From her very core, she wanted to destroy the Villalobos cartel, but she had to be honest. "Sam, this investigation will be highly dangerous. We'll be going up against a ruthless and well-funded organization."

Sam did not answer right away, letting the comment hang in the air as his steady gaze remained on hers. "Veranda, I'm not sure how much you know about me, but I want to make something very clear." He leaned forward. "I've been a cop for over thirty years. I've taken down street punks wearing a year's worth of my salary in gold chains and investment bankers with a net worth in the billions. I've been shot, stabbed, beat up, set up, and threatened with lawsuits. I'm not going to let some glorified dope slinger escape justice for what he's done."

So this is Sam Stark, she thought, *and he won't back down despite the odds.* Just like her.

Veranda grinned. "Then let's do this."

6

WHEN VERANDA AND SAM arrived back at Sam's corner cubicle in the Violent Crimes Bureau, a note stuck to his chair directed them to the conference room for a squad meeting.

Veranda did not underestimate the importance of this step. She would meet her new team for the first time. She had been on several units since joining the force thirteen years ago. First as a new patrol officer, or "booter" as they were called, then as a Property Crimes detective where she earned her chops in investigations, and finally, in Narcotics.

Each squad had its own small-group dynamics. There were leaders, followers, and sometimes saboteurs with hidden agendas. Seemingly innocent banter could be loaded with subtext. As part of the process of joining a team, she had to determine where she fit in.

On the Phoenix Police Department, homicides were investigated by an entire squad, each with its own sergeant, functioning as a team. Veranda wasn't surprised to learn that Sam, the senior detective on his squad, had the lead on this high-profile case. She expected the group to be comfortable with each other. They had all reached the pinnacle of their careers, attaining the status of Homicide Detective, where they would likely remain until retirement. For them, there was no longer a need to compete.

"Welcome to the war room," Sam said as he opened the door to the conference room.

Her eyes met several curious gazes. The rich smell of Thai food wafted to her as she spotted a cluster of white boxes in the middle of the long table.

"Everyone, this is Detective Veranda Cruz, on loan from DEB." Sam indicated an empty chair. "Have a seat. Looks like Frank scored some takeout from Thai Me Up. Just grab any box. I'll introduce you to our illustrious team."

Veranda slid a white carton and chopsticks in front of her and looked up at Sam, who remained standing. He pointed to the pale, slender dark-haired detective who had resembled a prairie dog popping out of its burrow earlier. "This is Steve Malloy. We call him Doc because he's spent so much time at autopsies he could pass for an ME." The group chuckled as Doc gave her a wave.

Sam moved on. "This is Frank Fujiyama." Frank grunted in her direction as he used chopsticks to push noodles into his mouth.

Sam shook his head. "He doesn't say much, so don't take his lack of interaction the wrong way."

"Hey," Frank said around a mouthful of Pad Thai. "When I've got something to say, I talk. Otherwise, I keep my trap shut."

"This," Sam indicated a striking blonde sitting across from Veranda, "is Marci Blane."

Marci raised a sardonic eyebrow at Sam. "What are you planning to say about me? Better watch it." The others grinned as a low "woooo" went around the room.

Sam held his arms out wide, fingers splayed. "Not saying a word. Got a keen sense of survival."

He turned to the last unfamiliar face. "This is Tony Sanchez, Brooklyn born and raised."

"Yo," Tony said. "Welcome to Paradise Lost."

Sam took the chair next to Veranda and whispered in her ear. "Whatever you do, don't ask Doc how he's doing because he'll tell you in excruciating detail." She raised her eyebrows and he winked. "A little knowledge is a dangerous thing."

"Anyway, you're full of shit," Marci resumed an interrupted conversation with Tony. "You've lived in Phoenix for twenty-five years. Your body acclimated a long time ago."

Tony leveled his chopsticks at her. "I could live here a hundred fuckin' years and still never get used to these summers, which last from April through October, by the way."

"It's a mental thing. Mind over matter," Frank said.

Marci snorted. "If that's the case, then Tony's a lost cause." She pointed at various parts of his body as she spoke. "Hairy knuckles calloused from dragging on the ground. Sloped forehead accented with unibrow. Slack jaw and vacant expression." Everyone burst out laughing.

Tony grinned. "Go ahead and yuk it up. You guys will be sweating your balls off when I'm retired back East. I'm counting the days."

"And so are we," Frank said.

The group chuckled again as Tony held up a middle finger to the room at large.

A few quiet moments passed while they ate, then Marci tapped Doc's arm. "What's the fastest way to heal a muscle strain?"

Doc looked anxious. "Are you sure it's muscular? What are your symptoms?"

Marci sighed. "It's definitely a muscle strain." She rubbed her right bicep. "I finally got my red belt last night."

"Hey," Veranda straightened. "I've kickboxed for years, but I've been considering martial arts. Do you like it?"

Marci nodded. "You should give it a try. I study karate. Come to my dojo sometime."

Silence fell as the men looked back and forth between Marci and Veranda. Marci sighed and rolled her eyes at her compatriots. "Let me interpret for you, Veranda. They're imagining the two of us in a naked mud wrestling match right now."

Frank put down his chopsticks and bobbed his head. "Oh, hell yeah."

"Their brains are jammed in overdrive," Marci continued, smiling at Veranda, "because they also know I prefer girls."

All eyes cut to Veranda. "Sorry guys," she said. "Not gonna happen."

Tony guffawed and looked at Marci. "A swing and a miss."

Marci ran her fingers through her long blond hair and licked her lips seductively as she batted her eyes at Tony. "You're just jealous because I get hotter chicks than you," she purred.

"Ouch," Doc said as everyone snickered.

Veranda felt right at home. The banter reminded her of similar conversations she had shared over the years with other long-standing teams. This squad had invited her into their circle. There was no mistaking their outreach and acceptance.

The conference room door opened and Sergeant Jackson walked in followed by two other men. The atmosphere in the room palpably changed as the laughter died out.

"As you were," Jackson said and turned to Veranda. "Detective Cruz, this is Lieutenant Aldridge and Commander Webster." Veranda leaned across the table and shook hands with both men. "Let's start

45

the briefing." There was some jockeying of chairs as everyone made room for the brass.

Lieutenant Aldridge addressed the room. "First, let's have a report from those of you who already received assignments, then Detective Cruz can give us an overview of the cartel. We'll begin with the crime scene."

Sam stood and walked to the front of the room holding his notebook. "Due to the high-profile nature of the case, we managed to push the autopsy to the front of the line. The ME will do it first thing tomorrow morning." He pulled his half-glasses out of his shirt pocket and flipped open the small spiral-bound pad. "While we wait for official tests, Crime Scene processed the scene and did a preliminary examination of the body. The victim's throat was slashed, which appears to be the cause of death."

Sam's eyes traveled down the page. "There were injuries all over the upper body, probably due to being kicked or beaten. The left side of the chest had a fresh burn showing the head of a wolf. Looks like he was branded." Several people grimaced.

Veranda shuddered as she thought of Flaco's last hours. The small amount of chicken panang she'd eaten now churned in her stomach. Even though she had seen the images earlier, they evoked a fresh wave of revulsion toward the cartel. *How could they be so savage?*

"Any trace evidence?" Lieutenant Aldridge asked.

"No latent prints, but samples of hair, fiber, blood and various secretions were all collected. Everything went to the lab. They'll check for a match and get back to us. If there's no initial hit, at least we'll be ready if we come up with a suspect for comparison."

Veranda recalled that Bartolo had been arrested many years ago for a felony narcotics charge. After his Armani-suited lawyer had gotten it busted down to a misdemeanor, Bartolo spent a minimal amount of time in jail as a first time offender. His DNA, however, remained in the database. If Bartolo hadn't taken proper precautions when dealing with Flaco…

She blinked as she realized Sam had sat down and Marci now stood in front of the table, a thin stack of papers in her hand. Veranda had missed the beginning of Marci's report.

"…so I was able to get fairly high resolution images from the lab," Marci said, and stepped forward to hand part of the stack to Sergeant Jackson, who distributed them.

Veranda glanced down at the page and recognized color images of the Drug Enforcement Bureau parking lot. Several photos had been isolated from the surveillance cameras positioned around the perimeter of the building.

Marci waited until everyone had a sheet. "Notice the still frame on the upper right-hand corner. The video forensics guys were able to get a partial on the rear license plate of the pickup truck that transported the body for the dump job."

Everyone leaned forward to scrutinize the image.

"We got the make and model of the truck from the front grille and fender on the previous shot." She smiled. "I cross-referenced the partial plate with trucks of that make and model and obtained only two matches in Arizona. One belongs to a seventy-five-year-old rancher in Yuma. The other one came back to this." Marci gave another set of documents to the sergeant.

When Veranda received her copy, she blurted, "Ponte Vista Construction!"

All eyes turned to her. She jabbed the paper with her finger. "That's one of the Villalobos cartel front companies. Whoever was driving really screwed up. We can actually put one of their vehicles at the scene." Her pulse quickened at the significance of the mistake.

"We can do better than that," Marci said, recapturing everyone's attention. "I ran another check and found two traffic citations over the past eighteen months for that vehicle. The driver was the same each time." Apparently enjoying the tension in the room before her bomb detonated, Marci handed the last of her stack to Jackson, who duly passed it around.

Veranda pumped her fist in the air as soon as she spotted the black-and-white copy of the Motor Vehicle Division photo. "That's Pablo!"

Commander Webster cleared his throat. "Detective Cruz, perhaps now would be a good time for you to give us an overview of the Villalobos cartel and how this Pablo fits into it."

Veranda's nerves thrummed with excitement as she sprang from her seat and strode to the white board, which took up most of one wall. She picked up a black marker. "The best way for me to explain this is to make an organizational chart. PSB has my case files, including a detailed schematic complete with photos of key players and connecting lines going down about six levels, but I can show you the basics."

She drew a large rectangle in the top middle spot and wrote *EL LOBO* inside the box. "For those of you who don't know, *el lobo* means 'the wolf' in Spanish. The head of the cartel is Hector Villalobos, but he's called *El Lobo* by everyone. This comes from their surname Villalobos, which means 'Village of Wolves' or 'City of Wolves.'"

"So that's the reason for the wolf brand on the victim's chest?" Sergeant Jackson asked.

"Yes, the Villalobos family crest has a gold background with two black wolves reared up on their hind legs. They've adopted the black wolf as their symbol. They stamp it on bales and packages of narcotics to identify their product."

Veranda turned to face the group. "Upper-level members of the group get wolf tattoos over their hearts and wear wolf-themed jewelry. When they reach the inner circle, they're awarded a dagger encrusted with gem-stones and inlaid in gold with a wolf design. At the highest level, family members have the distinction of carrying a gold-plated fifty-caliber Desert Eagle pistol with customized wolf's head ebony grips."

"And here I felt lucky getting to keep my service Glock when I retire," Tony said under his breath.

Lieutenant Aldridge scooted his chair closer to the white board. "Please continue with the org chart, Detective."

"The internal structure of the organization is patterned as something of a hybrid between a paramilitary group and a wolf pack."

Veranda drew four boxes below the first with lines linking them. "The second tier is Hector's four children, who are all adults now. He named them alphabetically by birth order."

"Seriously?" Frank asked.

"Hector is getting on in years and wants to retire and buy his own island. He raised his children to take over the empire. From what I'm told, it was supposed to go to Adolfo, the oldest, but Bartolo is so vicious that he's taken over as heir to the throne. *El Lobo* hasn't formally announced it yet, but it's common knowledge that Bartolo is being groomed."

A grin spread across Sam's face. "So, the big bad wolf wants to pack it in and enjoy a cozy retirement. I wonder if his pension plan is as good as ours."

She smiled back. "His pension plan is his kids. They have to step up so daddy wolf won't have to run the cartel and, of course, they each want to be the new head *Lobo*."

"Perhaps we can use that to our advantage," Sam said, stroking his mustache. "Maybe someone else in the family wouldn't mind seeing Bartolo go away for murder."

Veranda's smile vanished. "If another sibling wants a change in the pecking order, it will probably involve bloodshed. Hector gave each child a specific part of the cartel to manage according to their talents. Each of the four is considered a top lieutenant in the organization." Veranda wrote in the box farthest to the left.

"First, there's Adolfo. He's the finance guy and has a degree in accounting. He oversees loan sharking, including collections. He also handles money laundering, using fronts and fences. We believe he dabbles in counterfeiting and identity theft. His direct subordinate is a computer whiz and hacking expert."

She moved to the next box. "Second is Bartolo. He was in the top ten percent of his law school class and uses knowledge of criminal procedure to help him run the narcotics trade. This includes everything from farmers with grow operations in Mexico and South America all the way to their distribution network throughout the southwestern United States. He's trying to expand to the north and east as well."

The marker squeaked as she filled in another name in the next box. "Carlos is responsible for their human trafficking operations. His coyotes smuggle people over the border. After they arrive in Phoenix, sometimes they're held in drop houses while their families back in Mexico are forced to pay ransom for their release. If a woman's family can't afford the ransom, she goes to his network of pimps to work off her transport fee. There are a few locations in Phoenix we suspect are actually brothels and we've been trying to get enough evidence for a search warrant."

She moved to the right as she spoke, covering the length of the board. "Last, but definitely not least, is Daria, who is in charge of weapons and explosives. She arranges for shipments of arms to Mexico and handles a web of straw purchasers and other suppliers to feed a growing demand. She also procures the customized guns and daggers for the upper echelon. She's studied weaponry and built a factory in Mexico to manufacture ammunition and explosives." She paused.

"It took months to get a photo of her. She protects her privacy and is usually surrounded by armed guards."

The room fell silent. Veranda had been speaking for quite some time. She looked around the table, unsure about her presentation. "Our federal partners helped gather this intel." Her eyebrows drew together. "Did I miss anything?"

Jackson recovered first. "Detective Cruz, this organization is incredibly sophisticated. This is the bear—excuse me—wolf you've been poking?" He had a look of wonder on his face. "It's amazing you're still alive."

She lifted a shoulder. "Cartels are hesitant to kill a law enforcement officer in the US, although it has been known to happen. They know it would bring too much heat down on them, so they usually find other ways to work around interdictions. In my case, they definitely got me out of DEB and off their tail ... or so they think."

"I take it Bartolo has been your main focus?" Commander Webster asked.

"Yes, and Pablo is his top sergeant. He's responsible for a network of distributors and he takes orders directly from Bartolo."

Webster steepled his fingers. "We need to get this Pablo on his own to interrogate him. Perhaps we can convince him to cooperate."

Despite her excitement, Veranda had to be straight with them. "Sir, even if we manage to take Pablo into custody, I doubt we can offer anything that will turn him."

"I realize it's a long shot, Detective, but we need to try. If Pablo goes on record that Bartolo ordered the hit, we'll have them both for murder. If not, we're no worse off. We've certainly got enough evidence from the video and the citations to bring Pablo in."

Sergeant Jackson stood to address the group as Veranda took her seat. He looked at Sam. "You and Veranda locate Pablo. Identify his residence and any places he frequents on a regular basis." Sam nodded.

The sergeant turned to Marci. "You and Frank start writing. We need an affidavit for an arrest warrant for Pablo and search warrants for his domicile and vehicle as well as a buccal swab for DNA. Touch base with Sam and Veranda to see if they come up with anything else that needs a look."

Jackson addressed the room. "I'm headed to the Maricopa County prosecutor's office. We need authorization to make a deal and I want one of the assistant prosecutors in on the ground floor on this one."

"How about me?" Doc asked.

"You and Tony swing by the Resource Bureau and meet with SAU to brief them so they can work up a tactical ops plan to apprehend Pablo."

Veranda was glad to see they were taking no chances. Protocol for arresting a high-level cartel member included SWAT-trained officers from the Special Assignment Unit. She had seen firsthand the type of firepower cartel members routinely carried, and a detective's .45-caliber Glock was no match for a fully automatic AK-47 assault rifle.

———————

Veranda flew backward as Jake's foot connected with her ribs. She sprawled across the padded gym floor and gulped air.

Jake sauntered over and looked down at her. "Where are you, Cruz?" He put a hand on his hip. "Cuz you're sure as hell not here tonight."

"Fuck you, Jake." She grunted as she regained her feet. "I've got a few things on my mind." She had begged her kickboxing instructor to stay late so she could work off pent-up frustration. It had seemed like a good idea, but after spending the last twenty minutes punching his fist with her face, she reconsidered her decision.

Jake talked to give her a chance to catch her breath. "Fighting is about control. If your opponent can get in your head, he's already won."

Sweat ran in rivulets down her spine as she put up gloved hands. Jake was right. She was distracted tonight. She reflected on the afternoon spent knocking on doors with Sam, trying to get terrified people to talk about Pablo. It took hours, but they finally got an address.

She shook her head to clear her mind. "You ready?"

Jake chuckled. "For what you're bringing tonight? Yeah, I'm ready."

That pissed her off. She was sure it was what her kickboxing instructor had intended. She feinted with a left jab and switched to a roundhouse kick, nearly catching him in the jaw.

"Now we're talking." He grinned from behind his headgear. "Let's dance."

The gym smelled of sweat socks and disinfectant. She let the sights and sounds permeate her senses to ground herself in the present. An image of Bartolo's face kept intruding on her thoughts. She couldn't let it distract her. *Use it to your advantage.*

She pictured Bartolo in Jake's place and gathered energy inside her body until it coiled like a spring. In an explosive move, she lunged, hitting his upper body and head with a rapid series of blows from her fists. She lifted one knee to gain momentum, then planted her foot and thrust the other leg into his midsection, knocking him to the floor.

He rolled away before she could kick him again, bouncing back up to a fighter's stance. His mocking tone, gone. His eyes, narrowed slits.

She saw his arm muscles tighten in preparation for a hook, and blocked it easily.

"Well, well, the little girl is ready to play."

She knew what he was doing. He had been her instructor for many years. He had sensed early on that her weakness was her temper. If he could rile her, she would lose her composure and fight blindly, in a state of rage. Over the years, he had taught her to harness her anger and wield it as a weapon. She understood that a skilled opponent would use her emotions against her, and had learned to look past any jeers or taunts he might throw at her.

She sensed her opportunity and lashed out at his chin. He bent his knees to dodge the blow and she swept his feet from under him. This time he stayed down.

"Damn, Cruz, I don't know who I'm sparring with tonight. First you're distracted, then you act like you want to disembowel me."

She grinned. "You've taught me well."

"Seriously, though," he said, getting up. "What's on your mind?"

"It's this guy at work." She had never told Jake she was a cop. From the time of her undercover days in DEB, she had been careful not to let anyone in her regular life know so she would not jeopardize her cases.

Jake wiped the sweat from his brow with the back of a gloved hand. "You mean the guy who killed your informant and dumped his body in the parking lot where you work?"

She gawked at him.

He sighed. "I watch the news, Veranda."

"What was I thinking?" She threw her hands in the air. "Of course everyone knows who I am and what I do now."

"It wasn't a huge shock for me. You always trained like you thought you might be fighting for your life someday. A lot of women come in here looking to lose a few pounds and get in shape, but you were always driven. Motivated. Fierce as a warrior."

The observation made her uncomfortable. To change the subject, she asked a question. "Now that you know who I'm up against, do you have any professional advice?"

He walked over and peered directly into her eyes. "Fight like a girl."

"What the hell is that supposed to mean?"

"If you ever find yourself in a combat situation with a man, don't try to duke it out. Use the inherent strengths women have." He frowned. "Outsmart him, and kick the shit out of him."

"This particular man has a personal army at his disposal."

Jake shrugged. "You could just give up and let him sell his drugs all over the country."

"You know I could never do that."

"Then fight him with everything you've got."

After depleting her energy in the last round with her instructor, she felt drained. "I just hope it's enough."

"Not like you to indulge in self-pity, Cruz. This sounds a bit personal."

"Jake, you have no idea how personal this battle is." Nor did anyone else. She would do everything in her power to ensure that the link between her family and the cartel remained buried in the past.

7

Villalobos family compound, Mexico

BARTOLO PACED IN FRONT of his father's intricately carved mahogany desk. The glow of an antique lamp spilled over the ivory desk set on its polished surface. Moonlight poured in through the mullioned office windows. Shadows formed sharp angles across the opulent room.

He had barely napped on the family jet before it landed on the runway south of the compound. He hated to appear before his father with a stubbled jaw and rumpled suit, but one did not ignore a summons from Hector Villalobos.

"Why the emergency meeting?" Bartolo asked.

"Sit down, *mi'jo*," *El Lobo* said quietly.

He always grew concerned when his father's voice softened. Never a good sign. Yelling was better. He sat forward in the overstuffed leather chair facing the desk. *"Papá, I—"*

Hector held up a hand. "Enough."

Bartolo held his tongue as his father pushed back from his desk and stood. Hands clasped behind his back, he slowly crossed the room and glanced upward. Bartolo followed his father's gaze up the mahogany paneled walls to rest on the Villalobos family crest. The massive shield, plated in twenty-four-karat gold, featured a pair of upright ebony wolves intricately rendered in the metalwork.

Hector switched to Spanish. "I had this crest hand-tooled by craftsmen from a nearby village." He continued to stare at the shield as he spoke. "Do you know why I researched our lineage and spent a small fortune to re-create our ancient coat of arms?"

"Because you wanted to ensure we remembered our heritage," Bartolo said.

Eyes flashing, Hector whirled to face his son. "Exactly! We are not of common stock. We are the descendants of Spanish nobility. Our branch of the family came to the New World as conquistadors. The land was ours to take. The people, ours to rule." His expression darkened. "Over the centuries, our ancestors squandered their wealth. By the time I was born, the only thing my father passed on to me was a noble birthright." He clenched a fist. "I grew up poor, but vowed that my children would have the best of everything." His face contorted into a grim smile. "I forged a new empire and reclaimed our destiny."

Bartolo had always felt his father got dramatic when describing their family history. He didn't share his father's beliefs about noble bloodlines. He saw *El Lobo* as a man who used brute savagery coupled with business acumen to claw his way to the top, then cloaked himself with a veneer of respectability by citing manifest destiny. Of course, he would never dare to say this aloud.

Hector tightened his fist until the knuckles whitened. "I will not allow the foolish actions of one of my children to jeopardize all I have created. You were reckless as a young boy, but I thought you would outgrow your hotheaded nature." He jabbed a finger at Bartolo. "I have heard reports that you use cocaine."

A trickle of sweat coursed down the back of Bartolo's neck as he wondered who had informed on him. He met his father's eyes and tried to look affronted. "Lies, *Papá*, from those who are jealous of me."

"The drugs we sell are for the weak who cannot accept their lot in life. Not for my children. You will not lead this family if you are an addict. I forbid it." Hector lapsed into silence.

Bartolo tried to ease his father's concerns. "I can run our business. After all, I caught the snitch and identified the person targeting our shipments. Then I—"

"Then you took it upon yourself to try to solve the problem, and instead created a hundred new ones. The only saving grace is that our police mole keeps us informed. He told me how you revealed the identity of the detective who ran the task force to the media." His eyes narrowed. "I should have heard about it from you, not from a satellite news feed from Phoenix."

"I had to act quickly once I knew her name." Bartolo ran a hand through his thick, curly hair. "That *puta* cost me a fortune."

Hector surveyed his son before speaking. "I had one of my men check into her history. He discovered something in her background that is of great concern to me. I contacted our police mole today to help me get more answers." He murmured almost to himself, "You call her a whore, but she is much more than that. She is a threat."

Bartolo was confused. "*Papá*, I've already taken care of her. She can't cause any more trouble for us."

His father gave him a derisive look. "After you got her thrown out of Narcotics, she was assigned to investigate her snitch's death. Now she will try to charge you for his murder."

Shock ripped through him. He had thought Detective Cruz would be terminated after such a serious breach of security. At the very least, he expected her to be suspended. His plan had backfired, putting him in jeopardy. "She cannot tie me to the killing."

Hector's expression hardened. "Again, you are woefully uninformed. Fortunately, the mole told me what is going on, which gives us time to tie up loose ends."

Bartolo's gaze snapped up to meet his father's. "Loose ends?"

"Bartolo, Bartolo," his father said on a weary sigh. "Pablo is like another son to me. He served our family business for many years. He made a simple blunder, but he did so on your orders, carrying out your plan. Now you have put us all at risk."

Bartolo's heart raced. "What blunder?"

"The mole gave me a full report. Surveillance cameras captured images of Pablo's truck. The police have identified him as the driver and obtained warrants for his arrest. That is why I summoned you here."

Realization crashed in on him, tightening his throat. "*Papá*, there must be another way we can ... " He trailed off as he looked into *El Lobo's* pitiless lupine eyes.

"You must take care of this personally, Bartolo. It is your fault as well as his." Hector pierced him with an unrelenting gaze. "This time there must be no mistakes."

Bartolo lowered his head. He had always depended on Pablo, his most loyal sergeant.

Hector continued, "Take Pablo far out into the desert. Leave no evidence. Burn his body when you are finished."

Bartolo understood that this was *his* punishment as much as Pablo's. *El Lobo* often used harsh lessons to teach his children. Even when quite young, they had watched executions to ingrain the consequences of disloyalty or failure. When she was eight years old, Bartolo's sister,

Daria, had been forced to drown her kitten after Hector discovered she had stolen a cat toy from a store. She had wept for hours. After that, Bartolo had never seen her shed a tear again.

Now his father had ordered him to murder his right-hand man. Bartolo allowed himself a moment to grieve the prospect of the loss, then steeled himself as he straightened in his seat. "I'll see to it immediately upon my return to Phoenix, *Papá.*"

"Call me when it is done, and I will tell you what I learned about Detective Cruz."

Bartolo stood to leave. Every muscle in his body tensed. This was all her fault. Because of her, he would have the blood of his second-in-command on his hands. He could not allow Pablo's death to go unavenged.

As he turned toward the massive office doors, a glint crept into his eyes. Whatever his father had uncovered about her past, he would dig further to find out everything he could about Veranda Cruz. Flaco had told him she had used her resources to study him for two years. While she'd gathered intelligence, he hadn't been aware of her existence. Now he would turn the tables and learn her secrets, exploiting them to settle his personal score with the *puta* police detective. He would bring her to her knees.

8

SAM RAISED THE NIGHT vision binoculars to his eyes as Veranda stuffed the last of the fast food wrappers into a bag and tucked it under the front seat of the Impala. Kickboxing always left her ravenous, and she had worked her way through a foot-long spicy Italian sub over the past few hours.

She looked at Sam's profile silhouetted in the faint predawn light. "Why do you think Lieutenant Aldridge denied your request for surveillance on Pablo's house?"

Sam lowered his arms and turned to her. "Aldridge is a desk jockey. His biggest concern is overtime and fuel expenses. I heard he got his ass handed to him by Fiscal Management because Homicide is way over budget."

"I had no idea you Homicide guys had to count staples and paperclips like the rest of the department."

"If the public only knew. Sometimes it feels like the accountants are in charge."

"Tell me about it. If it weren't for the money we get from our asset seizures, our listening equipment would consist of two cups and a string."

Sam chuckled. "In situations like these, I've learned to trust my instincts. There are ways around the bean counters." He went back to looking through the binoculars.

"Like a freelance stakeout. No ops plan and no backup." She grinned. "This has some serious *caca* potential."

Sam cut his eyes to her. "You still on board?"

"Wouldn't be here if I wasn't."

"Good, because Pablo may have heard we're looking for him. We put out a lot of feelers today to get a bead on his location. What time is it?"

Veranda checked the dash clock. "Almost four. SAU should set up the command post in an hour."

"I'm not gonna be happy until this asshole is in custody. He's our only lead."

"Yeah, and he's—hey, what's that?" Veranda pointed down the street as Sam cursed.

A light came on inside Pablo's house. Veranda squinted as the door to the carport opened and a shadowy figure stepped out.

"It's Pablo," Sam said, binoculars protruding from beneath his bushy eyebrows. "He threw a duffel bag into that BMW before he got behind the wheel."

The dark sports car backed out of the driveway. She buckled her seat belt. "We can't lose him."

"On it." Sam tossed the binoculars in the back seat and cranked the engine. "I'll hang back, but he'll make us soon. Nobody's up yet, it's a ghost town."

"You want me to call for backup?"

"Hell yes, he could have a rocket launcher in that bag for all we know."

She snatched the microphone and keyed it. "Charlie thirty-four, requesting nine-oh-seven for a homicide suspect." She used Sam's coded designator so the dispatcher would know a Homicide unit was requesting backup.

A smooth female voice responded immediately. "Charlie thirty-four, go ahead."

"We're in an unmarked silver Impala following a black BMW sedan westbound on Roosevelt approaching Ninth Street. Driver of the vehicle is Pablo Moreno. We have a warrant for homicide. Suspect known to carry multiple weapons. We need a felony vehicle stop, air support, and K-9."

The dispatcher responded with an order for everyone on the channel to suspend routine radio traffic. "All units, ten-twelve. Units in the area of Central City, South Mountain, and Estrella Mountain precincts, assistance needed with a felony vehicle stop. Suspect wanted for homicide and considered armed and dangerous. Charlie unit, please provide current location and suspect description."

Veranda rapidly delivered the information as they made several sharp turns.

Sam jerked the steering wheel hard to the left. "Shit! He's made us."

The BMW shot forward and careened around a corner. The Impala's tires squealed as Sam struggled to keep up.

Veranda keyed the mike again. "Charlie thirty-four, suspect has identified us and is actively fleeing. We are now in pursuit. Suspect is westbound on West Van Buren turning south on First Street heading toward the Warehouse District."

The dispatcher picked up the pace. "Any patrol supervisor in the vicinity, please respond."

A gruff male voice answered. "Forty-two King, I'm monitoring. I need two units to take over for the Charlie unit and the rest to run parallel routes and set up bull's-eye perimeters. Is the air unit up?"

The dispatcher responded. "Air unit is coming from Deer Valley, ETA six minutes. Two K-9's are en route."

Veranda struggled to keep herself in her seat, clutching the door handle with her right hand as they skidded around a tight turn. She held the mike in her left hand, calling out changes in direction for responding patrol cars to intercept Pablo. Spinning the steering wheel, Sam grimaced as the Impala fishtailed around corners.

Suddenly, the BMW slid sideways, screeching to a halt in the middle of the road across their path. The driver powered the window down. The muzzle of an AK-47 poked out.

Sam stomped on the brakes. The staccato sound of automatic gunfire thundered in Veranda's ears as a barrage of bullets slammed into the Impala's windshield. Jagged circles fractured around entry holes in the glass as rounds hit the seat cushion next to her shoulder and face.

Veranda ducked beneath the dashboard with the microphone. "Shots fired! Thirteen hundred West Lincoln Avenue." The dispatcher broadcasted an emergency tone and a nine-nine-nine *officer needs help* code. Veranda yanked her Glock out of its hip holster and glanced at Sam. "You hit?"

Pulling out his gun, Sam shook his head. They both popped up, leaned out the side windows, and opened fire on the BMW. Adrenalin rocketed through Veranda's body. Time slowed. Her senses dimmed to exclude anything that did not affect her immediate survival. The deafening gun blasts, the scent of burning rubber and smoking brake pads, and the taste of blood in her mouth from a bitten lip receded into the background. Her vision constricted into a circle of light and focused on her muzzle flashes. The momentary glare illuminated each bullet as it slammed into the driver's door of the BMW.

The AK-47's barrel appeared in the window again. Another fusillade of shots ripped through the Impala's hood. Sam and Veranda hunkered back down under the dash, seeking the protection of the engine block.

"You still okay?" Sam asked. "That was full auto."

Over the ringing in her ears, Veranda heard tires screech and a powerful engine roar off.

Sam scrambled back into his seat and slammed his foot on the accelerator pedal as Veranda fumbled for the microphone. The Impala sputtered, clunked, and died. Sam twisted the key in the ignition. Nothing.

"All responding units," Veranda said into the radio. "We've taken fire. Suspect is in possession of a fully automatic weapon. We have no injuries, but our car is disabled. We cannot pursue. Suspect vehicle last seen southbound on Thirteenth Avenue heading toward Buckeye Road."

"Shit!" Sam slammed his palms against the steering wheel. "We'll be lucky if we ever see that asshole outside of Mexico."

"Forty-two King," the patrol supervisor's calm voice carried over the radio. "Dispatcher to provide last location and direction of travel to helicopter and K-9. Responding units lock down the perimeter."

A male voice rose above the sound of whirring helicopter blades, "This is Air Four. We're on your frequency. Still en route, ETA three minutes."

Veranda listened to sporadic radio traffic as everyone in the area attempted to spot and contain the fleeing BMW.

Sam's shoulders slumped. "They can't find him. Must've dumped his car somewhere out of sight."

Veranda closed her eyes and leaned back against the headrest. "Yep, this is definitely the *caca* scenario. We lost our only lead while we were on an unauthorized stakeout, our car looks like it just came back from Fallujah"—she rubbed her temples—"and I've already got PSB up my ass."

Sam glanced at her. "Just leave the supervisors and PSB ferrets to me."

"Fine for you to say. You're not on double secret probation."

"Trust me. I've been in worse situations. Let me do the talking."

Her hands trembled slightly as the last of the adrenalin left her body. As she came down hard, she reflected on the significance of Pablo's escape. Without him, they were back to square one. They still hadn't found out where Flaco had been killed, so there was no crime scene to examine. The warehouse where the tractor-trailer had been going was empty by the time the tactical team made entry. She couldn't get traction on this investigation.

Another question surfaced in her mind. How had Pablo known to leave before dawn? The cartel seemed to be one step ahead of her at every turn. With Pablo gone, Bartolo had slipped through her fingers again.

9

"HOW LONG HAVE THEY been in there?" Veranda's knee bounced as she sat in the vacant cubicle next to Sam's.

Sam glanced at his watch. "About an hour. Shouldn't be much longer."

Exhausted but wired from too much coffee, Veranda stood to peer at Commander Webster's closed office door. She heard raised voices, then the door swung open and Lieutenant Aldridge stalked out, Sergeants Diaz and Jackson on his heels.

Jackson veered toward her. "Cruz, Stark, come with me." He pivoted and headed to his office.

Sam rose and ambled through the cubicle maze with Veranda in tow. His body language was relaxed as he cast a knowing smile over his shoulder.

They sat in two frayed chairs facing the sergeant's desk while he closed the door and folded his lanky body into his seat. "Commander Webster persuaded PSB that your escapade earlier this morning was warranted."

Sam crossed his arms over his chest. "The commander backed us up because we were right. None of this would have happened if we'd gotten approval for the undercover stakeout I requested."

Jackson's eyes narrowed a fraction. "The fact that you were proven correct and that we now need Detective Cruz's help finding the suspect played a large part in the commander's decision."

"I've already provided intel to the SAU guys on every possible safe house where the cartel might have stashed Pablo," Veranda threw in.

Jackson inclined his head a fraction. "Given the amount of damage caused to your vehicle, and the use of deadly force, there will be an investigation." Veranda started to speak, but Jackson talked over her. "PSB will not, however, be looking at you two for insubordination, which means you both can keep your badges and stay on the case."

"Glad that's settled." Sam moved to stand.

Jackson held up a hand. "Stay where you are, Stark. Lieutenant Aldridge was furious that you violated his orders. He wanted your hides."

"Which brings up a question." Sam leaned forward in his chair. "Why didn't he authorize a stakeout and do this the right way? We'd have Pablo in custody and I'd still have my car."

"It's the city's car," Jackson said. "The lieutenant had valid reasons." He extended a finger on his raised hand to enumerate each point. "We had no reason to believe Pablo knew we were on to him. We were scheduled to begin surveillance at oh five hundred hours anyway. Most importantly, the identities of any undercover Narcotics detectives we might use on a stakeout—as well as their vehicle descriptions—may have already been compromised by Flaco."

"Let's not forget"—Sam held up a finger and adopted a sarcastic tone—"the overtime cost for an overnight callout of an entire surveillance team."

Jackson bristled. "The point is that it's not your place to second-guess a direct order."

"Even if I was right and that order allowed our only suspect to get away?"

"You're getting a pass this time, Stark. Don't push it."

Sam and Veranda stood and left the office. He grinned down at her. "Told you we'd be okay."

She opened her mouth to thank him when she saw Diaz waiting for them and the words died on her lips.

"I need a word with you, Detective Cruz."

Maybe next time I'll picture him when I spar with Jake. "I already gave you my official statement about the stakeout."

"This is about the other investigation." He glanced at Sam. "You can wait for her back at your desk."

Sam's jaw muscles tightened. "I don't appreciate being sent to my room ... Sergeant."

Diaz took a step toward Sam. "Either I speak to Detective Cruz alone now, or I take her over to PSB and turn on the recorder for an official statement. Again."

Veranda had no interest in another interrogation session with Diaz in one of the PSB rooms. "It's okay, Sam. I'd rather get it out of the way here."

Sam continued to glare at Diaz for a moment, then turned and walked through the maze of cubicles. Diaz led her to a nearby alcove where they could speak privately.

Veranda looked up into eyes that were so dark they were almost black. She could not read his expression. "What is it now, Sergeant?"

"How long was Flaco dealing at South Phoenix High before you recruited him?"

Her pulse spiked up. What had Diaz discovered? She paused, pretending to search her memory. "I'm not exactly sure. I think he told me he'd been there awhile. Why?"

"Something about South Phoenix High clicked in my mind when I was going over my notes last night. I Googled the school and found a news story from a couple of months before your first contact with Flaco. Turns out a different cartel dealer was arrested for selling drugs to the students. It made the news because one of the kids died after overdosing on heroin." He leaned in, as if anticipating a reaction.

With a show of indifference, she shrugged. "That must have been why Sonny Dever asked me to keep an eye on the vehicle traffic. Makes sense to me."

"Is there more you want to tell me?"

"No." Sensing that she needed more of a reply, she added, "If I remember anything else, I'll let you know."

Nerves on edge, Veranda turned to find Sam. Diaz was getting close. If he kept ferreting around, he would stumble on the truth.

10

SAM AND VERANDA DROVE out of the headquarters parking lot in a sun-bleached, dented Chevy Malibu.

"Jackson knows I like Impalas, so he made sure I got the crappiest POS Malibu in the loaner fleet," Sam said.

"I'm just glad we're still on the case after that clusterfuck this morning."

Sam grunted. "We're going to have to get some sleep, but I need to eat first and then I'll drop you at your place. It's almost lunchtime already. You know someplace we can get good Mexican food?"

Veranda gave him a wide smile. "I know a great little place in South Phoenix. Head over the bridge and I'll tell you how to get there." She could already taste *Mamá*'s carne asada.

———

Veranda scooted into the well-worn cushion of the corner booth. A dose of her mother's cooking was the best tonic for her frazzled nerves.

Sam slid in opposite her. "I didn't know *Casa Cruz Cocina* was your family's restaurant. Heard good things but never got a chance to try it."

"You're in for a treat if you like authentic Mexican food. My mother, aunts, and uncles get up before dawn every morning to make the food fresh. Some places use frozen stuff they buy at wholesale stores. *Mamá* says she would close the restaurant before she would serve prepackaged food to our customers."

As Sam pulled reading glasses from his shirt pocket and picked up a menu, Veranda noticed a handsome silver band with intricately worked symmetrical designs on the third finger of his left hand. "That's a very nice ring."

Sam glanced down. "My wife, Sarah, gave this to me last year for our twentieth anniversary. Handcrafted by a Navajo artisan on the reservation. She loves Native American jewelry. A stickler about only buying authentic stuff from local artists." He turned his hand over. "I get a lot of compliments on this."

Veranda smiled when her mother approached. "Sam, this is my mother, Lorena Cruz-Gomez."

Lorena scowled and plunked down a small bowl of salsa and a basket of tortilla chips. "Excuse us one moment, please." She pulled her daughter up from the table whispering, "Come with me."

Veranda flashed an embarrassed grimace back at Sam as her mother tugged her toward the kitchen. "*Mamá*, that was so rude. What are you doing?"

Lorena dragged her daughter into the kitchen and let the doors swing shut. Veranda's Uncle Rico and Aunt Juana stood by the gleaming stainless steel countertops, hands on hips. Her mother joined them. All glared at her.

"What's going on?" She demanded.

Her uncle spoke first. "*Mi'ja*, he is too old for you."

Aunt Juana chimed in, "That *cochino viejo* could pass for your father. It's disgraceful."

As understanding dawned, Veranda burst out laughing. "He's *not* a dirty old man. He's my new partner." She shrugged. "And besides, he's married."

Lorena gasped as her hand flew to her mouth. Aunt Juana crossed herself. Uncle Rico muttered a stream of obscenities under his breath in Spanish.

Veranda held up both hands. "Let me explain. There's nothing between Sam and me except work." They still stared at her, so she sighed and went on, "I never got a chance to tell you all that I've been transferred to the Violent Crimes Bureau. That man you just called a *cochino viejo* is the most respected Homicide detective on the Department. He's training me because he's the best."

"*Ay, mi'ja,*" Lorena smiled and swept her into a tight hug. "Some of our customers tell us your name is on the news. Something about that dreadful Villalobos cartel." Her mother shuddered. "We do not have time to watch TV, so what we got was bits and pieces. Then when we did not hear from you ... "

"I left you a voicemail telling you I was okay. Knew you'd worry."

"I know, but I need to talk to you about it." Lorena reached up to run her fingertips over her heavy silver choker. A sure sign that she was worried.

"*Mamá,* I don't have time now. I'm going straight home after we eat." She yawned. "Haven't slept all night."

"Of course," Uncle Rico gently pulled her out of her mother's embrace and began ushering her back to the table. "You must be tired. Now please introduce us to this famous detective."

Sam looked up as the foursome arrived at the corner booth.

"Detective Sam Stark." Veranda motioned to her family. "You've already met my mother." This time Lorena beamed at him as her daughter pointed to each of the others in turn. "This is my tío Rico and my tía Juana."

Sam began to laugh and tried to turn it into a cough. "I'm sorry, but did you say Tijuana?"

"No." Veranda smiled. "*Tía* means 'aunt' in Spanish. You could say she's my Aunt Jane. Tijuana is a city in Mexico. It's not actually pronounced the same because it comes from a Native American word, not Spanish. Most Anglos say 'tee-ya-wana' when they should say 'tee-whana.'"

"And before you ask"—her uncle's eyes twinkled with amusement—"I am her rich uncle. That's what *tío rico* means in Spanish."

"A family joke," Veranda rolled her eyes. "Because my tío Rico worked hard for every penny he has."

"Like the rest of the family," her uncle said. "Proud of it too."

Sam had risen as they spoke and shook all of their hands. "Pleased to meet you, or should I say, *mucho gusto.*"

They smiled as Veranda took her seat. "Would you like a recommendation, Sam?" she asked.

"Please. What's the house specialty?"

"You have to try my mother's green chile tamales, and I'll have street tacos with carne asada." She handed the menus to Lorena, who turned toward the kitchen with her brother and sister.

When they were out of earshot, Veranda leaned across the table and lowered her voice. "I'm sorry about the way my mother acted earlier, but they … well … misunderstood the nature of our relationship."

"Ah, I see," Sam stroked his mustache. "You set them straight?"

"Of course. That's why you're not lying unconscious in the street right now after a close encounter with a cast iron skillet."

Sam chuckled. "I like your family. They're a lot like mine."

"You haven't seen one of our celebrations. The whole crowd gathers on the family property. Years ago when the restaurant started doing well, my mother bought a few acres next to South Mountain. Over the years, my aunts and uncles each built their own *casita*. That way, they could have their own home but raise their families together on the land."

Veranda looked up. "This is my kid sister, Gabriela. She's in high school and just started working here this summer."

Gabriela gave them a shy smile as she placed two glasses of ice water on the table.

Veranda grinned back. "So, are you ready to go back to school next month, Gabby? Will you see that boy again? What was his name?"

Gabriela blushed. "Steve." She fidgeted with her apron. "We're just friends. We see each other in youth group at church."

Veranda picked up her water and glanced at Sam. "Gabby is beautiful but extremely shy. Every boy in school is sniffing around, and we're very protective."

"I can see why," Sam said.

Gabriela seemed determined to change the subject. "By the way, Veranda, that arson guy came back in here first thing this morning."

That brought her up short. She tensed. "What did he say?"

This time it was Gabriela who grinned. "He said the fire was accidental and asked if we replaced the ductwork over the stove."

Veranda let out a relieved breath. "What did *Mamá* say?"

"She told him we did. Dad took care of it last night."

"What fire are you talking about?" Sam asked.

Veranda picked up her napkin. "There was a grease fire in the kitchen early yesterday morning. An arson investigator from the Fire Department came out to determine how it started."

"And ... " Gabriela's grin grew mischievous as she lowered her voice. "He asked *Mamá* about you. I heard the whole conversation."

"What did he want to know about me?"

Gabriela seemed to enjoy turning the tables on her big sister. "He wanted to know if you came into the restaurant a lot." She twisted a strand of hair around her finger. "Sounds like he wants to bump into you again."

"Oh no." Veranda felt her stomach lurch. "What did *Mamá* say to him?"

Gabriela looked up as if trying to recall the exact words. "Let's see, there was something about how you came in to help on evenings when you weren't working because you had no man in your life."

Sam snorted into his water as Veranda groaned.

Gabriela, in apparent relish, dropped her strand of hair and tapped her chin. "Hmmmm. I think I remember the phrase, 'That one will never give me grandchildren.'"

Veranda put her elbows on the table, face in her palms. "Take my gun and shoot me. It would be less painful than this."

Sam looked at Gabriela. "So what did the fireman do?"

"He left."

Veranda spoke through her hands, head still down. "Of course he did. He probably ran out of here like the place was on fire again."

Gabby cast a furtive glance toward the kitchen. "*Mamá* made me promise, so I can't tell you what she did, but I think you'll see the fireman again."

Sam laughed. "Glad I'm happily married."

Veranda peered up at him through her fingers. "My mother's on a mission. She has the whole family recruiting potential husbands for me. I try to explain that I want to focus on my career, but will she listen?"

Gabriela stifled a snigger. "*Mamá* is worried because you're over thirty."

Veranda lifted her head from her hands and jabbed a finger at her sister. "Don't laugh, Gabby, you're next."

"I'm only fourteen. Once I have my *quinceañera,* I figure I've got a good ten years before *Mamá* starts on me. In the meantime, she can focus on you." She giggled and fled to the kitchen.

Sam watched her go. "She's funny and she's cute."

"Cute? She's gorgeous. And her body. All long legs and smooth skin. Our family thinks she could be a model if she overcame her shyness. She has the looks and grace for it."

Sam eyed Veranda. "I can see the family resemblance."

She ignored the indirect compliment. "That's surprising because she's actually only my half sister."

"Your half sister?"

"My father died many years ago in Mexico when my mother was still pregnant with me. Years later, she married again and had two children. Gabriela is the youngest." Veranda wasn't sure why she had spoken so openly about her family history, but something about Sam made her feel comfortable.

"You were born in Mexico, then?"

"No, my mother came to the United States before she gave birth to me. She brought her brothers and sisters with her." Veranda did not add that they had to flee for their lives in the middle of the night with only what they could carry.

Gabby reappeared, snapped open a folding stand next to their table, and balanced a tray on it. The aroma of fresh herbs and spices wafted to Veranda's nose. Gabby grasped Sam's plate with a towel and put it in front of him. Sam bent to sniff the tamales nestled in corn husks. Veranda's mouth watered as Gabby placed her order of street tacos on the table. Famished, she practically dove into her favorite dish.

After they ate in comparative silence, Sam dabbed at his mouth with a cloth napkin. "Those were the most delicious tamales I've ever eaten."

"*Mamá* uses only the best ingredients. She gets grass-fed beef shipped direct from a ranch in Cornville, and goes to Safford for cheese. She also makes the best *masa*. You can't have decent tamales without good *masa*."

"Now I won't be able to eat any other Mexican food."

Veranda glowed with pride. She had worked in the restaurant when she turned fourteen until entering the police academy. The experience had prepared her well. She learned how to handle belligerent drunks, quell family disputes and spot patrons planning to run out on their checks. In short—how to read people.

Sam reached out to stop Veranda as she delved into her pocket. "I've got this, Veranda."

"They won't take your money for the food," she pulled out a wad of cash and tossed it on the table. "But I like to leave enormous tips for Gabby and then sneak out. I remember what it was like."

"Let's go. I'm beat. I'll drop you off at your place on my way home."

"When do you want to get together again?"

"I'll swing by to pick you up in about four hours. I know that's not long to sleep, but I don't want to lose too much time."

"I'm with you. There's a BOLO out for Pablo, and I'd like to look at some of his regular hangouts this evening in case he turns up."

"Every minute Pablo is on the loose decreases the odds we'll catch him. The cartel will find a way to sneak him across the border."

"Sam, something is bothering me about our investigation."

"What do you mean?"

"Have you noticed that Bartolo has been one step ahead of us at every turn since the interdiction? He smoked out my CI and killed him, got me thrown out of DEB, and as a result the task force was disbanded." She paused as they walked to the parking lot. "And I'm sure he was the one who told our only viable lead to run."

"Are you saying Bartolo has an inside track?"

She opened the door to the Malibu. "I'm saying there's something we're missing." Wait a minute!" She smacked a palm to her forehead. "I can't believe I didn't think of this until now." She looked at Sam. "How did Bartolo know where to dump Flaco's body? I was careful never to let any of my CIs know where our facility was located."

Sam got behind the wheel and she slid into the front passenger seat beside him. The black vinyl burned her skin through her T-shirt. She was careful not to touch the scorching metal on the seat belt buckles as she clicked them into place.

Sam started the engine and turned the AC on high. "We discussed that in VCB before you arrived. Our squad assumed your CI found out where you worked and told Bartolo."

She shook her head. "Not possible. It's drilled into our heads from day one at DEB to check for surveillance and make sure we're not followed. We take no chances that might give our identities away. We don't even say hello to other cops we bump into while we're undercover."

Sam drove out of the lot. "You describe the cartel as a pretty sophisticated organization. Maybe they found a way to hack into our database."

"The DEB files are kept separate. The facility's address is listed under a phony business."

"Okay, now I see your point. Bartolo knows things he shouldn't. And we can't plug up the hole if we can't find the leak."

They both lapsed into silence. She kept turning over facts in her mind. Grasping for a conclusion that seemed just out of reach. How much had Flaco revealed to the cartel before he died? She was certain he would have told Bartolo she had him in her crosshairs. Flaco might have even explained *why* she targeted him.

A cold sweat stippled her brow. In the flurry of activity over the past two days, she had not stopped to consider all of the information Flaco knew about her family and her past. She swallowed hard. Bartolo might now be in possession of her secret.

11

VERANDA BOLTED UPRIGHT IN her bed as a siren blared. Covered in perspiration, her heart pounded as she snatched her cell phone from the night stand and switched off the alarm. She had chosen a wailing police siren as her wakeup sound. It usually didn't bother her, but the noise had interrupted a nightmare. A wolf chased her through dark woods, its slavering jaws stretched wide as it prepared to strike. As the dream faded, she noticed a message icon blinking on her phone. She released a ragged breath and tapped the screen to access the voicemail message her mother had left two hours earlier.

"*Mi'ja.*" Lorena sounded anxious. "I need to talk to you. There are things you should know. Please come see me soon."

Veranda, still groggy from her fitful sleep, shook her head to clear it. She would barely have enough time to shower and get dressed before Sam arrived to pick her up. Her mother would have to wait.

In a daze, she shuffled into the bathroom and turned on the shower. Stepping under the hot water, she tried to figure out what was on her

81

mother's mind. Veranda remembered when she'd first mentioned she wanted to become a police officer thirteen years ago to follow in her father's footsteps. She had not been told much about her father, but knew he had been a federal law enforcement officer in Mexico, and that her aunts and uncles described him as a very brave man.

Veranda could still see the color drain from her mother's face when she told her she had applied for the Phoenix Police Department. Lorena begged her to reconsider, then sat her down to tell her the story of how her father died.

Before Veranda was born, Ernesto and Lorena Hidalgo lived in a modest home in a small town on the outskirts of Mexico City. Lorena's five younger siblings moved in with them when their parents died from a virulent flu epidemic. Ernesto, a detective with the Federal Judicial Police, investigated several brutal slayings committed by the newly formed Villalobos cartel. On the verge of indicting *El Lobo*, Ernesto was murdered and his office destroyed by fire. Ernesto's coworker called Lorena to warn her that Hector Villalobos was coming for her. Lorena, pregnant with Veranda, awakened her younger brothers and sisters and the group fled across the border, where they were granted asylum and ultimately became US citizens. Lorena reverted to her maiden name, Cruz, to make it harder for *El Lobo* to track her.

If her mother thought this knowledge would deter Veranda, she had been dead wrong. It only honed Veranda's desire for justice to a fine point aimed directly at the cartel that murdered her father in cold blood. She became determined to finish what Ernesto had started.

Once hired by the PPD, Veranda concealed her family's history with *El Lobo*, certain the Department would see a conflict of interest and not allow her to pursue the cartel's drug trafficking business. For the same reason, she kept quiet about how she really met Flaco. It would all probably come out someday, especially if Sergeant Diaz proved to be as persistent as he seemed.

Thoughts of the PSB sergeant's questions earlier that day caused Veranda's mind to return to her current situation. Sam would arrive soon. She turned the water off and toweled down her wet skin. She stepped out of the shower, pulled a satin bathrobe from its hook and wrapped it around her damp body.

Something caught her eye and her gazed flicked to the foggy bathroom mirror. A torrent of shock cascaded through her body as she focused on one thought: *Get your gun.* As usual, she had left it on the nightstand with her cell phone while she slept. Since she lived alone, she didn't secure the weapon.

She dropped her towel and inched toward her bedroom. Water dripped from her wet hair. She snatched her Glock from the nightstand and checked to be sure the magazine was still in place. Crouching down, she crept back into the bathroom. The fog had dissipated. A stylized logo was emblazoned in bright red lipstick across the mirror over the sink. The same image she had seen stamped on kilos of heroin. A wolf's head.

Someone from the cartel was in her house.

12

VERANDA YANKED HER FRONT door open at the sound of Sam's knock. His eyes widened as he took her in. Clad only in her robe, she held her Glock at her side. His mouth opened, but she pressed an index finger to her lips.

Sam jerked his service weapon from the pancake holster at his waist. Veranda motioned forward and sank into a tactical stance, knowing Sam would understand that she wanted him to conduct a strategic search of the premises with her.

The pair worked their way methodically through the house, back to back, clearing each room as they went. When they finally reached the bathroom, she stood from her crouched position and gestured to the mirror. "This is what I saw when I came out of the shower a few minutes ago."

Sam examined the image. "Looks like whoever did it left." He pointed to a tube of lipstick next to a hairbrush on the counter. "Is this yours?"

"Yes. I keep it in the top drawer with my brush. Someone must have taken them out."

Sam faced her. "Was it just this drawing and the envelope in the kitchen?"

"Envelope?"

"Letter-sized, manila, wolf logo, stuck into a cutting board with a carving knife."

Veranda's skin got clammy again. "I was looking for someone hiding. Didn't see that."

She followed Sam into the kitchen and spotted a beige envelope impaled by one of her knives onto a thick butcher's block. "We shouldn't touch it," she said.

He withdrew latex gloves from his back pocket and snapped them on. "I know the forensics guys will get their boxers in a wad, but this may be time-sensitive. We need to see what's inside."

"Do you think it's explosive?"

"No, but if you want to wait outside, I'll understand."

She didn't argue and didn't budge as she watched Sam carefully extricate the envelope from the blade. He opened it and pulled out a sheet of photo paper. She stepped beside him and peered over his elbow.

It was a picture of a male body sprawled on the sandy desert ground near a cluster of red rocks. The corpse was stripped to the waist, revealing a wolf tattoo over the heart. A gunshot wound smaller than a dime in the center of the forehead did not distort his features.

"Pablo," she breathed.

"Shit," Sam said through clenched teeth. "He'd be alive if we'd caught him this morning." He turned the picture over. "Nothing on the back."

She passed a hand through her damp hair. "This envelope and the drawing on the mirror weren't here when I came home. Someone broke into my house while I was asleep and left that stuff. They didn't need to leave a note. The message is loud and clear. They knew Pablo was a loose end and they've taken care of him."

Sam shook the envelope. "There's something else in here." A single unlit matchstick tumbled out, landing on the countertop. They both squinted at it. "Do you know what this means?"

She shrugged. "No idea."

He met her gaze. "You okay?"

Her flimsy bathrobe felt nonexistent. She felt vulnerable. Exposed. "I'm more angry than upset right now. I'll feel better once I get some clothes on."

"Don't touch anything in the bathroom. I'll stay out here and make phone calls. They'll go over every inch of this place."

———————

Forty-five minutes later, Veranda sat in Lieutenant Aldridge's Tahoe parked at the curb in front of her house. Commander Webster was in the front passenger seat next to Aldridge, who was behind the wheel. Veranda sat in the middle row between Sam and Sergeant Jackson. Marci and Doc were in the third row of seats in the back part of the vehicle. The team held their impromptu meeting in the air-conditioned SUV to avoid the intense outdoor heat.

The commander jumped when someone knocked on the front passenger door window. He cursed and powered it down. "What is it, Sergeant?"

Diaz stood on the sidewalk next to the door, iPad in hand. "Lieutenant Aldridge notified me that Detective Cruz's home was burglarized and that the cartel might be involved."

All eyes turned to the driver's seat. Aldridge reddened. "I felt it was important to keep PSB apprised of all developments. This may have a bearing on his investigation."

"That's why I came out immediately," Diaz said. "I can't conduct inquiries in the dark."

Heads in the car swiveled to Commander Webster. He looked annoyed. "There's a seat in the back row."

Marci and Doc slid over to make room for Diaz as he climbed in. Veranda avoided his gaze and looked toward the windshield.

Lieutenant Aldridge addressed the group. "After this blatant attack, we need to consider Detective Cruz's safety. We should reassign her to the Property Room, where she can consult with Detective Stark as needed and remain in the building at all times."

Veranda's nerves, already frayed after the burglary, snapped. "I won't go the Property Room!"

Her words hung in the air.

Diaz cleared his throat. "Actually, I want to go further than that." He paused. "I've put in a recommendation to move you into a safe house where you will stay until the investigation is completed."

Veranda's pulse ratcheted up. She swiveled to face Diaz. "You want to put me under house arrest?" She clenched her hands to prevent herself from throttling him. *The bastard!*

As if he sensed she was on the verge of violence, Sam spoke. "I need Detective Cruz with me. She can best help the investigation on the front lines where things are happening. We barely have any traction on this case and we've got to keep our momentum."

"You won't make headway if you're constantly dealing with threats and attacks," Diaz countered. "Detective Cruz is more of a liability to your investigation than an asset."

Marci narrowed her eyes at Diaz. "So, you expect the little woman to wring her hands and wait by the phone for the big, strong men to tell her it's safe to come out?"

Doc groaned as every eye turned to Marci. Her comment created the tension of an armed bomb inside the vehicle. And no one knew which wire to cut without causing an explosion.

Commander Webster broke the silence. "Detective Blane, no one is questioning Detective Cruz's abilities. We all know she's an experienced investigator and has the most expertise about the suspect. As her commander, I have to weigh the risks and benefits of her continued involvement in this case." He addressed Veranda. "You mentioned at our briefing that cartels don't usually target individual police officers in the States. Why do you think this happened?"

Veranda composed her thoughts. Her next words were critical to her position on the Homicide squad. "I believe Bartolo may have gone rogue. From everything I know about *El Lobo*, he would never sanction this break-in. He knows it would put his organization on everyone's radar."

"Is this move out of character for Bartolo?" Sam asked.

She recalled Flaco's comments to her a few days before his death. "According to my CI, everyone in the cartel avoided dealing directly with Bartolo. They knew he did drugs and was getting more paranoid all the time." She didn't add that even Bartolo's top sergeants were rumored to be afraid of his increasingly violent outbursts. No sense giving Diaz more ammunition for his campaign to lock her away.

Aldridge peered around his headrest to question her. "Are you saying Bartolo is acting on his own?"

"Likely. Nothing else makes sense."

"An irrational drug lord has targeted one of our officers," Diaz said. "That's reason enough for extreme precautions." He turned to glare at Marci. "I would say the same thing if Detective Cruz was a man, by the way."

Marci snorted and rolled her eyes.

"I've reached a decision," Commander Webster said. "I agree with Sergeant Diaz that we need to implement measures to ensure Detective Cruz's safety." Veranda opened her mouth, but Webster held up a hand. "However, I also agree with Detective Stark that we have the best chance of arresting Bartolo if she remains on the Homicide squad."

He gave Veranda a stern look. "You will move into a safe house immediately. Sergeant Jackson will know your whereabouts at all times." He glanced at the back row of seats. "And you will apprise Sergeant Diaz of any developments in the case."

Veranda slumped in her seat. It was a relief to keep working with Sam, but Diaz's comments still rankled. He seemed to dog her every move.

She reflected on her situation. A few days ago, her career was on track. She was the respected leader of her team, a seasoned veteran at the top of her game. She was in control.

Bartolo had pulled the rug out from under her. Now she was the rookie in Homicide. Her base of power, gone. Her life, disrupted. She had to battle on several fronts just to keep her badge. A knot formed in the pit of her stomach as another realization hit her. Something she had learned in her kickboxing classes. Bartolo was keeping her off balance. Not giving her time to recover from the onslaught of blows. As soon as she'd staggered back to her feet from his left jab, he sent her reeling with a right cross.

If he kept it up, he would win.

13

Villalobos family
compound, Mexico

ADOLFO VILLALOBOS WAITED IN the anteroom outside his father's office. He had called to schedule a private meeting with *El Lobo*, explaining that the information he had was too sensitive to provide over the phone. To his surprise, his father told him to fly to Mexico immediately to discuss the matter, instructing him to retrieve a package from the mole's drop point and bring it with him on the family jet. Adolfo had located a brick-sized parcel wrapped in brown paper and sealed in a tamper-proof plastic bag at the clandestine location where the mole occasionally left materials for pickup by the cartel. His father had assured him it wasn't contraband, but he would not divulge the contents. Instead, he threatened Adolfo not to break the seal on the packaging.

Adolfo ruminated as he held the parcel in his lap. Now was the time to further his plan. He glanced at his Rolex, certain his father kept him waiting on purpose—a deliberate show of his status as alpha.

Adolfo looked down at the carpet and was reminded of an incident from his childhood that occurred in this very room more than two decades ago. The four Villalobos children were waiting to speak to their father. Adolfo had been doodling to pass the time when Bartolo snatched his favorite pen from his hand. Adolfo's stomach twisted into knots as the memory flooded back.

"Kick his ass!" Carlos shouted over the din of his two older brothers locked in combat. Adolfo's nose bled freely onto the imported Persian carpet. Bartolo swept Adolfo's legs out from under him with a swift kick. The two younger siblings, Carlos and Daria, backed up to make space as they eagerly watched Bartolo pounce, pinning his older brother down with his heavier bulk. Adolfo cried out as his brother's fist smashed into his unprotected face, his nose making an ominous crunch. The younger children whooped and jumped.

El Lobo opened his office door and walked into the room. "What is going on here?" He did not shout, but all action ceased as soon as he spoke.

Bartolo looked up. "We were just settling an argument, Papá."

Their father gazed down at the scene in front of him. He seemed to assess each child. Bartolo was astride Adolfo's chest with a look of fierce determination. Carlos quivered with excitement, his eyes full of bloodlust. Daria, the youngest, could not suppress a giggle. And Adolfo, the oldest, quietly sobbed.

Adolfo saw his father slowly stroke his goatee. "Well, finish it then." He crossed the room to take a seat and watch his children.

Adolfo's nose had been broken in two places that day. His father had not allowed him to have it treated, saying he wanted him to see the result of weakness every time he looked in the mirror. Adolfo rubbed his crooked nose reflexively as the door to the inner sanctum creaked open.

His father's butler emerged and held the door open for him. Adolfo strode inside and the man bowed his way out of the office, firmly shutting the massive twin doors, leaving Adolfo alone with *El Lobo* in oppressive silence. His father took his customary seat behind the ornate desk and gestured to the leather chairs that faced it.

As Adolfo sat, he glimpsed the taxidermy stuffed wolf in the corner behind his father. Positioned on its hind legs, the enormous creature towered over seven feet tall. Its black fur bristled and fierce amber eyes blazed above razor sharp teeth bared in a predatory snarl. The wolf appeared to spring from the shadows to tear out the throat of any visitor who displeased *El Lobo*. Adolfo knew the animal had been placed behind Hector to face the visitor's chairs for precisely this effect. The wolf was vicious, feral, and deadly—like the man in front of it.

Adolfo shuddered. "I'm sorry to bring you disturbing news, *Papá*, but I felt you had to know."

Hector extended his arm across the enormous desk and addressed his son in Spanish. "Before we get to that, give me the package."

Adolfo rose to put the parcel in his father's hand and sat down again. His jaw hardened as he pondered the contents of the package. Why didn't his father trust him with information that the mole, an outsider, clearly had? He concealed his irritation and waited.

His father placed the package on the corner of the desk and met his eyes. "What involves the family or the business matters greatly to me, and you said you have news about both."

Adolfo took a deep breath. He had to proceed with care, project just the right note of brotherly concern while he laid the groundwork for his strategy. "I'm worried about Bartolo, *Papá*. The mole briefed me on the information he provided to you about my brother's recent... activity. This is part of a larger problem." He smoothed a crease in his slacks. "As you know, Bartolo decided to deliver a personal message to that Phoenix detective after he disposed of Pablo."

Hector's dark eyes were inscrutable. "Go on."

"Bartolo may have left forensic evidence behind when he broke into her house. The things he did made no sense. He drew our wolf emblem on her bathroom mirror using her lipstick, and left a photo of Pablo's body in her kitchen."

A muscle rippled in Hector's jaw. A sure sign that Bartolo had indeed acted without his father's knowledge. "Your brother's behavior angers me, but I will turn it to my advantage." His dark brows drew together. "I am already aware of the break-in. Do not waste my time."

Adolfo hastened to respond. "I'm concerned that Bartolo is becoming obsessed with this detective. She could have awakened and found him there. Shot him. Arrested him. He's not thinking clearly—"

Hector held up a hand and his son fell silent. "You said you also had news about the business?"

He affected a grimace. "Unfortunately, yes. I was going over our accounts and there are irregularities with Bartolo's part of the operation. Even after I deducted the losses we took due to Detective Cruz's task force, there was a substantial shortfall."

Sweat gathered in Adolfo's palms. The next part was critical. He locked eyes with his father and arranged his face into a look of deep concern. "*Papá*, I believe Bartolo embezzled money from his portion of our family account. I have documentation if you wish to review it."

"How much?"

"Two million US."

Silence.

"*Papá*, if I may?" Adolfo spoke softly. When he got no response, he hazarded, "Perhaps you might order Bartolo back to Mexico. Right now he handles our narcotics distribution from Phoenix, but he could oversee the grow operation here in Mexico instead." He swallowed. "Temporarily, until the storm passes." He folded his hands so they would not shake. "Then he could go back to Phoenix and take over his old position."

"And who"—Hector's baritone voice dropped to a rumbling whisper—"should be entrusted to run Bartolo's Phoenix operation in his absence? Pablo is gone too."

Adolfo dug a finger inside his starched collar to loosen it. "I could step in. It would also give me a chance to rectify his accounts. My area of responsibility, our finances, are in perfect order. My subordinates are very efficient and can keep things running smoothly while I divide my time."

"It would seem you wish to change your place in the pack, *mi'jo*." Hector eyed his son as he stroked his goatee. "Perhaps you will live up to your name after all."

Adolfo straightened at the reference to his given name. As the first born son, he'd been christened Adolfo, from the Latin *adolphus*, meaning "noble wolf." *El Lobo* had expected his eldest son to take over the family business. That had been the plan until Bartolo had systematically undermined him over the years. Bartolo took every opportunity to humiliate him and denigrate his accomplishments until he lost his favored status.

Hector rolled an ivory letter opener between his fingers. "Despite your assurances that you are ready to take over for your brother, I am not prepared to make such a move yet. I have many things to consider."

"What do you mean?"

"The embezzlement troubles me. Bartolo can buy anything he wants." Hector shook his head. "Why steal money when you are rich?"

Adolfo decided to drive the wedge in further. "Maybe he's planning something he hasn't told you about."

The flash of anger in his father's eyes told Adolfo he had hit the mark. "You accuse Bartolo of acting against me?"

He was in danger of going too far. "I'm not sure what's going on, but he is being very ... erratic. I hear he takes drugs. That could be it."

Hector studied the signet ring on his right hand. It bore the Villalobos family crest. "There might be an explanation for your brother's behavior toward Veranda Cruz. I gave him some information this morning. Perhaps he overreacted to the news."

Adolfo had not expected this. His stomach roiled with anger at the idea that his younger brother had been entrusted with a secret. "What did you tell him, *Papá*?"

Hector leaned forward, fixing his dark gaze upon his son. "Even the preliminary facts I gave Bartolo upset him. I will not share them with anyone else until I have the whole picture."

Adolfo raised his chin. "I'm not Bartolo. I can be trusted with sensitive information."

"Echoes from the past can reverberate into the future, *mi'jo*. This is an important lesson for you to learn, as I see you are willing to set in motion a chain of events that could change our family's fortunes forever."

Adolfo was used to his father's dramatic speeches. For *El Lobo*, every struggle was a fight to the death, and every obstacle, a Herculean challenge. This time, however, Adolfo sensed that what his father withheld could alter his plans. "I understand."

"No, you do not. But you soon will." His father leaned back in his chair. "This morning Bartolo called after he killed Pablo. At that time, I told him what I had learned about Detective Veranda Cruz." Hector returned the letter opener to its place on the desktop. "A check into her background revealed something ... remarkable about her history. Something I doubt she even knows."

"What is that?"

Hector rested his elbows on his desk and steepled his fingers. "I don't have all of the answers yet myself, but I am trying to fill in the missing pieces. When the time comes, I will explain."

———————

Thirty minutes later, Adolfo sank into the white leather seat on the family jet as it taxied down the runway of the airstrip next to the Villalobos compound. A leggy brunette strolled over to offer him a wine list to peruse during takeoff. He waved her away and she teetered on high heels to the front of the cabin and buckled herself in the jump seat.

His mind raced. The visit to the compound had been a partial success. He had managed to undermine Bartolo's position with their father, but he was still not sure of his place in the pack.

An idea began to form. He could take over all US operations if he garnered support from Carlos and Daria. He would start the propaganda campaign as soon as he returned to Phoenix. The only thing that stood in his way was Bartolo and, after what he gathered from his father's cryptic comments, possibly Veranda Cruz. He would figure out a way to eliminate both of them without drawing suspicion.

As he considered various plans in turn, awareness washed over him. He was reliving his childhood memory. They were all grown up now, but *El Lobo* still stood by to see which of his children would be the victor as they battled amongst themselves.

He vowed to himself that this time the outcome would be different.

14

VERANDA ALMOST COLLIDED WITH Sergeant Diaz as he blocked her path to the Violent Crimes Bureau conference room door. "I'm not finished with you yet, Detective Cruz." He stepped closer, his nose nearly touching hers.

She pointed over his shoulder. "I need to get into the war room. The entire team is waiting for me."

"Would you prefer to go over to PSB and have this conversation with a voice recorder on?"

She planted her hands on her hips at the threat of another official interrogation. "Look, I didn't deliberately exclude you. It's just that PSB was not the first thing that popped into my mind when someone broke into my house."

He relaxed slightly and lowered his voice. "Detective, I told you to keep me apprised of all developments. I find out from Lieutenant Aldridge about the shootout with Pablo. And about your burglary. *You* need to be the one to brief me, and do it in a timely manner."

"It won't happen again, Sergeant."

Now that the tension had eased, their stance felt too close. Almost intimate. The wood and spice scent of his aftershave filled her nostrils.

His eyes traveled down to her mouth. He seemed to sense the awkwardness and stepped back. "By the way, Detective Johnson filed his paperwork. There will be no criminal charges placed against you for shooting the truck driver during the interdiction."

She blew out a sigh.

"Before you get too relaxed, I'm still conducting the administrative investigation into whether you followed proper procedure during that incident."

Her face fell. "Right."

"Now that we understand each other, you can go into the meeting." He turned and opened the door to the conference room. "But I'm coming in with you."

All eyes turned to Veranda as she strode in. Head held high, she did not betray the inner turmoil her confrontation with Diaz had caused. She sat in the empty chair next to Sam, who scowled at the PSB sergeant taking a seat on the opposite side of the room.

Sergeant Jackson stood. "All involved teams are ready to report our progress to date. Before we get to today's incident, let's update the other related investigations." He turned to an olive-skinned man with thinning dark hair and a scraggly mustache. "Detective Johnson, you have the floor."

Johnson stood and flipped his notepad open. His voice had the rasp of a two-pack-a-day smoker. "The criminal investigation of Detective Cruz for the fatal shooting of the cartel truck driver, Oscar Ramirez, is concluded. The Prosecutor's office was notified through chain of command that no probable cause exists for an arrest. They have elected not to pursue an indictment." He looked at Veranda. "Criminally, you're clear."

She felt everyone glance her way and made a point of staring steadily back at Johnson. "I'm still following up on Ramirez's burner phone," he said. "Our forensic techs are working on it, but they're encountering problems. The phone appears to have been purchased recently and was only used to contact one phone number."

"That's good news," Tony said. "You can ping the location of the other cell phone."

Johnson shook his head. "It's been deactivated."

Marci sat forward. "Then you can get a phone dump on the second number. It's got to belong to someone in the cartel."

"We already subpoenaed the service provider for all of the data from the second phone," Johnson said. "But it'll take a couple of days to get a printout, and that's rushing it through due to exigent circumstances."

"So where do we stand?" Commander Webster asked.

"We can't retrieve any texts or phone numbers from the second phone yet, but we're working another angle. Both phones were bought in a lot with ten others at a local electronics store. We're in the process of cross-referencing the serial numbers to see if any of the cartel front company credit cards we know of were used to make the purchase. If so, we'll try to get a subpoena to do a dump on the other ten phones in the group." An excited murmur went around the room.

"That's going to take some time, so don't get too excited. It's a long shot." Johnson closed his notebook before he sat back down.

Sergeant Jackson looked at Doc. "You attended Flaco's autopsy this morning. Could you give us a quick overview?"

Doc stood, adjusted his glasses, and pulled out a thin binder. "Proximate cause of death was a slashing incised wound to the left side of the neck from the midline to the back that severed the jugular vein, carotid sheath, and artery and all tissue down to the spine, including the trachea and larynx. Immediate cause of death was exsanguination."

He flipped to the next page. "The ME found antemortem trauma in the form of contusions over much of the upper body. This is believed to have been caused by a blunt instrument. The left side of the sternum sustained a burn approximately ten centimeters in diameter depicting the head of a wolf apparently caused by the application of a heated branding iron."

Veranda winced at the mention of the wolf logo seared on Flaco's chest. If not for her, he would never have spied on Bartolo. Or suffered such a gruesome death.

"Anything different from what Crime Scene found?" Aldridge asked.

"Nothing substantive," Doc said and sat down. "We'll get the first toxicology results next week."

Veranda forced her mind to remain objective. She could grieve Flaco's death, and her role in it, later. For now, she had to focus on the facts and how they fit together.

Sergeant Jackson turned to Marci. "Any updates on the investigation into Pablo Moreno?"

Marci stood. "When Frank and I executed the warrant to search Moreno's domicile, we located ten grand in cash hidden in a shoe in his closet."

Sam leaned to whisper in Veranda's ear. "Why do they always hide stuff in their shoes? Do they think the smell will scare us off?" She grinned.

"He must've been in such a hurry to leave that he forgot about it," Marci continued. "We think it was a secondary emergency stash. We still haven't located his body or his vehicle, but we got some prints, fiber, and DNA. The lab has them in the hopper to run against the database. Of course, his house wasn't the crime scene, so it may not be much use. Also, his laptop computer was missing, so he must've grabbed it when he ran."

Jackson stood again. "If no one else has anything to add about our previous investigation, I'd like to move on to today's incident at Detective Cruz's house." He paused. When no one spoke, he turned to Veranda. "A photograph of our key suspect, apparently deceased from a gunshot wound, was left behind by whoever burglarized your home. Based on that, and the logo drawn on your bathroom mirror, we are wrapping this incident into our ongoing homicide investigation." He nodded at Webster. "The commander has authorized this."

Due to her experience in property crimes before going to DEB, Veranda was aware that other detectives would normally handle a residential burglary case. It made sense to her that the Homicide squad would investigate this incident due to the circumstances.

Sam fidgeted in his seat. Used to his calm demeanor, she wondered why he seemed agitated.

Jackson looked around the table. "I touched base with the Crime Scene supervisor earlier. The techs are still at the scene, and they expect to be there all day. We'll have another briefing tomorrow, and I've requested a representative from their unit to attend and provide a report of their initial findings."

Sam seemed unable to contain himself any longer. "Sergeant, let's quit chewing on the gristle and get to the meat." The room grew quiet. "Everyone here knows Bartolo broke into Veranda's house." He paused. "Or sent one of his cronies to do it."

"Your point being?" Jackson asked.

"Let's go rattle his cage." Sam looked around the table as if seeking support.

Aldridge drummed his fingers. "What do you propose?"

Sam leaned forward, his face red. "I propose going to his house and making sure he understands we know what he did and we're not going to put up with his bullshit."

Aldridge flattened his hand on the table and straightened in his chair. "Detective Stark, we don't have probable cause to arrest Bartolo or anyone else. That logo on the mirror is hardly sufficient to—"

Sam didn't wait for the lieutenant to finish. "I'm not saying we arrest him. I want to do a knock and talk."

Veranda turned the proposal over in her mind. There was no need for a warrant to conduct a consensual interview with a person of interest in an investigation. If Bartolo incriminated himself or decided to make an admission, they could stop and Mirandize him. That, of course, would never happen. Sam must have another objective.

"Look," Sam said. "He thinks he's untouchable. I want him to understand that the law applies to everyone. I also believe he's coming loose around the edges. Face-to-face contact at this point might make him get careless and make a mistake."

"Or it could make him come after Detective Cruz again," Diaz said.

Marci waited a beat before she spoke. "I like Sam's idea. I say we take the offensive. At least he'll know we can't be intimidated."

"I agree," Veranda said. "We need to take the fight to him. He's been yanking our strings from the outset. It's time to put him on notice." Sam gave her an approving nod.

Commander Webster cleared his throat. "Detective Stark, you bring up an interesting suggestion. This is not your average situation, however. I'm sure Bartolo Villalobos has his attorney on speed dial, and there's no way to catch him off guard with the kind of security detail he has at his disposal. I'll consult with the Prosecutor's Office before we go forward with this. I should have an answer for our briefing tomorrow."

Jackson stood, taking the floor again. "That's it for now. Everyone remember to report to the range for semi-annual qualification tomorrow morning." A chorus of groans traveled around the room.

Doc looked shocked. "With all this going on?"

Jackson sighed. "The range is booked months in advance. This is your time slot. It'll take less than an hour and it's required to keep your law enforcement certification." His tone brooked no argument.

As they stood to leave, Jackson spoke again. "A final note. Not to leave this room. We authorized a safe house for Detective Cruz while the investigation proceeds."

She had no interest in packing up and moving into a safe house. Doing so felt like running and hiding to her. The squad filed out of the conference room behind Commander Webster. She mulled it over as she trailed behind, then turned and went back into the war room.

"Detective Cruz," Aldridge said to her as he motioned to Jackson and Diaz. "The two Sergeants and I were staying behind to discuss your living arrangements."

"That's why I came back in," Veranda spoke quickly. "It really won't be necessary. I'll be extra vigilant from now on, and—"

"It's not up for debate, Detective," Sergeant Jackson interjected, handing her a piece of paper and a door key.

She glanced down at the address in Central Phoenix scrawled in black ink across the page and sighed.

Sam was waiting for her in the hallway when she walked out. "You look irritated."

"Tried to talk them out of the safe house." She showed him the paper. "No luck."

"You need help packing? We can grab a bite and I'll follow you to your place."

"I appreciate that, but I'm not hungry. I'll just…" She smacked her forehead. "Oh, shit!"

"What's wrong?"

"Today is my mother's birthday. With all the crap that happened this morning, I totally forgot." She looked up at Sam. "Every year they close the restaurant for the evening and have a huge party on the family property in South Phoenix. I've got to be there."

"When does it start?"

She glanced at her watch. "Right about now. I've got to get to my house and pack my stuff before I go to the party." A thought occurred to her. "I need to remember to get her birthday gift out of my closet." She turned. "See you at the range tomorrow."

———

Veranda pulled up to her house. A lump caught in her throat at the sight of crime scene tape around her property. She waved to her next door neighbor, Mrs. O'Shea, who darted back into her house and slammed the door. Veranda sighed and walked to the edge of the tape to speak to the uniformed officer stationed at the walkway to the front door.

She pulled out her ID. "Detective Cruz. This is my house."

He nodded. "They told me you'd be coming. Stand by while I get one of the CSI techs."

She waited while he disappeared around the side yard. The lump in her throat turned to ice as she considered how her personal space had been violated. She mentally added another score to Bartolo's tally. In addition to everything else, he had now successfully ejected her from her home. What else would he take from her?

A petite woman in white Tyvek coveralls emerged from the front door and followed the patrol officer to meet Veranda. "We were advised that you need to pack some belongings to relocate," the Crime Scene technician said.

"Yes, I won't need much. Can I go in?"

"Sure, we're finished in the master bedroom." She held out a plastic package with a folded crime scene suit. "But first you'll need to gown up."

Veranda tore open the clear wrapping and stepped into the coverall, fastening it over her clothes. She bent to tug matching booties over her shoes. She resented having to take such precautions to enter her own home. This was her sanctuary. Her place of peace and tranquility. Not wanting the CSI tech to see she was rankled, she plastered a smile on her face. "All set."

Once inside, she made quick work of stuffing two suitcases with business clothes, casual wear and shoes. She grabbed her black nylon go-bag that contained her tactical gear and gun belt to use at the range the next day. Spotting the little box covered in bright pink wrapping on the closet shelf, she slipped it in the duffel's side pocket. Hair products and a few cosmetics rounded out her packing. As she left, she made a silent vow to repay Bartolo in kind. She would drive him out of *his* home. In handcuffs.

15

AN HOUR LATE TO her mother's party, Veranda had to park among the line of cars and trucks along the gravel driveway leading to her family's cluster of homes. She nosed in behind her cousin Chuy's flashy purple Monte Carlo, tricked out with orange flames on the fenders and oversized exhaust pipes. Chuy owned a garage and had a reputation for eye-catching rides. She could at least be grateful he didn't bring the low-rider. The little ones loved the modified Coupe de Ville and begged Chuy to jump it up and down and hit the horn, which played "La Cucaracha." She chuckled at the memory of children dancing around the car and laughing.

Her shoes crunched on the rocks as she approached the yard. She loved coming to the three-acre corner lot in South Phoenix near the mountain. Over the years, she had watched each of her aunts and uncles build a *casita* on the land as they married and had children.

Now five homes nestled together on the property with a large open space for family gatherings in the center. This was the most loving environment Veranda could imagine. This site had seen weddings, holiday celebrations, *quinceañeras,* and even memorial gatherings after funerals. Her family had laughed, rejoiced, and wept together here.

Mariachi music filled the air and the scent of exotic spices wafted to her as she entered the interior courtyard at the center of the *casitas.* Every year, friends, relatives, and neighbors gathered to celebrate *Mamá*'s birthday. Veranda's mother was revered as the matriarch of their family and a compassionate presence in the community.

Her mother beckoned her. "You're late, *mi'ja.*"

"*Ay, Mamá*, things were a little … hectic at work today." No way was she going to tell the truth. Her mother would run to church and light enough candles to burn down a small village.

"Father Sanchez already gave the blessing, and everyone is eating."

Veranda stepped forward to embrace her mother. *"Feliz cumpleaños, Mamá."* She handed her the wrapped gift. "Happy birthday."

"You did not need to get me a present."

"Go ahead and open it now, *Mamá.*"

Smiling, Lorena unwrapped the box and opened the lid. "This is beautiful, *mi'ja.*" She pulled out a set of intricately worked earrings in the design of a cross using colorful beads.

"I got them at the church bazaar. They came from their mission to Africa. There are ladies in the village who make jewelry from local materials and sell the items to fund safe water programs." She knew her mother would appreciate the meaning behind the gift.

Her mother hugged her. "I will wear these with pride. Thank you, *mi'ja.*" She kept her arm around her daughter's shoulders and pulled her aside before they drew near the crowd gathered at the tables that dotted the lawn. "Veranda, did you get the message I left you on your phone?"

Veranda's face warmed as the guilt that only a mother could bestow rushed through her. "Yes, *Mamá*, but I got involved in an investigation and never had a private moment to call you."

"I must talk to you, *mi'ja*, about something very important."

"Everyone's here for your birthday, *Mamá*. It can wait until another time."

"No!" Her mother, who rarely used such a sharp tone with Veranda, quickly looked around to be sure she had not attracted attention by raising her voice. "Talk to me before you leave this party."

"Fine." Veranda wondered what could have upset her mother. "I promise."

Her mother put on a smile and strolled with Veranda toward the massive pavilion that took up most of the communal space. Her stepfather, Miguel Gomez, owned a construction business with twenty-two employees. Seven years ago, he and his men built the structure out of discarded lumber. He even installed a misting system with eight overhead fans and a fire pit so that they could have gatherings in any season.

Miguel approached, arms open to envelop her in a hug. "So nice to see you, Veranda."

"You too. What a great turnout. There must be close to a hundred people this year."

Miguel nodded. "Everyone loves your mother." He looked at Lorena with warmth in his eyes.

Her mother smiled back at him, then turned to Veranda. "I have a surprise for you."

Veranda's antennae went up. Her mother's smile had turned mischievous. "What's going on? I don't like surprises."

Lorena took Veranda's hand and escorted her around chairs and partygoers until they arrived at the center table Miguel had hewn

108

from reclaimed barn doors. She stopped, a bit stunned. Captain Cole Anderson from the Fire Department sat in front of a plate heaped with enchiladas.

He grinned and stood. "When I stopped by the restaurant to tell your mother I'd closed the investigation into the fire, she was kind enough to invite me to her party."

Veranda whirled to narrow her eyes at her mother, who affected a look of concern. "I must check on dessert in the oven, *mi'ja*. I do not want another kitchen fire." Lorena scurried toward the house.

Veranda rolled her eyes and plopped down on the picnic-style bench next to Anderson. "I had no idea my mother asked you to come. I hope she didn't strong-arm you."

"Are you kidding? I've been having a great time. Everyone has made me feel welcome. Besides, I've been told I'm not the only non-family member here."

She grabbed a slice of quesadilla from a nearby platter. "This is an annual community event. It gets bigger every time. Last year, one of the candidates running for the City Council showed up, claiming to be in touch with the Latino community." She rolled her eyes. "My uncles told him that if he could eat *Mamá*'s extra spicy picante sauce, he'd get our vote." She bit into the warm tortilla and groaned with pleasure as the gooey melted cheese touched her tongue.

Anderson lifted a bottle of water from an ice bucket and handed it to her. "What happened?"

"He ate the sauce and won the election." She looked around. "But I don't see him back this year for more."

Anderson laughed. "What's in the sauce?"

"The hottest peppers north of the border. We love it, but most *gringos* can't take the heat."

He winked. "I like spicy things."

Veranda opened her mouth to comment, but she was interrupted by a tap on her shoulder. "Father Sanchez, I'm so glad you could make it." Praying he hadn't overheard Anderson's somewhat suggestive remark, she stood and pecked the priest's cheek. "Please join us, Father."

He wore a traditional black short-sleeve shirt with a clerical collar. A silver crucifix on a thick chain dangled down to his chest. He shook his head. "I'm leaving to visit a sick parishioner. I just wanted to say goodbye since I missed you earlier."

"Had to work late." Veranda said taking a sip from the water bottle.

He wore a look of understanding. "I saw the stories about you on the news. I'm sure you've been very busy." He turned to Anderson. "Lorena told me you have a special guest tonight."

Veranda almost spit out her water. Is this what priests meant when they talked about mortification? Or was this purgatory? "Father, I don't know exactly what she told you but we're just colleagues." She turned her flaming face to Anderson. "Captain Anderson, this is Father Sanchez."

Anderson stood and shook the priest's outstretched hand. "Pleased to meet you." He leaned in and dropped his voice to a conspiratorial whisper. "I think Lorena may be getting ahead of her daughter where I'm concerned." He darted a glance at Veranda. "But give me some time and I'll work on Veranda. I can be very ... persuasive."

A wave of embarrassment washed through her as she eyed Anderson. *He's enjoying this.* She turned to the priest. "Father, we've had this conversation before. I've got some things to do before I'm ready to settle down."

Father Sanchez patted her arm. "Don't worry. I won't get my hopes up too quickly."

Veranda watched the priest turn to go before leveling a hard stare on Anderson. "What was that all about?"

His cheeks dimpled as he grinned down at her. "Getting in good with your mother and Father Sanchez can't hurt my chances." He craned his neck to look around. "Haven't met your stepfather yet though."

"*Ay, Dios mio.*" She flung her arms in the air. "You have no idea what you're messing with. A Latina mother is a force of nature. Put that together with the family priest and you'll end up walking down the aisle faster than you can say chimichanga." She lifted her chin. "My mother does not believe in casual flings."

His blue eyes focused on her. "Neither do I."

Still recovering from the intensity of Anderson's gaze as well as his words, she was caught off-guard by her tío Rico. He jerked her by the elbow, then pulled her onto a nearby dance floor made of heavy wooden planks. She laughed as her uncle stomped in time with the music and spun her around. The band, dressed in full mariachi regalia, clapped and whistled as they danced. She pulled her hair free from its ponytail and twirled faster. Shouts of *"Arriba!"* filled the yard. She caught a glimpse of Anderson leaning against a corner post of the pavilion, watching her every move.

Soon the pavilion was packed with gyrating bodies. Her other uncles, Juan and Felipe, pulled their wives onto the floor and joined Uncle Rico to dance. She treasured her family. They could be boisterous, loud, even interfering. And even so, she loved every one of them.

When the band took a break, she joined her relatives at their table and beckoned Anderson over to make introductions. As it turned out, her mother had already done the honors with the exception of her stepfather, who was up on a ladder checking one of the fans that hung from the pavilion's high ceiling.

Anderson leaned over to whisper in her ear. "Can you teach me to dance like that?"

She looked him up and down. "I don't know," she said. "I'll have to check out your moves to see if you've got what it takes." She shrugged. "For me, it's in the blood."

Tío Juan sipped a Corona. "This is what we're missing from our lunch service downtown." He spread his arms. "Dancing!" He and Felipe laughed.

Veranda looked at Anderson as she gestured at Juan and Felipe. "They have a food truck. Since the Spanish word for truck is *camión*, and since their last name is also Cruz, they named it *Casa Cruz Camión*. Six days a week in downtown Phoenix, they sell the best fast food in the city."

"No, *mi'jita*. The best in Arizona," Felipe said.

Juan plopped his beer down on the table. "At least until the inspector shuts us down."

Veranda leaned forward. "What are you talking about? You always pass inspection."

"Yeah," Juan said, "but they got a new guy. He comes to our truck Friday afternoon, automatically thinking we don't speak English. So he yells everything real loud and puts an *o* on the end of every other word."

Felipe screwed up his face and yelled. "Does this truck-o have a valid-o permit-o?" He accompanied this with gestures pantomiming a driver turning a wheel and a person holding a piece of paper.

Everyone around them laughed, but Anderson looked appalled. "No way."

"Welcome to my world, man," Juan said.

"What did you do?" Anderson asked.

Felipe chuckled. "Well, I didn't want to disappoint him, so I looked real confused and said, *No comprendo*."

Anderson raised his eyebrows. "You didn't pass your inspection?"

Felipe grinned. "Juan came out of the truck and showed him our paperwork. He got up real close to the inspector and shouted, 'Here-o is the permit-o.' The guy was pissed."

Anderson joined in the laughter as Juan and Felipe clicked their beer bottles in a toast.

"My only question is this," Juan said. "When he inspects the noodle truck, does he holler at them with a fake Chinese accent?"

Veranda stole a sip from Felipe's beer. "You two have the funniest stories."

Felipe shrugged. "You gotta have a sense of humor. Otherwise, you take life too serious." He looked at Juan. "We had enough trouble for two lifetimes. It was hard growing up. We only made it because of your mother."

Juan looked at Anderson when he spoke. "It was hard on this one too." He jerked a thumb at Veranda. "She pretty much raised herself while the rest of us cooked all night and sold burritos at construction sites during the day."

"That's why she started the kickboxing," Felipe said. "She had to look after herself because we were always out working. I didn't find out until years later how many fights she used to get into."

Veranda squirmed on the bench and pointed at her uncles. "They were my heroes. First they sold burritos out of the back of an old pickup, then got a food truck and expanded the menu, then a restaurant." She swept a hand out to encompass the property. "All of this is because of hard work."

Anderson gave her a warm smile. "And the best food in Arizona, I'm told."

She grinned back, impressed. *He definitely knows how to get in good with the relatives.* Her uncles gave approving nods to Anderson. She would have to watch out for this one. He had figured out that the way to her heart was through her family.

She excused herself and went into the kitchen to help bring out dessert. She found her mother layering sliced strawberries over a *tres leches* cake. Veranda's mouth watered as she looked at the decadent treat. "*Mamá*, can I help you with that?"

"I can do this, *mi'ja*, but you could sprinkle some more sugar on those churros."

Veranda crossed to the counter where a platter was heaped with an enormous pile of warm churros. She grabbed the sifter and began dusting them with powdered sugar. "Everyone's having a great time."

"Yes, and because of that I realize my birthday party is no time to have a serious talk with you." She sliced another strawberry. "You are right. It will have to wait."

"*Mamá*, I've never seen you this agitated. I can't imagine what could make you so upset."

"Let me ask you this." Lorena put her hands on her hips. "What is the real reason you were too busy to return my call?"

It was as if her mother sensed she hid something. "Like I said, things got busy at work."

Lorena shook her head. "Secrets and lies, *mi'ja*. They breed trouble." She turned back to the cake and picked up the sliced strawberries. "I see now that I have taught you too well how to hide the truth." She looked at Veranda over her shoulder. "No more."

"*Mamá*, what are you talking about?"

"Soon, I will tell you something I should have told you long ago."

"What is it about?"

"Do not be in too much of a hurry to hear what I have to say. It is not good news." Eyes filled with regret, she turned to face Veranda. "After our talk, things will never be the same."

16

VERANDA'S RIGHT HAND HOVERED above the grip of her holstered .45 caliber Glock. She wore her darkest shooting glasses to shield her eyes from the early-morning glare as she focused on the space fifteen yards in front of her. Knees slightly bent, muscles tensed to react, she drew in a steadying breath and waited for her cue.

The range master's voice carried over the loudspeaker affixed to the tower behind her. "Twelve rounds, six seconds." *Floom!* The target swiveled to reveal the silhouette of a man pointing a gun at her.

The sharp staccato of rapid gunfire on the line penetrated Veranda's ear protection. Each of her rounds punched a hole in the center ring marking the middle of the dark figure's chest. With a swish, the targets canted sideways again.

"Shit," Tony said from the next firing position to her right. "No way was that six seconds."

Veranda grinned. *Looks like he's about to spend some money.* Before they started their semi-annual qualification course, Sam explained to

Veranda that their squad tradition was for the person with the worst score to buy lunch for the team. The person with the best score got to pick the restaurant.

Without taking her eyes off the target, Veranda slid her thumb back, pressed the release button, and dumped her empty magazine. Weapon still trained straight ahead, she used her left hand to whip a loaded one out of its holder on her belt, shove it into the magazine well, and check to be sure it was seated. The entire process of reloading took her less than two seconds.

Moments later, the boards swiveled to face the group again, and shooting resumed. The range master directed all segments of the qualification course from the tower behind them. Each of her squad members approached closer to the targets at every interval, finally stopping at the three-yard line.

Veranda cut her eyes to Sam's target to the other side of her. Tight shot grouping. *Guess he took his Geritol today.*

The range master announced their final segment. "Two rounds, two seconds." Most police shootings occur in close proximity, and certification included rapid-fire, close-range drills.

Bam, bam! This time, the target boards did not turn to the side, but stayed in place for scoring. After glancing at hers, she ambled over to inspect Sam's target. His last two bullets had been center mass. Perfect.

She and Sam slid their ear covers off their heads to rest around their necks, then strolled down the line to watch the firearms instructors score the rest of the squad. They got to Tony first.

Sam rested a hand on the grip of his holstered pistol. "Damn, Tony, whose target were you shooting at?"

Tony looked sulky. "Bastards kept short-timing us."

Marci had a sly grin on her face when they approached. Her silhouette included several shots in the groin area.

"Holy shit, Marci," Frank said. "Just looking at that makes my boys shrivel up."

Marci opened her blue eyes wide in feigned innocence. "Oops. Did a couple of mine go a tad low?"

They moved to Frank's target, which Veranda thought looked pretty good. Finally, they ended with Doc.

He rubbed his nose. "Sinuses are messed up this morning. Couldn't see a freakin' thing."

"Yeah, right," Tony said. "Let's go clean our guns."

The squad walked to the open-sided stucco armory with its cement floor and metal roof painted terra-cotta orange. Once inside, they stood side-by-side to disassemble their weapons on the metal counter that ran the length of the building.

Marci took a bottle of gun oil out of the storage cabinet and brought it over to share with Veranda. "Did you get moved into the safe house okay yesterday?"

"Yes. And I didn't like waking up in a strange bed."

"You should have let us help," Tony said.

Veranda shrugged. "Only had a couple of small bags. Won't be there long anyway."

Frank grabbed a barrel brush from the cabinet. "Why is that?"

She pushed the lock down and released the slide from the frame. As she separated the components of her weapon, the scent of heated metal, oil, and gunpowder tingled in her nose and left a metallic taste on her tongue. "Because Bartolo will be in jail."

Sam picked up his pistol and ratcheted the slide of his empty Glock a few times to spread oil on the rails. "I like your attitude."

As they finished up, one of the range instructors Veranda recognized came up behind Sam and clapped him on the shoulder. "Sam Stark! I can't believe it."

Sam's rugged face split into a grin. "How you doing, Greg?"

"Fantastic. I've only got six months left in DROP."

Sam put down his weapon. "That's not possible."

Greg slung an arm around Sam's shoulders and addressed the squad. "Sam was my training officer when I was a booter."

Veranda surveyed Greg. He was muscular with a slight trace of love handles and a close-cropped afro suffused with gray. *He has to be pushing fifty. And Sam trained him?*

Greg dropped his arm. "When Sam and I rode together, we both had wheel guns. Try qualifying with those."

Veranda shook her head. *They carried revolvers.* "Did you guys wear a pair of six-shooters and ride horses?"

Sam chuckled as he looked at his squad. "Laugh while you can. We've got new recruits coming on every year who want to take your slots in Homicide."

Frank pointed at a group jogging toward them in tight formation. "Speaking of which, here they come."

As they passed in lock step, they glanced at the shed and shouted, "Morning, staff!"

Sam turned to Greg. "You still make them say that?"

Greg shrugged. "Promotes respect for senior officers. You should appreciate that."

Marci's lips curled into a smile. "Looks like they're headed for Hemorrhoid Hill."

Veranda remembered running up the peak located just behind the shooting range. It was a steep incline that punished even the most physically fit in the arid desert heat. "Poor bastards."

"Nobody forced them to sign up for the police academy." Greg showed the same level of compassion Veranda remembered in her instructors when she was a recruit.

"Everyone got fresh ammo?" Greg asked. When they all nodded, he put up a hand. "You're done. The targets have been scored and everyone passed." He glanced at Veranda. "Cruz had the highest score." He looked at Sam. "You gave her a run for her money though. Only one round out." He turned to Doc. "Malloy had the lowest score."

Tony pumped his fist. "Fuckin A, I'm not buying lunch!"

Marci gave him a sardonic look. "Real class, Tony."

"Hey, I had to buy last time."

Marci softened her voice and patted Tony's shoulder. "Remember how I told you to shave your knuckles so the hair wouldn't impede the trigger?" She glanced down at his hand. "It worked."

Tony rolled his eyes as the others laughed. "Hilarious, Marci."

Sam addressed the group as they walked toward their cars. He took on a serious expression. "I want you guys to know that I intend to push hard for us to interview Bartolo. I'd like your support at the briefing today."

"Sounds like the commander is okay with it if the Prosecutor's Office will sign off on it," Frank said.

Sam looked grim. "Depends on who you ask over there. Some of the county attorneys get real queasy about gray areas."

"I don't see a gray area," Marci said. "You have every right to interview anyone who comes up in your case." She waved a hand. "Of course, if he refuses to talk to you…"

Sam stopped at the door to his dented Malibu. "That would be a gray area. See you all in the war room."

Veranda drove out of the lot and stopped behind the other detectives' cars to wait for the main gate to open. They had all driven straight from their respective homes, and Veranda enjoyed wearing her black cargo pants and boots again. Anyone shooting at the range was allowed to wear tactical clothing, including detectives, who would not be expected to get their business clothes covered in dust and smeared with gun oil.

She glanced to her left and admired the rust-colored metal obelisk bearing the Phoenix Police Academy symbol. The tall structure was set on a three-tier square stone base. Each tier bore a word. *Pride. Honor. Integrity.* It was no accident that these principles were placed underneath the obelisk. They were the foundation of police service. She always took stock of her career when she passed through the gate. If the day came that she ever felt she did not represent these ideals, she would turn in her gun and badge.

———————

Veranda guzzled her second bottle of chilled water at the war room table in the Violent Crimes Bureau. All of the Homicide squad was in the room, along with the brass. She noticed a new face across the room and assumed it was someone from the Crime Scene Unit.

"Damn this friggin heat." Tony rubbed a cold bottle against the back of his neck before he cracked it open.

Sergeant Jackson looked unmoved. "You were out for less than an hour, and it was still early." He addressed the group. "Thank you for coming straight from the range. I wanted to have this briefing as soon as possible so we could get a jump on our day. We have a lot to do."

Jackson gestured to the opposite end of the table. "This is Technician Wallace. He's a forensic specialist with the Crime Scene Unit. I asked him to come this morning to give us a briefing."

The tall, wiry man with thinning auburn hair got to his feet. He cleared his throat and looked uncomfortable. "It's still early, and I want to make sure everyone understands that this is not a full report, but we've got some preliminary information from our initial investigation of the scene." He cast a nervous glance at Webster, as if he was concerned that the commander would be angry CSI hadn't completed their analysis in less than twenty-four hours.

Wallace pushed his thick glasses higher on the bridge of his nose. "These are a few photos from Detective Cruz's house."

Someone dimmed the lights as he touched a button on a remote for a laptop computer in the center of the conference table. A photograph of the front of Veranda's two-bedroom bungalow appeared on the white board. He clicked the remote again.

The lurid image of a wolf's head drawn on her bathroom mirror glared at them. "We verified that the detective's own lipstick was used to draw this. The suspect left the tube of lipstick on the countertop adjacent to her hairbrush, which may have been moved as he searched for a particular shade of red." He glanced around the room. "There were no latent prints on either item, which leads us to conclude the perpetrator wore gloves. We lifted several prints from around the house and have already eliminated those of police employees. No hits from any of the fingerprint databases."

Veranda's stomach clenched. She had been completely vulnerable in her sleep. Her Glock would be under her pillow tonight. Whether she managed to get any sleep or not, she would be ready.

The technician pressed his remote and a photo of Veranda's back door replaced the wolf. "We believe the point of entry was at the rear of the house. There are some pry marks on the door. The electrostatic dust print lifter obtained shoe prints from that location and several other points in the house."

He looked at Veranda. "We'll need to know who else has been in your house recently for elimination purposes, unless you wear a men's eleven and a half wide." There was a slight chuckle that died quickly. "We already took Detective Stark's shoe prints for comparison."

Pressing the remote again, he pointed at the image on the whiteboard. "This is the envelope found impaled by a knife in the butcher's block in the kitchen. The photo paper used is common color inkjet printer stock. No latent fingerprints on the photo paper."

He addressed Veranda a second time. "Again, Detective, we may need to take prints from any visitors for elimination purposes."

She inclined her head. "It will just be my relatives. Don't have much of a social life lately."

"We collected various hair and fiber samples to submit for comparison to the database." He tapped the remote again and a picture of a single unlit match appeared. "The match in the envelope is a standard cardboard bar style, detached from the rest of the matchbook and cover. We have it in our Ninhydrin unit to see if we get any latent evidence."

He leaned forward and closed the lid of the laptop. The lights in the room came back up. "That's a brief overview of what we have for now. Our guys are still working in the lab."

Jackson thanked Wallace, who looked relieved to sit down. "I'm sure there will be more information to follow. In the meantime, I met with Detective Johnson an hour ago to review his findings on Oscar Ramirez's burner phone."

Veranda recalled that Ramirez, the tractor-trailer driver she shot during the botched interdiction, had a cell phone on his person that was recovered and sent for analysis.

Jackson went on. "As you may recall, our electronics and forensics guys did a phone dump. There were no text messages and they harvested only one phone number, so they subpoenaed the service provider for data from the number that Ramirez called."

Veranda sat forward. "Did the printout come in yet?" She knew that such subpoenas, which normally took weeks, could be expedited in emergency situations.

Jackson held up a sheaf of papers. "It came in yesterday and we got several new phone numbers from it, which will require additional subpoenas." He frowned. "But the forensics unit can't crack the code on the text messages in the printout. All of the sent and received texts seem to be both encrypted and written in Spanish."

Veranda slapped her palm on the table. "Why didn't you tell me about this?" The room fell silent. She knew she should watch her tongue, but this was the kind of needless compartmentalization of information that bogged down investigations when she worked with federal agencies on the task force. She hadn't expected it on her own department.

She injected calm into her tone. "Flaco gave me the cartel's encryption ciphers. If you had told me about this, I could have decoded and translated the messages for you as soon as we received them."

Lieutenant Aldridge spoke. "Detective Cruz, we followed procedure. Until recently, you were under criminal investigation for shooting the suspect who carried the cell phone that led us to the encoded messages. It would have been an outrageous breach of protocol to turn evidence over to you under those circumstances."

Veranda squinted to prevent herself from rolling her eyes. *Sam's right. Aldridge is a desk jockey. He couldn't see the big picture if someone painted it on the side of a skyscraper.* "If I had access to the information from that device, we might be a lot further along in our investigation. How recent were the last phone calls and texts on that printout?"

"The cartel must have assumed the phone was compromised, because all transmissions ceased early yesterday morning after zero-three-thirty-hours," Jackson said.

She extended her hand. "Now that I'm not going to be charged with murder, can I have a look at the printout?"

Jackson picked up a manila envelope lying next to his notepad. "I made an extra copy for Detective Johnson's files."

Commander Webster signaled Jackson. "Give it to Detective Cruz." He turned to her. "If you're successful decoding the messages, I want you to translate them and provide me a copy immediately."

She nodded at the commander and took the envelope.

"Now that we have that out of the way," Commander Webster said, "I'll brief you on my conversation with the Prosecutor's Office."

The room grew quiet.

"He said he will authorize the knock and talk provided we do a reconnaissance first to ensure the safety of our detectives. He doesn't want us walking into an armed camp without current information about the layout and he wants backup staged nearby." Webster looked at Sam. "I wholeheartedly agreed."

Veranda sat forward. "Bartolo's listed residence is a mansion in Paradise Valley. I have the address in my folder from DEB. The last intel I had was that he stays there regularly."

Marci snorted. "Figures he would live in PV with all the other bazillionaires. I mean, why live in the city where his dealers sling dope on street corners?"

"Is his mansion near Camelback Mountain?" Frank asked.

"It is," Veranda said. "I've seen it on satellite photos."

"Can we use those satellite photos to do the recon?" Jackson asked.

Veranda shook her head. "We need a real-time look."

Jackson leaned back with a thoughtful expression. "What about the chopper?"

"Too noisy," she said. "Bartolo has countersurveillance. We don't want to attract too much attention until we're ready to make contact. That way, he won't beef up security before we get there."

Commander Webster spoke into the silence. "Before anyone asks, we don't have our mini-drone program up and running yet, so that's not an option either."

Sam stroked his mustache. "Sounds like the best way to do this is old school. We need to get an eyeball on his place."

"Excellent." Frank looked excited. "I hike Echo Canyon all the time. I can take you guys up the trail where we can get a perfect vantage point to see the whole area."

Veranda caught his enthusiasm. "That would work. His place butts up against the base of the mountain."

Everyone turned to Commander Webster. "Sounds feasible, especially if Frank hikes the trail regularly. I don't want to see any of you on the local news tonight getting rescued because of heat stroke."

"I'll take care of my team," Frank said.

"This is only supposed to be a recon," Webster said. "I want you to call me with your plan of approach after you get a look. My assumption would be that it's impossible to catch him by surprise. He'll have guards and a security system at his residence."

Sam smiled. "I have no intention of surprising him, Commander. I want him to know we're coming—just not too soon."

Webster stood, indicating they were dismissed. "You may as well keep your range gear on and head out now before the midday sun cooks you." He turned to Aldridge. "Why don't you lend them your Tahoe, Lieutenant? They can travel together."

Veranda grabbed the envelope and followed Sam out of the war room. "I'll just take this printout over to my desk. Shouldn't take me long to decode the messages."

Sam looked down at her. "Veranda, every minute we wait the sun gets higher in the sky and the temperature climbs. We're not all experienced hikers like Frank." He glanced at the packet in her hands. "There will be some downtime when we come off the mountain. We'll have to get cleaned up before we drop in on Bartolo. You can go through it then."

She tucked the envelope under her arm. "You're right. It can wait. Pablo can't get any deader than he already is, and I don't know what other information will still be pertinent since the cartel isn't sending messages or making calls to this number anymore."

———————

Veranda sat in the front passenger seat as Frank drove past the gate into the Echo Canyon Recreation Area and maneuvered Aldridge's Tahoe into the parking lot at the base of the trail. She checked her watch. "Still morning, but the sun's already blazing."

Frank pulled into a parking space. "Now you see why I insisted we wear our range hats and put sunblock on. The place we're going is only about a forty-five-minute hike, but you can get in trouble fast in the summer if you aren't prepared." He handed them each four bottles of water and a protein bar.

Frank pointed toward the trailhead. "There's a case in point." They watched as a heavyset man in his fifties struck out on the hardened dirt path. He wore a black tank top, nylon shorts, and flip-flops. "That dude has an eight-ounce bottle of water. And he probably thinks he's going to the farthest peak, which will take him all day at that pace." The man ambled along, his puffy face already reddening with the exertion.

"Yep," Sam said. "We'll see him on the news tonight loaded into a basket swinging under a helicopter."

Veranda got into line with the group as they started up the dusty trail. Twisted mesquite trees and short scraggly bushes dotted the rocky ground. She couldn't detect even a wisp of a cloud in the cerulean blue sky as the unforgiving sun beat down on them.

Tony brought up the rear. "This is fuckin' miserable. I can't believe tourists come here to do this for fun. Feels like a death march to me."

Frank called back to him from the front. "The tourists hike the entire trail. We're only going as far as the camel's nose. You should be grateful."

Veranda tilted her head back to take in the first, and lowest, peak. Camelback Mountain got its name from its resemblance to a camel kneeling on the ground with its head down. The largest peaks were in the camel's hump. The site they had selected for reconnaissance was at the camel's nose below its head. Frank was right; it could have been a much longer and steeper hike.

Tony shaded his eyes with his hand and squinted up. "Look, there's a buzzard circling overhead. Looking for lunch."

Frank's retort carried in the still air. "You should be scared, Tony. If that bird flies low enough, it'll get a whiff of your cheap cologne and think you already died. Probably start pecking your eyes out."

Veranda laughed with the others, enjoying the camaraderie of the banter. In the excitement of working the case, she had almost forgotten her assignment would end soon. She had come to think of this group as her team. She was surprised when a knot formed in her throat. It would be hard to leave them behind. And where would she go? Probably back to a precinct to work a beat. She enjoyed patrol, but her passion was investigation.

Veranda rarely hiked, but she loved the bleak beauty of desert mountains. The trail switchbacked around massive boulders as they climbed up the lowest peak. Coppery brown outcroppings jutted out at odd angles. Vegetation grew sparser the higher she went, with only a few hardy bushes peeking out from among the rocks. Tiny lizards darted across her path, scampering into holes at her approach. Despite its barren appearance and unforgiving terrain, life was everywhere in the desert, if you looked closely.

When they reached the shade of an enormous boulder, Frank stopped them for a water break, ordering them to eat their protein bars.

Sam pointed up the trail. "Not much farther."

———————

Veranda reached the observation point first. She plunged a hand into the roomy side pocket of her cargo pants, pulled out her binoculars, and scanned the panorama below. The area was called Paradise Valley for good reason. Surrounded by desert, it featured lush vegetation and looked like an oasis sprinkled with mansions on oversized private lots.

Sam came up next to her and looked through his own binoculars. "Which one is Bartolo's place?"

She dialed her lenses to focus on a Mediterranean-style estate with a terra-cotta tile roof that sprawled over the largest lot. She pointed it out to the others.

"Of course," Sam muttered. "The biggest one."

Veranda studied the wraparound observation deck where she spotted a telescope. As she watched, a man exited a covered portion of the terrace and walked the perimeter of the roof. "Looks like a guard making the rounds." The man did not look up in their direction before he disappeared inside.

Sam chuckled. "Damn, you just can't get good help."

Veranda swung her binoculars to the back yard. Her gaze took in the negative-edge pool with attached hot tub, fire pit, and putting green. The front of the house featured an enormous three-tiered fountain surrounded by a travertine courtyard. Palm trees lined the entire length of the cobblestone driveway, which ended in a guard shack next to a massive wrought iron gate.

Doc gave a low whistle. "It's got everything but a moat and a dragon."

Marci angled her binoculars to the right. "He doesn't need a dragon when he has that."

Veranda had noticed it too. "What is that thing?" A guard had just stepped into view around the side of the house with a dog on a tight leash. The beast looked like a wolf.

Doc's voice went up a notch. "That can't be a wolf. It's not legal to keep them as pets."

Veranda's tone was derisive. "It's probably a hybrid Bartolo's passing off as a Malamute or something. It's just like him to bend the law so he can own a wolf."

Sam put his arms down and turned to the group. "Let's sum up what we've got." The others stopped watching and gathered in a circle. "There's no way Bartolo isn't going to see us coming a mile away."

Veranda pushed back a lock of hair that had escaped her ponytail. "The guard at the gate will ID us and ask us what our business is as soon as we pull up."

Sam didn't look concerned. "That's fine. It's not about the element of surprise. This is to let Bartolo know we're not intimidated by his toys or his goons and that we'll continue to investigate him no matter what."

Veranda arched an eyebrow. "So we just want to piss him off?"

"Exactly."

"I'm all in favor of that," Marci said. "But is there any danger of an overreaction from his goon squad?"

Sam shook his head. "Not the way I intend to play it. Veranda and I will approach the house alone, so it doesn't look like the SWAT team is coming with an arrest warrant or anything. In this kind of situation, low-key works best."

"Makes sense," Doc said.

Sam continued. "We'll need to let the Paradise Valley Police Department know that we're here on official business though. I know the chief. I'll give him a call and explain that it's a knock and talk only, and we don't expect trouble. I'm sure he knows Bartolo lives there and exactly who he is, but since Bartolo's not committing crimes in PV, there's nothing his force can do about it."

"Oh, I'm sure he's the model resident around here," Veranda said. "Keeps to himself. Doesn't make trouble. Ideal neighbor as long as you don't send your kids to his house to trick or treat or sell Girl Scout cookies."

————————

Veranda maneuvered the Tahoe through downtown traffic as she listened to Sam's cell phone conversation on speaker. He'd called Commander Webster to advise him what they'd found and gotten approval for their planned interview with Bartolo. Webster said he would pre-alert the SAU tactical team and request a contingent to stage a couple of miles from the mansion. As Sam disconnected, she drove into a parking lot crowded with a cluster of gourmet food trucks offering fare from around the globe. She had decided to cash in her reward for scoring highest at the range by visiting her Uncle Juan and Felipe's truck in downtown Phoenix on the way back to headquarters. The team sat on a nearby patch of grass, where they ate burritos wrapped in foil. Her heart soared when they all raved about the taste. Doc was overjoyed at the prices.

"You don't have to go to a fancy restaurant to get gourmet food," Veranda said. "You just have to know where to find the good stuff."

She drove the team to the garage at headquarters after their lunch. The sweaty, exhausted group traipsed into Sergeant Jackson's cramped office.

Jackson accepted the proffered key ring from Veranda and wrinkled his nose. "Why don't you all head home to clean up and change. We'll meet in the war room in three hours. I know that's not much time, but I want to get this interview with Bartolo wrapped up today." They nodded their agreement and left.

————

As Veranda pulled up to the two-bedroom stucco safe house in Central Phoenix, she realized it was not that different from her own place. But she could never think of it as home. She took out the piece of paper stating the entry code, unlocked the front door, and deactivated the alarm after stepping inside. The furniture looked like it came from a yard sale, and probably did. Veranda showered and changed into a navy blue pant suit with a white silk blouse. She scraped her long hair into a French twist high on the back of her head and slipped into a pair of black pumps.

She checked her watch. Plenty of time to review the printout from the cell phone service provider Sergeant Jackson had given her earlier. She retrieved the manila envelope, slid out the sheaf of papers, located the file that contained the encryption cipher, and started to translate the texts.

She flipped back to Sunday, right before the interdiction, and found an outgoing phone call to Oscar Ramirez's cell phone number. *That must have been the call telling Ramirez to change routes*. Sure enough, a half hour later, there was an outgoing text sent to a group of numbers. She deciphered the message. REPORT TO THE SECOND WAREHOUSE NOW. BOSS DISCOVERED A SNITCH.

Guilt clawed at Veranda. This message had instructed the entire group to attend Flaco's execution. She could tell by the way it was worded that Bartolo had not sent the text. *So this phone dump wasn't from Bartolo's phone*. Judging by the fact that the originator had sent orders on Bartolo's behalf, Veranda surmised the printout was from Pablo's cell phone. Bartolo's second-in-command would have the authority to summon his men.

This printout was a gold mine. They now knew every number in Bartolo's group and could subpoena the service provider for records from all of them. Even though it would take several days, she looked forward to the next batch of printouts from the other numbers. They would yield even more fruit. Unfortunately, because these were all burner phones, she couldn't use the information to make a case against Bartolo without a substantial amount of supporting evidence.

She continued through the pages, reading several innocuous texts that were not encrypted. Apparently, mundane messages about lunch or dinner didn't require security. Her finger traveled down to another coded text, an incoming message received on Monday. Veranda decoded it quickly. SHE'S BEEN TRANSFERRED TO HOMICIDE. NEED TO TALK. She put a star next to that number, certain it had to be Bartolo telling Pablo about her reassignment. *He found out two hours after I did.* Her skin prickled. That hadn't been in any media reports. Something was very wrong.

Her apprehension grew as she continued to work through the messages. When she decrypted and translated the final text, icy fingers of dread crept down her spine as the full realization of her situation crashed in on her. What would she do now? Pulse pounding, she glanced at her cell phone but didn't pick it up. Who could she call? She thought of Sam. Could she even tell him?

17

VERANDA THREADED THROUGH THE warren of cubicles in VCB to her borrowed desk. During the drive over, she had considered what she had learned from the printout. Her first inclination had been to keep the information to herself, but she realized that this problem was too great for her to deal with alone. She had come to the conclusion that if she couldn't trust Sam, there was no one on the entire department she could turn to.

She sat down and motioned to Sam. "Come here," she whispered.

Sam pushed back from his keyboard and crossed the narrow passageway to peer over her shoulder as she sat at her desk. "What's up?"

Veranda pointed at the sheet of paper in her hand. "I've decoded these texts from the printout Sergeant Jackson gave me. Fortunately, it's the same cipher they've been using for months, the one Flaco gave me."

"What do the messages say?"

She lowered her voice even further. "Look at this word." She touched the tip of her pen to the printout.

"*Topo*?"

"It means 'mole' in Spanish."

"I don't follow."

She had to remember that Sam couldn't read the message. "The text around it translates to 'Mole says police will watch your house at five. Arrest at six. Leave now. Meet at second warehouse.'" She raised her eyebrows. "The term 'mole' has the same meaning in Spanish as in English. It's used to refer to an imbedded spy."

He looked incredulous. "A cop? One of us?"

She nodded. "Remember when we couldn't figure out how Bartolo knew where to dump Flaco's body?"

A look of dawning comprehension crossed Sam's face. "Of course. Someone on the Department could have learned DEB's location and obtained a roster of employees assigned to work there."

She spoke quickly. "But they couldn't have accessed DEB's confidential informants or ops plans because they're kept in a separate database. That's why the interdictions were all successful." She tapped her chin. "So we know the mole doesn't work out of DEB."

"That last text you showed me." Sam's expression darkened. "Pablo was tipped off that we were about to arrest him."

She shook the page. "This explains everything."

Sam checked to see if anyone was within earshot. "Is there something in that printout that points to an ID on the mole?"

"Nothing. I looked through all of it."

Sam dragged his chair over. Head close to hers, he murmured, "Let's try to narrow it down."

She thought back over the past two years. "Like I said, it couldn't be anyone from DEB, or we wouldn't have had so many successful interdictions. The same is true for SAU. They were deployed with us on every major bust."

"Agreed. That leaves Homicide and any command staff personnel who get briefed on our investigation."

Something clicked in Veranda's brain. Briefings. "Wait," she said. "You should've heard Diaz ripping me a new one for not keeping him in the loop. He gets regular briefings on what I'm doing while he's investigating me, plus he keeps butting in to all of our meetings."

"Don't forget that he reports all of that information up his chain of command in PSB, so everyone above his pay grade has access to what he knows."

"Normally PSB would look into something like this mole thing. Who investigates PSB?"

Sam appeared to give it some thought. "I've got an idea." He glanced at his watch. "There's one person we can count on to be above suspicion. Stay here while I make a phone call."

"Hold on, Sam."

"What?"

"Commander Webster told me to immediately report any findings."

Sam put his hands on his hips. "I thought you narcs were world-class bullshit artists."

She put her palm to her chest in mock astonishment. "Are you telling me to blatantly disregard a direct order from a command staff officer?"

"Would you prefer to call Bartolo personally and tell him we cracked his code?"

She grinned. "If I had Bartolo's direct number, I'd ask him if he's ready for an orange jumpsuit."

Sam furrowed his brows. "That's just the kind of smart-ass attitude that drives coked-out drug lords over the edge." She could see a hint of a smile buried in his mustache. "We've still got half an hour until our meeting. Let me see what I can do."

Sam pulled his cell phone out and flicked through his address list. He tapped the screen and waited. "Hey there, stranger. I hope this isn't a bad time." He paused. "Well, I wouldn't call you directly if this wasn't important. I need to speak with you privately. It's urgent." Veranda held her breath until Sam nodded. "Okay. I'm bringing someone with me. We'll be there in two minutes." He disconnected and turned his attention to Veranda. "All set."

"Who was that?"

"An old friend." He stood and pushed his chair back to his desk. "Let's go."

She followed Sam in silence as he walked down the stairwell out of VCB. She thought he would leave through the lobby, but he kept going down below the first floor. She was completely perplexed when he entered the basement level. Then she remembered that the headquarters building, which housed VCB on the second floor and the executive offices on the fourth floor, also contained a fitness center in the basement. Sam pushed open the door to the gym.

The room was deserted except for an athletically built man in gray cut-off sweats and a white T-shirt soaked with perspiration, straddling a weight bench. As she drew closer, Veranda recognized the close-cropped salt-and-pepper hair and pale green eyes of Steven Tobias, whose official title was Chief of Police for the City of Phoenix.

"Please excuse my appearance." The chief mopped his forehead with a nearby towel. "When you told me it was urgent, I didn't want to make you wait until I showered."

Sam extended a hand. "Thank you for seeing us, Steve. I'm sorry it has to be under these circumstances."

The Chief wore a concerned expression as they shook hands.

Sam nodded at Veranda. "This is Detective Cruz, formerly of DEB and now on my squad."

The chief turned to shake her hand. "It's nice to put a face to the name I've been hearing so much about over the past few days."

Veranda shifted her feet, unsure which one of her fiascos he referred to. She grasped his hand briefly. "Pleased to meet you."

Sam looked at Veranda. "Chief Tobias and I went through the academy together. We were booters on the same patrol squad at the old Central City Precinct." He turned to the chief. "Thanks for seeing us on short notice."

"So tell me what's going on."

Sam came right to the point. "Steve, someone on our department is informing for the Villalobos cartel." He stated this as fact, not suspicion.

When the chief remained silent, he explained how Veranda had translated and decoded the texts from the printout of the phone dump on Pablo's cell. Chief Tobias listened closely, his penetrating gaze occasionally flicking to Veranda.

When Sam described how they eliminated all bureaus from suspicion except Violent Crimes, Professional Standards, and upper management, the chief broke his silence.

"I have full confidence in my executive staff, Sam."

Sam put both palms up. "I understand. You work closely with them every day. All I'm saying is we can't be sure about them yet because they have access to sensitive information about the murder investigation."

"As they should." Chief Tobias appeared to resent any suggestion that the upper echelon could be compromised.

Sam plowed on despite the growing tension. "They would be interested in this particular homicide because the suspect is high profile, at least in law enforcement circles."

The chief grew pensive. He absently picked up a dumbbell and began a set of curls. "So, if I take VCB and PSB off the table, I'll need someone else to look into this."

Veranda sighed with relief. Chief Tobias believed them and was ready to take action.

Sam waited in silence. The chief switched to the other arm, then stopped in mid-curl. "I've got the exact person for the job." He smiled broadly at Sam. "Ken Murphy."

Veranda hadn't heard of him, but Sam grinned in apparent recognition. "Commander Murphy."

"He's in the perfect position to handle this." The chief plopped the weight on the mat with a dull thud and reached for his cell phone on a nearby bench. "He's in charge of FIB."

Veranda considered this. Among its many other duties, the Family Investigations Bureau housed the Special Investigations Detail, a squad of detectives responsible for investigating criminal complaints against city employees.

She corrected her thought. Criminal complaints, that is, that didn't involve death. Those were investigated by the 9-9-8 Squad, as her fatal shooting had been. Any other kind of criminal activity fell under the purview of FIB.

This was even better than PSB. If criminal charges were brought against the mole, the case would already be in the right hands. Also, FIB had no involvement with any part of the investigation up to that point and therefore was above suspicion. The chief's reasoning impressed her.

"Ken is completely trustworthy," Tobias said.

Sam nodded. "But how are you going to get him away from his regular duties without explaining everything to his chain of command?"

A wide smile creased the chief's weathered face. "Sometimes it's good to be king. I'll just let Assistant Chief Delcore know that I need the FIB Commander for a special investigation." He spread his hands. "Done."

For the first time in her career, Veranda entertained the idea of going for promotion. It would be nice to be the one who called the shots. She never thought about what she would do after she brought down the cartel. She had been focused on that goal for so long she hadn't formed a plan for the future.

"Thank you, Steve," Sam said. "Detective Cruz and I are due at a briefing on the second floor. We aren't telling anyone in our chain we spoke to you."

"I understand." Chief Tobias picked up his phone. "I'll back you up when this comes out. But you'll need to give Murphy a full briefing ASAP."

"We're about to do a knock and talk with Bartolo Villalobos. I'll call Murphy as soon as I'm clear."

Chief Tobias pointed at Sam. "See that you do."

Sam grinned and turned to leave. As Veranda followed him up the stairwell, she thought about their predicament. "Sam, whoever the mole is would have told Bartolo that I have the printout by now."

"Which is why your expert bullshitting will come in handy in our briefing. You need to convince everyone that, despite your best efforts, you couldn't crack the code."

She waved a dismissive hand. "I can do that. But what about the fact that Bartolo already knows we're coming to see him?"

"Won't make a difference. We knew we weren't going to surprise him anyway."

They had arrived at the war room door. Veranda pushed it open and strode inside. As she looked at the faces around the table, a thought crept into her mind. *One of these people might be the mole.* It occurred to her that one of the most insidious things about having a spy in the Department was the way it sowed distrust. Made her suspicious of everyone around her.

Commander Webster called the meeting to order. "Paradise Valley police are aware of our interview." He inclined his head toward Sam. "Thank you for reaching out to them."

"Are you prepared to head out now?" Lieutenant Aldridge asked.

"It will just be Detective Cruz and me," Sam said. "Anything more than that and Bartolo's goons could overreact thinking we're serving a warrant."

Webster folded his hands on the table. "I concur. SAU is staged a few miles away, so no one will see them. They'll be monitoring your radio frequency if you need them." He turned to the others. "Sergeant Jackson has assignments for the rest of you while Detectives Stark and Cruz are gone."

Sam and Veranda pushed back from the table.

Jackson held up a hand. "Before you go, Detective Cruz, did you have any luck deciphering those texts?"

She drew her brows together. "I worked on that data for over an hour. Turns out the codes Flaco gave me were either wrong or obsolete." She shook her head. "I can understand why the forensics guys couldn't make heads or tails of it. Neither could I." She ended with a bright smile. "I want to keep trying though."

"Sure, keep the stuff. It's useless to us until we can read it." Jackson waved her off and she trailed Sam out the door.

"You definitely sold it," Sam muttered as they walked down the hall.

Unaccustomed to wearing pumps, Veranda was disturbed by the *clack* of her heels on the tile floor in the lobby as they left the building. *I'll never get used to these things.* She lengthened her stride to keep pace with Sam as they followed the sidewalk to the parking lot. "Let's go over our strategy for the interview. Unlike you, I haven't been in Homicide for fifteen years, and this is our first tag-team interrogation together." She glanced up at his rugged profile. "How do want to play it?"

"We don't have a warrant, so he has to agree to talk to us at the outset. That's our first challenge. Assuming he's at home." He reached the clunker Malibu, muttered something under his breath, and opened the door. "I'll take the lead, but feel free to jump in any time." He slid behind the wheel. "You know more about him and his background than I do, so watch his body language. You narcs are supposed to be good at reading people."

She opened the passenger door, eased into the scorching vinyl car seat and buckled herself in, wincing when her fingers touched the heated metal catch. "A necessary skill, but I've never met Bartolo in person, so I may not pick up on changes in his normal behavior patterns."

"Don't worry, I'll crank him up. You'll have plenty of opportunity to watch his reactions. I'm going to put that bastard on notice that his people may grovel to him, but he's going to take it up the ass like any other inmate when he goes to the pen." His jaw hardened. "Because that's where we're going to send him."

"You said you wanted to rattle his cage." She grinned. "That should do the trick. Bartolo's not used to answering to anyone but *El Lobo*. And the burglary of my house tells me he may not even be listening to his father anymore."

"I've been thinking about that. What does it mean when a rich, powerful drug lord goes rogue?"

She drew a deep breath. "It means we could be walking into a buzz saw."

18

VERANDA TILTED HER HEAD back to admire the elegant date palms that lined either side of Bartolo Villalobos's cobblestone driveway. A massive wrought-iron gate decorated with an elaborate shield blocked the main entrance.

"When they see us drive up in this beater, they'll think the lawn service is here," she said.

"Jackson won't let me have a decent car until he gets over that unauthorized stakeout we did," Sam said as he pulled up to the guard house, positioned on the left outside the gate. The closed-in structure bore a coat of arms that matched the one on the gate. She recognized the Villalobos family crest from her research into the cartel in DEB. Sam powered the window down as a muscular man wearing a black military-style uniform signaled them to stop.

Sam slid his credentials out of his pocket and held them up before the guard had a chance to request them. Veranda couldn't see a weapon on the gate sentry as he looked at the identification, but she assumed he was armed.

"Why are you here?" the guard asked in heavily accented English.

"To see Bartolo Villalobos."

"You cannot see him without an appointment."

Sam's jaw tightened. "This isn't a damned dentist's office. We're on official police business."

The guard sneered down at them. "Wait here."

Veranda grinned as the guard closed his window and picked up a phone. "Smooth, Sam."

"Pretentious bullshit doesn't sit well with me."

The guard opened his window. "Señor Villalobos will see you. You will drive around to the servants' entrance in the back." The gate glided open.

Sam pulled forward and followed the driveway around the fountain. He exited the circle onto a narrow lane that wound around the side of the Mediterranean-style mansion.

As they turned another corner of the estate, she spotted a tall burly man wearing dark sunglasses and a black tailored business suit. He stood at attention in front of the rear door with his hands behind his back. "Not the butler type," she said. "Looks like muscle."

The man's dark hair was gathered into a ponytail tied at the nape of his neck. His pockmarked face was inscrutable as he stepped forward when they ground to a halt. After they got out, the bodyguard approached Sam as if to frisk him.

Sam rested a palm on the butt of his gun. "Lay a hand on me and I'll shoot you where you stand."

The man stopped, then glanced at Veranda. She translated Sam's comment into Spanish in case he hadn't understood. He appeared to give the matter some thought.

Veranda rolled her eyes and spoke in Spanish again. "We're police. We carry guns. And there is no fucking way we're going to turn them over to you. So take us to your boss." She paused. "Now."

He gave her a withering stare but turned and strode to the back door.

Her shoes echoed on the travertine tile floor as they made their way down a cavernous hallway toward the front of the house, following their escort under soaring curved archways and past lush potted plants. Enormous oil paintings adorned the cream-colored walls.

The bodyguard opened a set of mahogany doors and stood to one side. Sam and Veranda entered a formal living room. Light glittered from a crystal chandelier hanging from the coffered ceiling. Bartolo sat on a chocolate brown leather chair. He dragged a hand through his unkempt mop of curls and removed his sunglasses, revealing red-rimmed eyes. His silk shirt clung to his body, showing signs of dampness. He didn't rise but gestured to his bodyguard. "*Gracias*, Camacho." Dismissed, the man closed the doors behind him as he left.

Bartolo's eyes traveled up and down Veranda. "The photo of you I saw on the news doesn't do you justice, Detective Cruz."

She would not let him see that his reference to her humiliating expulsion from DEB bothered her. She raised her head to meet his eyes. "It's nowhere near as attractive as your mug shot."

He gave a bark of laughter. "It is a pleasure to finally meet you in person."

So this was Bartolo Villalobos, she thought. Lord of the Underworld. Drug kingpin. Arch nemesis. He was taller than she imagined, with a powerful physique. He couldn't have been using very long. His body didn't have that wasted look she had come to associate with junkies. She studied his demeanor. He exuded arrogance, sitting on his overstuffed chair like it was a throne. She decided he was every bit the dangerous enemy he seemed.

Aware that Sam intended to take the lead, she remained quiet. Better to assess Bartolo before she continued.

He glanced over at Sam, as if barely interested, and raised an eyebrow. "And you are?"

"Detective Sam Stark. Homicide." Neither man made a move to shake hands.

Uninvited, Sam sat on the matching leather sofa opposite Bartolo. Veranda settled herself on the other end of the overstuffed cushion.

"Please, have a seat," Bartolo said in a sarcastic tone. "You mentioned official police business at the gate?"

"Let's not waste each other's time, Mr. Villalobos," Sam said. "You know why we're here."

"I have no idea. Why don't you enlighten me?"

"Three days ago Guillermo Valencia was murdered. His body was dumped in the Phoenix Police Drug Enforcement Bureau parking lot."

Hearing Sam mention Flaco's full name reminded Veranda that her informant had a family. He wasn't just a code name in a database. He was flesh and blood; too young to be a casualty in the drug wars. His death would always haunt her.

Bartolo knit his brows. "I saw a story about that on the news. In fact, that was how I recognized Detective Cruz." He cut a penetrating gaze to her before turning his eyes back to Sam. "I can't imagine why you would bring this up to me. I don't know the man."

"We suspect the person who drove the body to the parking lot was Pablo Moreno."

Bartolo's eyes narrowed a fraction. His jaw muscle twitched before he relaxed his features, as if to hide his reaction to the mention of Pablo.

Sam, apparently noticing the unguarded moment, continued. "Unfortunately, we never got a chance to interview Mr. Moreno. He disappeared after we chased him in his BMW through downtown Phoenix. Haven't seen him or his car since."

"You've had some bad luck."

"And now we have evidence that Mr. Moreno, like Mr. Valencia, was murdered," Sam said.

"What kind of evidence?"

"Someone left a photograph at a crime scene. It showed Mr. Moreno dead of an apparent gunshot wound."

Veranda knew Sam wouldn't give away too many details in case they were needed to corroborate a confession from Bartolo. Unlikely, but necessary for procedural reasons.

"Tragic. But what has this to do with me?"

"You're the common denominator," Sam said.

"How is that?"

"The pickup truck leaving the Drug Enforcement Bureau parking lot was registered to Ponte Vista Construction, a company affiliated with one of your ... business enterprises."

"I don't recall a company by that name. Perhaps we contracted with them to build one of our facilities."

Sam leaned forward. "Pablo Moreno received two traffic citations over the past eighteen months driving that pickup. Mr. Moreno was your employee."

Bartolo glanced up as if trying to remember an obscure detail. "I have no one by that name on my payroll."

"Then it's off the books," Sam said. "Either way, Moreno's employment with your company was corroborated by Guillermo Valencia."

Bartolo raised his eyebrows. "Didn't you say Mr. Valencia was dead? How can he corroborate anything?"

"Exactly." Sam paused a beat. "You silenced both of them."

Bartolo guffawed. "Prove it."

"I will, Mr. Villalobos. You're going to jail." Sam lowered his voice as his eyes bored into Bartolo's. "And no amount of money will change that fact."

Veranda sensed her moment. "That little stunt you pulled at my house will only tack years onto your sentence."

He turned to her. "Stunt?"

"You're attempt at intimidation didn't work," she said. "It's only going to bring more heat down on you."

Bartolo looked indignant. "Who's trying to intimidate who? You come into my home, my private property, with baseless accusations. Police harassment. This meeting is voluntary on my part and I'm about to end it." He lifted his chin. "I'm sure you're aware I have a law degree. I don't practice, but am quite familiar with my Constitutional rights."

Veranda snorted. "Excellent. You can be the jailhouse lawyer for your cell block. Maybe your future boyfriend will be impressed and treat you extra nice."

Bartolo's gaze iced over. "You have no idea who you're messing with."

She scooted to the edge of the couch cushion and leaned forward, invading his personal space. "Actually, I've seen a dossier with all sorts of information about you. For example, I know you own a Desert Eagle tiger-striped gold semiauto." She arched an eyebrow. "Fifty caliber seems a bit over the top though." She cocked her head to one side. "Are you compensating?"

"This interview is over. Get out." Bartolo shot to his feet, marched to the wall, and tapped a display panel. Seconds later, Camacho entered the room and stood at attention.

With his bodyguard in the room, Bartolo appeared to regain his composure. He jammed a fist onto each hip. "You're fishing. You don't have enough evidence for a warrant, and you're wasting my time." He looked at each of them in turn. "Camacho will show you out."

Veranda stood her ground and faced Bartolo. "This meeting might be over, but I'm not finished with you." She allowed her contempt to show as she glared at him.

Bartolo retraced his steps to stand directly in front of her. "You are quite right." He bent closer. "There is far more business between us."

She could sense the hook buried in his words but took the bait anyway. "What business are you talking about?"

A slow smile spread across Bartolo's face. "Does your partner know why you became a narc?"

Veranda's throat tightened. Bartolo had the look of someone cradling a bomb. What did he know about her? "Every cop wants to put away drug dealers. I'm no different."

"Oh, but you *are* different. Especially when it comes to dealers who sell in schools."

Sam stepped behind her. "What would you know about drugs in schools, Mr. Villalobos?"

"Only what I see on the news. Terrible to tempt young people with drugs." He cut his eyes back to Veranda. "And some of them are too weak to say no."

Her pulse pounded in her ears. "It's people like you who bring poison into our communities."

"Not that I'm a narcotics trafficker, but what they do isn't wrong." He took a hand from his hip and laid it on his chest. "They simply supply a demand. The drug trade is a risky business. The only reason to get involved is the constantly growing market." He dropped his hands to his sides. "Why don't you narcs focus on getting people in your community to quit buying drugs?" He cocked his head in imitation of her previous jab at him. "Oh, that's right. They won't stop. Their lack of self-control is their own fault." He smirked. "You should sponsor more treatment programs."

As her temper flared, she knew she was in danger of giving him the upper hand. "You can justify anything, can't you?"

"And so can you, Detective. Didn't I also hear on the news that you killed a man? I believe his name was Oscar Ramirez." He tapped his chin as if trying to recall something. "How many people did you say are dead this week? Three?"

"I don't have to justify my actions to you."

"But you must explain them to the people you work with. Otherwise, your situation will keep getting worse." He leveled his gaze back on her. "You can't keep hiding the truth."

The knot in her throat tightened. "What truth?"

"After your name came up in the news, I got curious. I've discovered a few pertinent facts about you," Bartolo said. "In fact, I know things you don't even suspect."

She had to turn the focus back to him. "The only thing you need to know about me is that my name will be on the affidavit for your arrest warrant."

Bartolo considered her for a long moment before he spoke. "There is an expression that comes to mind." He leaned so close his breath, reeking of cognac, fanned her face. "People who play with matches … get burned."

She pressed her lips into a tight line, refusing to respond to his thinly veiled threat.

Bartolo pivoted and left through a paneled wooden door on the far side of the room.

———

Veranda propped the visor midway down as the setting sun slanted into the windshield. Streaks of bright orange and gilded purple traversed the evening sky over Camelback Mountain. Once Sam drove past the front gate, she glanced at him. "Bartolo's parting shot about matches indicates he intends to burn me somehow. What do you think he has in mind?"

"Stands to reason it's related to that matchstick in the envelope with the photo of Pablo," Sam said. "Don't know what to make of it though."

"I don't either, but I have a bad feeling we're going to find out."

He cut his eyes to her. "What do you think Bartolo knows about you?"

"No idea." She looked out the window so he couldn't catch her expression. "I think he was trying to keep me off balance." She changed topics—another favorite tactic when she didn't want to answer a question. "Shouldn't we call Commander Webster?"

"I'll call him after I drop you off at your car and give him a quick briefing."

"Which brings me to the next issue. What about the mole? Could it be Commander Webster? How much are you planning to tell him when you call?"

"As little as possible." He shrugged. "We went in. We danced. We left. No developments."

"We still have to make arrangements to meet Commander Murphy so we can brief him about the mole. He needs to start the investigation right away."

"I'll call him after I talk to Webster." Sam made another turn. "I'll ask Murphy to meet us at Encanto Park first thing tomorrow. It's close to VCB, still cool, and practically deserted early in the morning."

"Let me know if he agrees. I can bring the printout to show him."

"I'll shoot you a text." He rubbed his neck. "It's been a long day and I'm tired and hungry. Sarah made lasagna. She'd like to meet you. You're welcome to come to my house for a bite."

Her stomach roiled at the thought of a heavy meal. "Thank you for the offer, but I'm not hungry after listening to Bartolo's line of bullshit. I'm going to finish unpacking."

"I almost forgot about the safe house."

"Which really isn't safe once the mole tells the cartel where it is."

"We need to keep up pretenses." His eyes held a sympathetic expression as he turned toward her. "Things will only get more complicated. We're working two investigations now and one of them is a secret."

"Commander Murphy will track down the mole, not us."

"True, but we'll help." Sam pulled into the VCB lot where her car was one of the few remaining.

"Thank you, Sam." She hoped her smile conveyed her gratitude. He had stood next to her to confront Bartolo. She had never worked with anyone like Sam before. A true partner in every sense. "For everything."

————

The sun had almost set when Veranda pulled into the driveway of the tiny stucco house in Central Phoenix. She trudged inside and deactivated the alarm. Unlike the splendor she had just witnessed, the place had the air of a vacant home haphazardly staged for quick sale.

She kicked off her pumps with a moan of pleasure and strolled to the galley-style kitchen. She tugged open the refrigerator door and scanned the array of leftovers from *Mamá*'s party. Despite the delicious food, her stomach rebelled at the idea of a meal. She wrinkled her nose as she recalled the smell of cognac on Bartolo's breath. Shuddering, she pulled out a beer and nudged the door shut with an elbow.

After a long pull, she wandered into what an optimistic realtor would have called the master suite, dug her accessory bag out of her suitcase in the closet, and headed to the bathroom. She blew out a sigh and arranged her makeup on the counter, resigned to the idea that she might be here a while. The safe house did not feel secure or welcoming to her.

As she hung up her clothes, she turned the problem of the mole over in her mind, unable to fathom who would betray the Department … or was it only a betrayal of her personally? Had the mole been around for years, or recruited recently to spy on her?

A thought hit her and she groaned as a fresh wave of guilt washed over her. She'd forgotten to call her mother. Again. Even if she had remembered, there hadn't been time for a serious conversation. And her mother wanted a personal visit. When would there be time for that? She glanced at the clock. Too late to call. *Mamá* rose early to start cooking and usually went to bed by sunset. It would have to wait for tomorrow.

She thought about what her mother said at the party. Her mother had accused Veranda of keeping secrets and telling lies. And hinted that she had done the same.

Her cell phone's vibration in her pocket interrupted her reverie. She glanced at Sam's terse message. ENCANTO @ 0630 TOMORROW. I'LL PICK YOU UP. She acknowledged the text.

That brought her back to her dilemma with Sam. Bartolo's comments made him suspect there was something she hadn't told him. And there was. How much longer could she keep her secret about why she had targeted the cartel?

She thought about Sergeant Diaz digging into her background as he investigated her shooting and sighed. Soon it would all come out anyway. Bartolo had made it clear that he knew why she'd recruited Flaco. He had also hinted that there was more he knew about her.

Should she confide in Sam before he found out from someone else? It pained her to keep secrets from him. When he learned the truth, he would know that she had kept critical information about her background from the Department for years. Would he understand why she did it, or would he have her thrown out of Homicide?

19

SHE AWOKE TO HER cell phone's rhythmic buzzing on the nightstand. Disoriented from the unfamiliar environment, she fumbled for the device so long that the call went to voicemail. She squinted blearily at the screen. Five in the morning. She touched the voicemail icon and heard her sister Gabby's frantic voice.

"Veranda, come to the restaurant right away. The fire department is here. It's burning to the ground. Mom is freaking out. Hurry!"

Dread pierced Veranda's heart as she sprang into action. Years of midnight callouts had trained her well. She showered, dressed in her tactical gear, and flew out the door in less than five minutes.

The Malibu's tires screeched as she careened around curves on deserted streets in the dim light of daybreak. She swerved into the restaurant parking lot and vaulted out of the car.

Fire engines, ladder trucks, and assorted rescue vehicles jutted at odd angles over the entire area. Red lights flashed as helmeted men in beige turnouts with reflective striping and black boots dragged thick hoses toward the flaming structure. Police patrol cars, blue lights rotating, abutted the fire apparatus. She had witnessed many fire scenes in her career, but they had never taken her breath away like this one did. She spun, searching for her family.

Finally she spotted her mother on the other side of the parking lot, speaking to someone. One of her mother's hands clutched her heavy silver necklace as she spoke to a tall blond man in a black golf shirt and khaki cargo pants. The man took notes on a metal clipboard.

Veranda called out and ran to her mother. "*Mamá*, is everyone okay?"

Her mother stopped talking and tapped the man on his arm, pointing at Veranda. Captain Anderson turned, his face lined with concern.

As soon as Veranda reached her, Lorena flung her arms around her daughter. "We are all safe, *mi'ja*. We got a call from the alarm company. Tío Rico came out and found—" She stretched an arm out to indicate the flaming building and burst into tears.

Veranda held her mother and looked up at Anderson. "Were you on call?"

He shook his head. "Got a callout from the Battalion Chief. He knew I already investigated this restaurant." He looked away, as if considering his next words. "The earlier incident was clearly accidental. I could see that grease had gradually built up in the cooking vent in the attic. All of the damage was contained to the inside of the vent, so there was no destruction to the attic itself. Classic grease fire."

She stroked her mother's hair. "And this fire?"

He glanced at the firefighters running back and forth, silhouetted by the bright wall of flames. "I won't know for sure until I determine the cause and origin, but this blaze ripped through the entire building." He gave her a dark look. "It's got all the earmarks of a fire fueled by accelerants."

It was strange to deal with him in an official capacity after their banter at her mother's party. He sounded so clinical. Had she spoken like that to victims when she investigated cases? As she continued to hold her mother, an image bubbled up to the surface of her conscious mind. Sam shaking a manila envelope as something tumbled onto her kitchen counter.

"The matchstick," she breathed.

"Pardon?" Anderson cupped a hand over his ear and leaned closer to hear her over the shouting firefighters and growling engines.

"I believe this is arson, and I have information for you."

They were joined by her aunt and uncles as well as a growing group of extended family. Gabby had put the word out and everyone responded. Veranda didn't want them to hear the terrifying details of her burglary.

She released her mother and turned to address her relatives. "Listen everyone, I need to speak to the arson investigator. I won't be long. Can you all wait for me over there?"

She pointed to a far corner of the parking lot next to an adjacent building. They murmured their assent and shuffled in that direction. She watched her tío Rico put an arm around her mother before she turned back to Anderson.

"I need five minutes to make some phone calls, then I'll join you," she said. He inclined his head and went to stand by one of the massive fire engines.

Veranda pulled her phone out and called Sam first. She quickly outlined what happened and what her suspicions were. "Sam, I think this is what that match in the manila envelope meant. It was a message, but we couldn't understand it until after the fact."

"It's also interesting that Bartolo specifically mentioned matches when we spoke to him. I'll make all of the necessary departmental notifications. Sounds like you're pretty busy at the scene."

"Thanks. I guess it doesn't matter what you say because it'll probably be all over the news anyway. The camera crews are here." She glanced over at Anderson. "By the way, Sam, there's an arson investigator from the Fire Department here. I'm going to bring him in the loop."

"Do you think he'll help us?"

"There's no time to explain why, but I trust him." She gave Sam a moment to digest this.

"Actually, the arson guy could come in handy," Sam said after a brief pause. "The mole won't have access to his investigative files and he may find some evidence we can use against Bartolo or the cartel. Just don't mention the mole. No one is supposed to know about that."

"Got it." She glanced at her watch. "Sam, there's no way I'm going to be finished here in time for our meeting with Commander Murphy at Encanto Park."

"I'll go. You can give him the deciphered text message printout later if he needs to see it."

She disconnected and stared at her phone for a long moment. She sighed, pulled a business card out of her pocket, and tapped in a number.

A groggy male voice answered. "Sergeant Diaz."

She did not apologize for waking him. "This is Detective Cruz. My family's restaurant is burning down and I'm at the scene with an arson investigator from the Fire Department. He believes the fire was deliberately set, and I agree."

"Was anyone hurt?"

Veranda paused, surprised by the concern in his voice. "No one was inside," she said. "Everyone is fine. The restaurant is a total loss though."

Her throat tightened as her gaze landed on the bright orange flames licking the morning sky.

"I'm so sorry, Veranda. I'll be right there. What's the name of the restaurant?"

He had never called her by her first name before, and sounded like he genuinely cared. Of course, it could be an act if he was the mole. "*Casa Cruz Cocina* in South Phoenix. There's no need for you to come out, I just called to notify you as requested." *Demanded, more like.*

His tone became more businesslike. "If it turns out to be arson, and targets your family, the cartel could be behind it. It will have a direct bearing on my investigation. I'll be there shortly." He disconnected.

Baffled by Diaz's abrupt change but too preoccupied to give it much thought, she found Anderson waiting for her where she'd left him. "I had to notify my chain of command. This fire probably involves an ongoing police investigation I'm involved in."

He began scribbling on a notebook clamped to a metal clipboard. "Why don't you start from the beginning?"

She explained about Flaco, the Villalobos cartel, Pablo, and the burglary of her home. She wasn't sure how much he may have already seen on the news, so she gave him a broad overview.

Anderson's sandy eyebrows drew closer together as she spoke. Finally, he looked up from his note pad. "You believe this asshole Bartolo set the fire as some sort of warning to you?"

"More like retribution. I think he's paying me back for interfering with his family business by destroying my family's business."

Anderson stared at her for a beat. "So you're basically at war with a drug cartel?"

"I used to think so … but the burglary and the fire are not standard operating procedure this side of the border. The cartels usually write off interdictions as part of the cost of doing business. This is much

157

more personal and targeted toward me. Makes me wonder if Bartolo is acting on his own."

He lowered the clipboard and took a step toward her. "I think you're in just as much danger whether it's an entire cartel or one lunatic drug lord." He was so close she could see faint stubble along his jawline. "Is your department taking care of you? I mean, do you have a security detail or anything?"

Veranda snorted. "We don't do stuff like that. I'm a cop. I take care of myself."

He waited until she tilted her head back to meet his eyes. "I'm serious. Your life is at risk."

———————

Veranda spent the next hour going over every detail of her morning. Commander Webster, Lieutenant Aldridge, Sergeant Jackson, and her entire Homicide squad all responded to the scene after Sam notified them about the fire. Sam arrived last, and whispered in Veranda's ear that Murphy had started his investigation into the identity of the mole.

She briefed her team about her assumption that the match left in her kitchen during the burglary was a message about torching the family restaurant. Veranda proposed that either the cartel had adopted the kind of tactics previously only seen south of the border, or Bartolo had gone rogue.

"Either way, someone's playing mind games with you now," Sam said.

"I think it's Bartolo acting on his own, and he's coming unglued," Aldridge said.

Veranda addressed her commander, "Boss, I'd like some time with my family. They've been through a lot."

"Go." Webster waved a hand. "Take the rest of the day off. We'll hit your cell if we need you."

She turned and strode to her family, clustered by the corner of the building next door. Their number had swelled past twenty as more relatives arrived. "Everyone!" She held up a hand to get their attention and the group fell silent.

"The fire is out now, but it's unclear how much damage there is. We can't go in until after the building is inspected. The worst-case scenario is that the restaurant is a total loss." She heard several gasps. "We have insurance. We can rebuild if we have to."

Her words rang out like a death knell for the family business. Her relatives exchanged anxious glances. Veranda could guess their thoughts. Closing down for the time it took to rebuild could spell financial disaster. Her heart ached as she watched them cross themselves, clasp hands, and pray.

She bowed her head but stood apart from her family. They prayed for deliverance. She prayed for forgiveness. *I brought this destruction into their lives.* Her relentless pursuit of Bartolo had done this. Oscar Ramirez, Flaco, and Pablo Moreno were all dead. Now her family's livelihood was at risk.

She raised her head and surveyed the scene. Firemen dragged hoses through sooty puddles of water. Fire trucks choked the street. The stench of charred wood assaulted her nostrils. Police directed traffic around a barricade. Surrounding business owners stood in front of their stores, hands on hips, shaking their heads.

She spotted the owner of Power Pawn, Marty Dander, in front of his seedy shop. She couldn't believe his store hadn't been incinerated years ago. Dander was the shadiest businessman in town. Angry customers threatened to bomb his place on a weekly basis. Her family referred to him as *la cucaracha*, the cockroach.

She froze. Her eyes traveled to his store's tiled roof. Her heart beat faster. A video surveillance camera pointed downward in the direction of the restaurant. After repeated vandalism, Dander had set up an elaborate system of cameras that covered not only his store and parking lot, but the street as well.

Veranda turned to her family. "I have to go and talk to the arson investigator. There's nothing more you can do here. Why don't you all go to *Mamá*'s house and I'll meet you there later."

Without waiting for their response, she picked out a group of firemen on the perimeter of the scene and jogged over to them. "Where is Captain Anderson?" she asked.

One of them pointed to a tall figure facing away from her, clipboard in hand. She walked up behind him and tapped his shoulder. He pivoted and looked surprised. "Detective Cruz. I thought you'd be tied up with your team."

"My commander gave me the day off, but I need to speak to you." She pointed across the street from the restaurant. "See that pawn shop? The owner, Marty Dander, is so crooked he has to screw his socks on. After thousands of dollars in damage from vandalism and constant death threats, he installed a very sophisticated video system. It covers half the block. I wouldn't be surprised if one or more of the cameras cover this location too."

Anderson followed her gaze to the short, pudgy man with a thin comb-over pulled back in a scraggly ponytail. "Is that Dander standing in front of the shop?"

"That's him."

Anderson tucked his clipboard under his arm. "I'd like to speak to him now, but I won't recognize any suspects or vehicles if he's got video. You're the expert on the cartel. Can you come with me?"

"You couldn't keep me away." Her mouth twisted into a wry smile. "Plus, you'll need help with Dander. Don't expect cooperation."

They walked across the street to join Dander. Since it was his investigation, Veranda let Anderson take the lead.

The fire captain towered over the squat proprietor, whose three-day growth spread down his double chin and into the neckline of his stained shirt. "I'm Captain Cole Anderson with the Phoenix Fire Department Arson Investigation Unit."

Dander gave him a curt nod. "So, you guys think this is arson, huh?"

"We investigate to determine the cause and origin of all suspicious fires."

Dander cut his beady eyes to Veranda. "What's she doing here?"

Anderson's jaw tightened. "She's assisting me on my investigation of this morning's fire."

Dander's eyes narrowed as he took in her black cargo pants and boots. "I remember when you used to wait tables at your mom's restaurant, but you're a cop now. I saw you on the news. You're mixed up with some drug killing." His jaw slackened as he turned widened eyes to Anderson. "Holy shit. She messed with a drug cartel and now they've torched her family's business. I want nothin' to do with this." He wrenched open the front door of the shop and darted inside.

Anderson and Veranda followed him.

Anderson began, "Mr. Dander—"

"Didn't see nothin'. Don't know nothin'. Can't help you."

Anderson ignored the interruption. "Your video cameras may have recorded something that could be useful to our investigation."

Dander looked up as if he could see the cameras perched on his roof. "Surveillance system's on the fritz. Hasn't worked for a week."

Veranda stepped around Anderson. "Bullshit, Dander." She put her hands on the counter and took in the glittering assortment of Rolex watches, heirloom jewelry, and gold coins. "How about I call

161

the pawn shop detail and get them down here? I'm sure they could carve out some time to go over your books and your inventory."

Dander put his hands on his hips, a defiant expression on his pallid face. "It'd take a lot of time to go through that footage. I got eight cameras around this place. Time spent helping you is time away from doing business, and for me … time's money."

Anderson glared at him. "What the hell are you talking about?"

Veranda glanced up at him. "He wants us to pay him for his trouble. Classic Dander shakedown." She pinned the shop owner with a fierce glare. "You don't have to spend your precious time. We'll go through the video files ourselves." When he continued to stare at her, she narrowed her eyes. "If you make me get a warrant, I'll come back with the entire pawn shop detail."

Dander threw up his hands. "The system connects to a laptop in the back room. Follow me." They trailed him as he stomped back to a cramped office stuffed with notebooks and dusty file cabinets in the rear of the shop. "Enjoy," he said and closed the door as he left.

Empty fast food containers lay on the floor next to the wastebasket. A wooden shelf affixed to one wall held an array of monitors above a relatively clear table. The screens displayed different views of the exterior and interior of the pawn shop.

She focused on one screen that showed the parking lot in front of the store. The angle was wide enough to include the street and the smoldering remains of her family's restaurant. "There! That one shows most of the restaurant."

Anderson put his clipboard down and leaned in to look at the monitor. He stood directly behind her and his chest brushed against her back. His chin touched the top of her head, causing a slight flutter in her belly. He pointed at a label beneath the screen. "DX-5. The monitors are labeled in order. We should be able to view that camera's feed from last night."

She ducked under his arm, slid into the chair behind the desk, and pulled Dander's laptop closer. Anderson dragged a stool beside her and sat down. "The files on the computer match the labels on the monitors."

She skimmed the mouse over its pad and clicked on the icon for the DX-5 monitor. A series of files with dates popped up. A color image from the vantage point of the pawn shop roof lit the screen. A date and time stamp in the lower right corner of the image began at 00:01 hours. One minute past midnight, before the fire.

Anderson leaned so close his words brushed her ear as he spoke. "If the date is right, that will be the night before last. We should fast forward to about twenty-one hundred hours or so."

She nodded and left-clicked the mouse over the FF triangle on the screen. Images whizzed by in a blur. She stopped at 21:00 and slowed down. The video file ended when she got to 00:00 hours. "Must have happened after midnight then." She closed the file and clicked on to-day's date. She sped forward from one minute past midnight.

Anderson clutched her wrist when the time stamp reached 01:22 hours. "Slow down."

A silhouette of a tall, athletic man came into view from the side of the frame, on the terra-cotta tiled roof of the restaurant, picking his way over to a tubular vent that protruded up from the peak.

Her body tensed as she watched the dark figure squat down near the vent. He pulled something from a side pocket and turned it upside down, returning it after a few seconds. In a moment, a tiny flame ig-nited a bright orange dot near his head. It didn't provide enough light to make out his face. The flame went out, but the circle continued to glow until the figure tossed it into the vent.

"Bingo," Anderson muttered. The silhouette retraced his steps sideways across the roof until he was out of the frame.

Veranda spoke over her shoulder. "What just happened?"

Anderson didn't move his hand from her wrist. "A good way to burn down a restaurant is to create a makeshift incendiary device. One favorite method is to wrap matches around a cigarette with a rubber band. Then all you have to do is light the end, take a few drags to get it going, then throw it into the attic vent. The matches will catch fire and ignite whatever fuel it touches. In this case, it looks like he took an accelerant out of a container in his pocket and poured it into the attic first."

She closed her eyes. "It would look like the fire is related to the grease fire we had earlier."

"Except that I have the training to tell the difference, and we have the technology to prove it was arson." He paused. "The video doesn't show who set the fire, but it can still be useful as evidence."

She sighed.

Still holding her wrist, he gave a gentle squeeze. "Trust me, Veranda. I know what to look for. I've investigated hundreds of fires. I won't stop until I nail this guy."

She looked into his crystal blue eyes. He was strong. Sincere. Dedicated to his job. A man she could relate to.

They jerked back at the sound of a raspy voice.

"Get a freakin' room." Dander stood in the doorway of the office, arms crossed.

She swiveled to glare at him. "Haven't you got some stolen merchandise to fence, Dander?"

He looked petulant. "Always busting my ass." He peered at the screen behind them. "So, did you spend all your time ogling each other back here or did you find anything?"

"We found some useful footage," Anderson said. "I have a thumb drive to download it from your laptop. We'll need to subpoena you if this goes to trial."

Dander reddened. "I'm not testifying in any case that involves a drug cartel."

The front door to the pawn shop chimed.

"Why don't you two leave? You've got what you came for, and I'm trying to run a business here," Dander said, turning toward the front of the shop. "I've got a customer."

"You mean victim," Veranda said to his retreating back.

Anderson tugged a thumb drive out of his pocket and inserted it into a port on the side of Dander's computer. "We should download files for the day before as well."

She clicked the file icons and dragged them to the folder for the portable drive. When the process was complete, she pulled out the drive and handed it to Anderson.

"I meant what I said, Veranda." He wrapped his hand around hers as he took the device. "I don't care who set the fire to your family's restaurant. I'll bring him in."

"I won't lie to you. Bartolo Villalobos is a dangerous man."

"The only thing I'm concerned about is your safety. It sounds like he's after you."

She pulled her hand away. "He's angry because my partner and I visited his home last night."

"What happened?"

"We did a knock and talk. I'm sure you arson investigators do those too."

"We follow the same investigative procedures you do. That's why we all get law enforcement certifications."

"Well this interview wasn't what I would call textbook procedure. By the time we finished, his *chonies* were in a wad and he made a comment about matches."

"Matches?" Anderson straightened. "What did he say?"

"He said that people who play with matches get burned."

Anderson leaned back in his chair. "If Bartolo is the person in the video who set the fire, then his comment may come back to bite him."

"What do you mean?"

"It's too technical to explain right now, but that video has given me a course of action for my on-scene investigation of the fire." He stood. "I need to get over to the restaurant and suit up."

She led Anderson to the front of the store to let Dander know they were leaving, giving him perfunctory thanks for what she could only loosely term cooperation. Dander grunted as he wiped a glass display case with a grimy rag.

"I've got to ask," Anderson said as the door swung shut behind them. "Would you really have called out the pawn detail to go over his entire inventory this morning?"

She cut him a look. "Hell no. It was a total bluff."

She was treated to a full display of Anderson's dimples as he grinned down at her.

They arrived at Anderson's white pickup truck in the restaurant parking lot. He opened the driver's door and reached inside. "Time for me to go through the scene. Thanks to that video, I know what to look for."

"I need to be with my family." She gave him a card. "My cell number is on the back. Call me if you find anything."

He brushed her fingers with his as he took the proffered card. "I will. Please be careful."

She strolled back to her car, pulled open the door, and slid into the front seat. Before she turned the key in the ignition, she paused to watch Anderson step into a beige turnout and thick black boots. She smiled to herself as he put on a white fire helmet and walked toward the restaurant. Her cell phone interrupted wayward thoughts about the handsome fireman when it vibrated against her waist in its clip. She tugged it out.

Her heart stopped. She had received a text message from Flaco's cell phone. *Impossible.* Flaco's body had been dumped in the DEB parking lot. His cell phone, never recovered. That meant the person who was using his phone was ...

She tapped the screen to open the message. Malevolent yellow eyes glared at her. She read the words beneath the image of a snarling black wolf.

YOU'RE BURNED.

20

VERANDA FORWARDED THE TEXT to Sam. Twenty seconds later, her phone buzzed. "What the hell was that?" Sam asked.

"Love note from Bartolo. Who else would send me a message like that with a picture of a black wolf? He used Flaco's cell phone, which had my contact info. Makes sense Bartolo kept it, but our tech guys found no activity when I gave them Flaco's number."

"If he's smart, he keeps it turned off. Probably activated it just to send you the text."

"And he knows we can't track his location if it's deactivated."

"What do you think about that text message?" Sam asked.

"Bartolo would have chosen those two words for a reason."

"There's the obvious reference to the fire at the restaurant, but I think there's more."

"He told us last night that people who play with matches get burned," she said. "He's letting me know he made good on his threat."

"There could be a third meaning. When someone who works undercover is exposed, he's been *burned*. Remember how Bartolo said he knew stuff about you?"

Sam was right, but Veranda didn't want to dwell on it. "Total bullshit. What could he know?"

Sam paused before he said, "You tell me, Veranda."

She needed to deflect Sam from his line of thinking. "You saw him. Odds are Bartolo was snorting coke when he sent that text. Everything he's doing is nuts." She raised her voice. "He went after my family!"

"You're right. I know this must be difficult." His tone softened. "You okay?"

"He wants to scare me." She tightened her grip on the phone. "But he's pissing me off instead."

"What do you think his end game is?"

"He sees me as a threat. I know more about his operation than anyone else. If I stopped working the case, he could use the mole to sabotage the investigation."

"He still doesn't seem to know we're aware of the mole."

"It's our only advantage. By the way, did you brief Commander Murphy about the fire?"

"I'm with him now. I'll show him the text message. We can try to track it, but I think it'll be a waste of time."

"Agreed. Besides, I want Bartolo to keep Flaco's phone. It might come in handy."

"How'd it go with the arson investigator?"

She switched gears. "That's the only bright spot. I briefed Captain Anderson about Bartolo, the burglary, and the two murders. I didn't mention the mole."

"About time we caught a break. The mole can't access the fire department's investigation. If the arson guy makes headway, Bartolo won't know about it."

"Which is good, because we found some interesting footage from a surveillance camera across the street from the restaurant." She outlined what they had downloaded from Dander's security system.

"I wish his face had been visible, but it sounds like the arson captain is optimistic about recovering some useful evidence." Sam paused. "You've been through a lot, Veranda. I'll drive tomorrow."

"Thanks, but that's not nec—"

"I'll be at the safe house to get you in the morning." He disconnected.

———

Fifteen minutes later, Veranda pulled into the driveway at her mother's house. The sound of many voices in an animated discussion reached her ears as she stepped through the front door of the largest *casita*.

Lorena stood in the living room, arms crossed, glaring at a crowd of relatives. "Miguel says it will take more than three months."

All heads turned to Veranda's stepfather, Miguel Gomez, whose eyes peered out from his rugged face, burnished from years of manual labor on construction sites in the desert sun. Dusty work boots propped by the front door, Miguel stood next to her mother in his socks.

He had met Veranda's mother eighteen years ago when she sold burritos out of a pickup near the job site where he worked construction. He had been a laborer then, but he saved his money until he had enough to start his own business. He married Lorena when Veranda started high school.

Miguel ran a hand through his salt-and-pepper hair. "It will be at least a month to get the permits through Zoning. Who knows how long the insurance company will take to give us a check. Then I have to clear the lot before I can start to rebuild anything."

"C'mon," tío Rico said. "We don't call you McGomez for nothing."

Everyone laughed. It was a family joke that Miguel could build a house out of toothpicks and duct tape. He was the Mexican McGyver.

"We're Mexican, so we don't need fancy tools to do the job," tía Juana said. "*And* we're American, so we fix our own problems."

Miguel put a calloused hand on his hip. "But the restaurant still needs to be built to code."

Lorena spoke over the din of voices offering suggestions to her husband. "Doesn't matter how fast Miguel does it. Our customers will start to eat at some other place. We will lose them forever."

"Wait a minute!" Tío Felipe looked excited. "Juan and I can bring our food truck to the restaurant parking lot. That way, we can still serve many of our regular customers until Miguel is done."

Tío Juan appeared to catch his brother's enthusiasm. "We could do a lot of the prep work here in Lorena's kitchen. We'd make fresh tortillas, marinate the meat, chop the veg, and do other stuff here, then take it to the food truck a few times a day." He spread his hands. "Not as good as having a building, but maybe enough to keep us going during construction."

Tío Felipe's grin lit the room. "We would finally live up to the restaurant's name. Our customers really would eat food from the Cruz home kitchen."

A cheer went up and other family members slapped Felipe and Juan on the back. Her uncles could make the difference between financial survival and bankruptcy for the restaurant.

Veranda's chest swelled with pride as her family began making plans for taking shifts in the food truck and rearranging the menu to suit the tiny galley kitchen. They were fighters. They would over-come this disaster and get back on their feet.

Unfortunately, they were not out of danger yet. Bartolo was a dark cloud looming over them. Veranda felt a tug on her sleeve, bringing her out of her reverie. Her mother's soulful eyes peered up at her.

"*Mi'ja*, I must speak to you now. It cannot wait."

"All right, *Mamá*."

"Let's go to my bedroom. We will be alone there."

Veranda studied her mother's face. She looked careworn, strain showing in the lines around her eyes and mouth. She followed Lorena into the corner room at the back of the house. Veranda closed the door behind them and sat beside her mother on the bed.

Lorena twisted her hands in her lap. "*Mi'ja*, I have many things to tell you. Difficult things."

Her mother had switched to Spanish. Lorena usually spoke English, only reverting to her native tongue when she wanted to be precise about what she communicated.

Her mother picked at a loose thread on the handmade bedspread. "Have you ever wondered why I named you Veranda?" Her voice was soft. "It is not a common name."

Veranda shrugged, answering in Spanish so that her mother could converse more comfortably. "I figured you thought it was pretty. Had a nice sound."

"No, *mi'ja*. That is not why."

Veranda wrinkled her brows. "Tell me then."

"I combined the Spanish words *ver* 'to see' and *andadura* 'path' in a way that had special meaning for me." She drew a deep breath. "It was to remind me to watch how your journey would go, which path you would choose."

Veranda was perplexed. Her mother had never spoken about this. "Isn't that true of every child?"

"Yes, but you were ... are ... special." She hesitated. "Do you remember what I told you about your father?"

"Of course." Veranda smiled.

From the time she was old enough to understand, her mother had told stories of her father, Ernesto Hidalgo. Ernesto, born into a wealthy family in the Mexican upper class, had attended law school and was expected to become a partner in the family's prestigious law firm. Ernesto had different ideas. He saw people suffer at the hands of brutal drug lords and decided to take on the cartels and the corrupt officials who allowed them to thrive. His family was outraged when he joined the Federal Judicial Police.

Lorena had described Ernesto as a principled man who sometimes referred to himself as a modern-day knight, a *caballero,* who would give his life to protect the people. Veranda had tried to live up to her father's legacy. He had been her inspiration to join the force.

Her mother met her eyes. *"Mi'ja,* you know how I told you that *El Lobo* killed your father and that the rest of us ran to the United States to escape him?"

"Of course I remember. It's one of the reasons I became a cop."

Her mother's hazel eyes, so much like her own, misted. "That is not the whole truth about what happened."

"Mamá, what does my father's death have to do with—"

Her mother rested her hand on Veranda's. "You must know everything. I believe your life is in danger." It was the second time Veranda heard that comment today, and it was much worse coming from her mother.

173

Lorena cleared her throat. "You always knew I was pregnant with you when I fled Mexico, but I never told you that I didn't *know* I was with child when I left."

Veranda could not understand why this was important, but she held her tongue.

Her mother lowered her voice and continued. "The first part of the story is true. Ernesto worked for the Federal Judicial Police Department and was about to arrest Hector Villalobos. This next part, I have never told you." Lorena drew a deep breath. "Hector worked for your father at the time."

"What?" Veranda could not stop herself from interjecting. "*El Lobo* was a *Federale*?"

Lorena nodded. "They both joined as idealistic young men. Hector came from a poor family in Mexico City. He had a hard childhood. When he became a police official, he thought he could clean up his community by arresting criminals. Over time, he saw those around him get promotions he felt he deserved. He thought it was because they took bribes or did favors for the cartels."

"Wait. How do you know all this about Hector?"

"Because I met him when I met Ernesto. They both came out to ask questions about a cartel shooting in my neighborhood. I was nineteen years old. The only witness. At least, the only one who would admit I saw who did it." Lorena smoothed her skirt. "Both men protected me while I prepared to testify. Eventually, the suspect was killed by his own cartel, so I did not have to go to court. Right after the case closed, Ernesto got a promotion. He was so excited. I remember when he came to tell me the news. He grabbed me and kissed me, then asked me to marry him." She blushed at the memory. "I said yes before he finished asking."

Veranda guessed what was coming. "Was Hector jealous?"

"Oh, yes. I was confused at first. I knew nothing of his feelings for me. They were not allowed to date me while I was a witness under their protection, so neither of them could say anything until the case was over. When he learned of our engagement, Hector felt that Ernesto had stolen both his promotion and his woman."

Veranda sat riveted. "What happened between my father and Hector?"

"Hector ended his friendship with Ernesto, who had become his supervisor due to the promotion. They worked together, but never spoke unless they had to. Over the next few months, Ernesto began to suspect that Hector was taking payoffs from cartels. I don't know all of the details, but Ernesto confided to me that he set a trap to catch a mole in their ranks."

Veranda swallowed hard. Her father had faced the same threat she did now. She leaned forward. "How did he catch the mole?"

"Ernesto gave out information to each person on his team separately. He swore them to secrecy, explaining that it could compromise a future mission if the cartel found out. All of the operations he described were different. That way, when the cartel took action, it would be obvious which team member's information was leaked."

Lorena looked pained. "Hector turned out to be the mole. Ernesto was devastated. He told his superiors about the investigation and got permission to charge Hector with conspiracy. The night before the arrest, Ernesto stayed late at the office, getting his paperwork in order. I was at home in bed. My younger brothers and sisters—your aunts and uncles lived with us—were asleep in their beds. I woke up with a knife at my throat." Lorena's hand crept up to the heavy silver necklace she always wore. Her fingers traced the outline of the cross etched into the metal. "It was Hector. He told me ... he said ... "

Veranda's heart ached to the point of bursting. She had taken statements from countless victims over the years. She read the telltale signs of repressed trauma in her mother's body. Downcast eyes, ragged breaths, hands in constant motion, and an overwhelming sense of shame and guilt that engulfed her. She knew what her mother was about to say and wanted to stop her, but she forced herself to remain silent. Once a wound this old and deep opened, it needed to bleed freely. A scab could reform over it later. Veranda stilled her body completely, allowing her mother to gather the strength to reveal her secret.

Lorena's eyes brimmed with unshed tears. "Hector said he had just killed Ernesto and that, as Ernesto lay dying, Hector told him he would have me."

"*Dios mio*," Veranda whispered.

Lorena crossed her arms and clutched them to her belly, folding in on herself. "Hector raped me. He held the knife against my throat so I would not cry out and wake my little brothers and sisters. I tried to push him off, and he sliced into my neck." Her hands traveled back up to her necklace again, this time circling around to release the catch.

Her mother pulled the heavy necklace away, revealing a two-inch, dark red, raised line on the side of her graceful neck. The earth shifted under Veranda's feet. She had never seen the scar before, although her mother mentioned it. "You always said you had a mark on your throat from a car accident before I was born."

Lorena shook her head. "I wear this jewelry to cover it. No one should have to see the ugliness."

"Oh, *Mamá*," Veranda clutched her mother's free hand. "Please don't say that. There is only beauty in you." When she saw her mother shake her head in denial, she posed another question to guide Lorena away from self-recrimination. "How did you get away?"

"Something must have awakened your tío Rico, because he snuck up behind Hector and hit him over the head with a pot from the kitchen." Lorena drew a shuddering breath, tears coursing down her cheeks. "Hector fell on top of me with his pants down around his knees. I pushed him off and grabbed his knife. I was about to plunge it into Hector when I saw your tía Maria standing in my bedroom door. She was only five years old." Lorena crossed herself. "It was a message from the Blessed Virgin that I should not become a murderer like Hector."

Tears stung Veranda's eyes.

"I woke the others and got them dressed. Hector's car was parked out front. I found the keys inside and we drove off with whatever we could carry. I did not find out until after I was in the United States two months later that I was pregnant."

Lorena finally raised her head to meet her daughter's eyes. The pain in her expression wrenched Veranda's heart. Still clutching the necklace, Lorena whispered, *"Mi'ja*, I must have become pregnant right before we ran. I don't know … that is … I … can't say … "

Blinding realization hit Veranda with the force of a punch to the gut. "You don't know who my father is, do you?"

21

BARTOLO STRODE ACROSS THE cramped living room of the dilapi-dated ranch-style house. His younger brother, Carlos, had rented the tiny home for one month. Situated on a large, secluded lot in an older neighborhood in the western part of Phoenix, it offered enough privacy to serve as a temporary way station for the cartel's human trafficking operation.

Carlos maintained several teams of coyotes, smugglers who brought people across the border illegally. Once in the United States, the coyotes took exhausted travelers to a central location where they awaited disbursement. Sometimes they were held for ransom until their families paid even more money to the cartel for their release.

Bartolo surveyed the twenty people huddled before him. He wrinkled his nose at the stench of sweat and fear that filled the room and turned to Carlos. "If I find one I like, you'll have to clean her up."

Carlos frowned. "There's a shower in the master bedroom."

Bartolo scanned the group again. His eyes rested on a woman clutching two girls tight against her body. He switched to Spanish. "How old are your daughters?"

The woman trembled. "Th-they are both fourteen years old."

"Ah, twins." Bartolo smiled. "Are they virgins?"

A gasp went around the room. A man in his fifties stepped beside the mother and her daughters. "Leave them alone!"

Bartolo, never taking his eyes from the girls, jerked his chin in the direction of the interloper. Carlos's second-in-command pushed away from the wall, strolled directly behind the man, and sank a dagger between his shoulder blades.

The man howled in pain as the coyote twisted the knife and wrenched it free. The man sank to his knees and collapsed on the floor. Eyes glassy. Face contorted in agony. A pool of blood oozed into the filthy carpet beneath him as he ceased writhing.

No one moved. The coyote sauntered back to his post against the wall.

Eyes still fixed on his prey, Bartolo continued as if there had been no interruption. "You were about to tell me whether your daughters are virgins?"

The girls sobbed into their mother's arms as she looked at him plaintively. "They are too young." She pried her daughters away from her, pushed them toward a woman standing next to her, then took a wobbly step toward Bartolo. "Take me."

Bartolo's lip curled. "I don't want a dried-up old woman." He glanced at the girls, who now clung to the other woman. "I want something young. Fresh. Unspoiled." He slid his index finger along his jaw. "In fact, I like the idea of twins. I will have them both."

"No!" Their mother threw herself at Bartolo's feet. "Please!"

Bartolo relished the drama. He viewed it as an exotic spice to arouse his appetite. "I will offer you a choice. I will agree not to take both of your daughters." He looked down at her. "But *you* have to decide which one I enjoy."

She gazed up in horror. "What?"

"If you don't choose which daughter you will give to me, then not only will I take them both, but every single man here will do the same."

Still on her knees, the woman cast a glance at her daughters.

They began to shriek. "No, *Mamá*, please!"

Bartolo laughed. This was more fun than he had anticipated. "You have one minute to decide."

While he waited, Carlos slid behind him and whispered in his ear in English. "You're cutting into my profits by taking a virgin from my stable."

The corners of Bartolo's eyes tightened. "It is my prerogative."

"The last time you took one of my girls, you beat her senseless. I had to wait a month for her to heal before she could start working off her transport fee."

"And since then she has made up for the loss of a month's wages." A smile spread across his stubbled face. "I remember her. She didn't want to do what she was told. I had to teach her obedience."

"You almost killed her, Bartolo."

"And ... ?"

Carlos sounded exasperated. "Just don't damage my merchandise this time."

"There is a price to pay for coming to the United States. As the saying goes, 'freedom isn't free.'"

"This is *my* part of the business you're messing with."

Bartolo spoke through clenched teeth. "If I say I want a virgin, you give her to me. If I beat her until she dies, you bury her body in the desert. If I cost you money, suck it up. Do I make myself clear?" He reverted to Spanish and looked at the mother, who now stroked her daughters' hair. "Time's up."

The mother's voice sounded strangled, as if she spoke around an enormous lump in her throat. "Please don't make me do this."

"I'm getting angry."

"Please, I will do anything you want."

"You did not do as you were told. As punishment, you must not only choose which daughter, but you will bring her to me." He held out his hand. "Now." He beckoned. "Or I take them both."

The woman crossed herself. "Mother Mary, forgive me for what I must do." She crept toward Bartolo. Both girls sobbed and clung to her. Tears streamed down her face as she used her right arm to force one of her daughters into his grasp.

———————

Across town, Adolfo pulled out his cell phone when he felt it buzz. "What is it, Carlos?"

"Bartolo, again." The strain in his youngest brother's voice was audible.

"Tell me."

"He took one of my girls at the drop house in West Phoenix. He looked totally coked out, as usual."

"He said he would stop using."

"He's losing control. You should have seen what he did to this girl. She's just a kid. I had to get one of my guys to take her to our private emergency clinic downtown. I don't know if she'll pull through."

Adolfo sensed the growing rift and took advantage. "Bartolo has become a liability."

"You mean because of his drug use?"

"Not just the drugs. He's been hotheaded since we were kids. Cocaine just makes it worse." Adolfo let that sink in before continuing. "I heard from our mole today that someone burned down the restaurant owned by that Phoenix detective's family."

"You mean Veranda Cruz? Was that Bartolo?"

"No doubt."

"Did he get approval to do that?"

Adolfo wanted Carlos to understand the stakes. To choose sides. "Bartolo is operating on his own." He paused for effect. "I'm going to call *Papá*. He must be told that we do not support Bartolo's actions. His drug use and reckless behavior put us all at risk."

"From what our mole tells us, Detective Cruz isn't the type to back down. Now that Bartolo has attacked her family, she'll never stop coming after him."

"And Bartolo is the same way. I wonder if either of them realizes this will only end when one of them is dead."

22

As THE MORNING SUN warmed the scarred surface of the dinette table in the safe house kitchen, Veranda pushed her half-eaten bowl of breakfast cereal away. She gulped her second cup of instant coffee as she assembled a makeshift gallery in front of her. To the right was a mugshot of Hector Villalobos, downloaded from Interpol when she was on the task force in DEB. To her left, a photograph of Ernesto Hidalgo, a childhood gift from her mother. Her makeup mirror stood in the center. Her eyes swiveled between her own face and that of the two men. She strained to see any likeness and blew out a sigh.

She looked exactly like her mother.

Could she have the blood of *El Lobo* coursing through her veins? She thought about her quick temper, her physical strength, her competitive streak. Villalobos traits. Then she recalled her devotion to her mother's family, her love of the restaurant and her fierce protectiveness. Qualities her mother had described in Ernesto Hidalgo. The man she thought of as her father.

Every belief she ever held about her past was in question. Was she the daughter of a brave defender of the people, or the offspring of a vicious killer? She thought of her poor mother, who had raised her without ever knowing the answer to that question. Lorena had kept her in the loving shelter of the family, despite the possibility that she was the child of her mortal enemy. Her very existence must have been a constant source of pain for her mother.

Then she remembered what Lorena had said about her name. *Veranda*. Watch the path she chooses. Even her name was a reminder that she could go in either direction.

Veranda balled her hands into fists as a new thought took shape in her mind. Did Hector know she might be his daughter? Had *El Lobo* told his children they might have a half sister? Was that what Bartolo was talking about at his house when he said he knew things about her?

Her cell phone buzzed with a text. Sam's message advised that he was in front of the safe house to pick her up.

Swallowing the lump in her throat, she stood and picked up her briefcase. She had a job to do. Questions about her parentage would have to wait. She had made a conscious decision to dress professionally today. In lieu of cargo pants and tactical boots, a pinstriped gray suit would instill confidence that she had made the transition from busting drug dealers to questioning homicide suspects. In the back of her mind, she acknowledged that the change in appearance was as much for herself as for her peers.

She pushed oversized sunglasses onto her nose as the sun blasted her eyes when she strode out the door. Sam waited at the curb, still driving the dreaded fleet Malibu.

He did not comment on her attire when she slid into the passenger seat. He cut his eyes to her. "What's wrong?"

So much for silent reflection. "Nothing." He frowned at her terse response. She sighed. "Except that my family is being pursued by a homicidal maniac."

He appeared pensive as he made his way north on 15th Avenue past the turnoff for headquarters. Veranda realized they weren't going to VCB, but she kept silent as he drove into the deserted parking lot of Encanto Park. He shut off the engine and got out of the vehicle.

Baffled, Veranda followed suit and circled around to him.

Mouth set in a grim line, he said, "Dammit, Veranda, I'm sick of this."

"Sick of what?"

"Let's walk. I'm too pissed off to sit still."

Brows furrowed, she fell into step beside him as he strode to the park's entrance. He continued toward one of the bridges spanning the canal that meandered through the property. Clearly, Sam was not here to admire the scenery. She lengthened her stride to keep up with him as he tramped up the bridge. He came to an abrupt halt when he reached the top. She almost collided with him as he pivoted to face her.

"You're holding out on me." His gray eyes turned to steel. "Have been since I met you that day in the mobile command vehicle."

"What do you mean?"

"I expect suspects to tell me half-truths and shade the facts, not my partner. There's something you're not telling me. I knew it when I interviewed you after the shooting, but I didn't call you on it because I didn't want Diaz up your ass."

She crossed her arms and stared back at him.

"And there's more," he said. "Bartolo Villalobos is coming after you like nothing I've ever seen before. And I've seen plenty. You're as obsessed with him as he is with you. What's really going on between you two?"

Veranda knew Sam was a seasoned detective. Decades of experience taught him to read people. Even her. She hesitated, wanting to

185

come clean. Realizing a confession could put his career in jeopardy as well as hers, she opted to deflect his questions instead. "I told you. He found out from Flaco I led the task force interdictions. Cost him millions in product and embarrassed him."

Sam waved a dismissive hand. "What else? What was he talking about when we went to his house?"

This was the moment. She couldn't bullshit Sam. He had seen through her from the start. She had to tell him what had set this whole chain of events in motion. Or she could refuse and lose his trust forever. She turned away from Sam to lean against the railing.

She heaved a sigh. "I've hidden the truth for so long, I'm not sure where to begin." Secrets and lies. Her mother's words replayed in her mind to remind her of her own subterfuge.

Sam's voice gentled. "Start at the beginning."

"If Diaz finds out—"

"I won't tell anyone." He gave her an appraising look. "As long as you didn't commit any crimes."

She stared at him. "I'm not guilty of any crime, it's just that ... " The silence stretched. *He's waiting me out.* She averted her gaze to a lone black swan floating toward them, bright red bill contrasting with ebony feathers. Ripples fanned out as it disappeared under the bridge beneath her feet. "I've never come clean about how I recruited Flaco."

"I thought you got sketchy on the details when Diaz and I asked about that after the shooting. Give me the rest of it."

She pushed away from the railing and they resumed their walk across the bridge. "My mother had two children with my stepfather, Miguel Gomez. Gabby is the youngest. I also had a half brother named Roberto, we called him Bobby."

Sam kept pace with her as they followed the path along the bank of the canal. She drew a deep breath. "Bobby was at South Phoenix

High School when he started hanging around some bad kids. This was years after I joined the force. I was a Property Crimes detective earning my investigative chops. Didn't have much time for Bobby."

Her mind filled with images of Bobby as a happy child, then guilt washed over her as they passed under the shadow of towering palm trees. "You've heard it before. Good kid gets in with the wrong crowd. Starts taking drugs..." Regret constricted her throat as her words trailed off. "My mother called me one night three years ago. Bobby was found in an alley across the street from his high school. Dead from an overdose. I never knew he was even using."

She fought to keep her voice measured. "They caught the dealer who sold the drugs to Bobby. He worked for the Villalobos cartel."

"Shit." Sam's voice was soft.

"I started angling for a position in the Drug Enforcement Bureau then. I worked property cases until my closure rate was the highest in the bureau. When an opening in Narcotics came up, I put in for it. Commander Montoya was in charge of DEB. He selected me, and I became the youngest narc on the department."

"How did you make inroads into the Villalobos network?"

"Started squeezing everyone I busted for info on the cartel. Didn't make much headway at first."

"I can imagine."

"Gabby had just started middle school, but she was on track to attend South Phoenix High like Bobby did. I figured it was my duty to keep drugs out of there." She shrugged. "So I drove through the area on my lunch break to check out the streets around the school. Sure enough, a dealer was slinging dope on a corner across from the school. I snatched him up on the spot."

"Flaco?"

She nodded. "I threatened him with enhanced penalties for selling drugs in a school zone. He got scared. Told me he had just graduated from lookout to dealer. Promoted to replace the previous guy."

"The one who sold Bobby the drugs?"

"Exactly. That's when it hit me. My brother's death was meaningless. Nothing had changed. The cartel just put another dealer out there to get the next batch of kids hooked. The Villalobos cartel carried on without even a hiccup."

Her throat tightened. "That's when I promised myself I would bring them down."

"And Flaco?"

"Flaco was still young. He wasn't a member of the Villalobos family, just a low-level employee at the time. I told him he could work off the charges if he registered as a confidential informant, and he did. After he became my CI, I told him about Bobby. I wanted him to understand what I was doing and why. He had a kid brother too. That's why he became a dealer, to get money for his family. Flaco and I developed an understanding."

"Did your supervisor know about Bobby?"

"Not one single person on the entire department knows about Bobby. We have a different last name. I use my mother's maiden name, Cruz. Gabby and Bobby use their father's last name, Gomez. We didn't share an address and Bobby was a lot younger than me. There was no obvious connection between us."

"Why all the secrecy?"

"What I did was no small thing. Do you think DEB would have let me lead a task force investigating the cartel responsible for the death of my own brother? I made the decision before I ever became a narc that my goal was to dismantle the cartel. If I told anyone why, I would never be allowed to do it."

Sam nodded. "Conflict of interest. Also, it could have given defense counsel some ammunition."

"That's why I never said anything to you before, Sam."

"We're partners. We're supposed to be honest with each other."

"Not about this. You could get into trouble for keeping my secret."

He stopped as they reached the foot of a second bridge. "Bottom line. Did you make lawful arrests when you were a narc?"

She looked him straight in the eye. "Every bust I made was legit."

Sam stroked his mustache.

"I'm in a bind though," she said. "Now that so much time has gone by, it's far too late to come clean. I had to leave out some pertinent details during my interview with Diaz. He's sniffing around like he smells another reason for my interest in the cartel's drug trafficking. He's not there yet, but he won't stop digging. Now I know why you refer to PSB as ferrets."

Sam hooked a thumb in his belt. "I don't give a crap about your motivation for going after any cartel. They're all a bunch of thugs who should be in jail. But I do need to know the background so I can see the big picture. Puts things in a different light." He looked thoughtful. "What does your family know about Flaco?"

"I've never told anyone the Villalobos cartel supplied the drugs that killed Bobby. My mother couldn't have taken it. Hell, I could barely take it."

"You said you told Flaco that Bobby was your kid brother?"

"Yes, to keep him informing for me after he worked off his charges."

"We can assume he told Bartolo before he died."

She bit back the dread that threatened to swamp her. Sam had come to the same inevitable conclusion that she had reached. "It's a safe bet the whole Villalobos clan is aware."

Sam started across the second bridge. "That means no more striking from the dark and then retreating behind cover until the next attack."

She furrowed her brows. "What are you saying?"

"That's how you narcs operate. Always the sneak attack. Cloak and dagger." He paused for a beat. "Never my style."

She rolled her eyes. "Your style involves dragging around a club and chiseling your reports on stone tablets."

He chuckled. "My old-school methods have put plenty of bad guys behind bars."

Sensing the unguarded moment, she put the question bluntly. "Are you going to tell anyone about Bobby?"

He stopped at the top of the bridge and turned to her. "Not unless I have to, but I'll clue you in first." He hesitated. "Is there anything else I need to know?"

Her stomach lurched as she thought about what her mother had just told her. She faced another decision. She spent a long moment scrutinizing Sam's watchful expression. What she had already told him was bad. The next part, worse.

She squared her shoulders. "There's something I just found out. Something shocking my mother told me last night."

He started down the other side of the bridge. Veranda sensed he was giving her time to compose her thoughts. As they followed the path around the other side of the canal, she decided to start with what he already knew. "Do you remember when we ate lunch at *Casa Cruz Cocina* and you met my family?"

"They're hard to forget."

"You recall that I explained how my mother came to the States when she was still pregnant with me?"

"Yes."

"Last night my mother told me things I never knew about our family's true history." Once she began talking, the words rushed out. She confided every detail of her mother's story. Sam listened in silence as she unburdened herself.

When she finished, he waited a long moment before speaking. "This would be a lot to take in for anybody. With everything that's going on right now, you've got to be a bit scared and a lot pissed off." His features hardened. "I know I sure as hell am. I never need extra motivation to take down a killer like Bartolo, but now I'll be damned if I'm gonna stop until that asshole is behind bars doing a life stretch." He paused. "And then we'll see about the rest of his family."

A lump formed in her throat and she blinked away the tears beginning to bead in her eyes. She quickened her pace. "This has always been *my* fight. I was alone, even when I was part of a team. After what you've seen, I can't believe you're willing to take on a deadly adversary like the cartel with me." She held up her hand when he stretched out an arm toward her. "Don't you dare give me a hug. I'm holding it together, but if you show me the slightest bit of compassion, I'll lose it."

They arrived back at the parking lot. Veranda felt a sense of true partnership with Sam. She had confided her darkest secret and, instead of judging her, he had shown concern and a willingness to stand beside her.

Another thought was uppermost in her mind. "Do you think this prevents me from working the case with you?" She held her breath as she waited for his answer.

"Just the opposite. This makes you the most valuable member of the team."

She exhaled with a sigh of relief. "How so?"

"Now that I know the background, I believe Bartolo's comment during our interview means he found out about your possible blood ties."

"How does that help us?"

"It explains a lot about Bartolo's behavior. Lately, he's been acting more like an obsessed stalker than the leader of a criminal enterprise."

"Stalker?"

"The body dumped with a personal message to you. The break-in at your house while you were asleep. The attack on people close to you. The personal text message." He spread his hands. "Classic stalking behavior."

She hadn't looked at it that way, but she agreed with his assessment. Bartolo had acted irrationally. Nothing he did made good business sense for the cartel. "Are you saying he's become obsessed with me?"

"That's exactly what I'm saying. And I'd like to use it to our advantage. You need to be front and center." He dug out his car keys and tossed them to her. "In fact, from here on out, you're in the driver's seat."

23

VERANDA PUSHED OPEN THE war room door and stopped short at the sight of Captain Anderson at the far end of the table, engrossed in conversation with Lieutenant Aldridge. She darted a glance over her shoulder at Sam, standing behind her. She and Sam had discussed the importance of the restaurant arson investigation remaining separate from the VCB investigation. She should have clued Anderson in about the mole. He would never have come, and if he did, he would be careful about what he said. Now, the mole would be in on all of their findings. Her eyes traveled around the room. Her squad, her supervisory chain of command, and Sergeant Diaz were all present. *Might as well make it a conference call with Bartolo.* She concealed her dismay and took a seat near the door. Sam slid into the next chair down.

Sergeant Jackson called the meeting to order over his steaming PPD coffee mug. "Some of you may not be familiar with our guest." He gestured to Anderson. "This is Captain Cole Anderson, arson investigator with the Phoenix Fire Department."

Anderson gave Veranda a businesslike nod of recognition.

Jackson waited for murmured greetings to die down. "Captain Anderson is in charge of the investigation into yesterday's fire, and he's here to give us a report of his initial findings. He advised Commander Webster yesterday that he found trace evidence at the fire scene. Lieutenant Aldridge invited him to brief us because we have reason to believe the arsonist is Bartolo Villalobos or one of his men. Captain Anderson, the floor is yours."

Anderson stood and picked up a remote for a laptop. He wore a white polo shirt with blue jeans. A fire department ID dangled from a lanyard around his neck.

As the lights dimmed, he clicked the remote. An image of her family's restaurant flashed up on the whiteboard. Veranda's heart somersaulted. The two walls that remained amid a sea of rubble were charred black. Her family's dreams were reduced to smoldering ruins. She blinked to focus on Anderson's words.

"I have concluded the preliminary investigation into the fire at *Casa Cruz Cocina* in South Phoenix." He met Veranda's eyes briefly before he continued. "The primary goal of an arson investigation is to determine the cause and origin of a fire. In this case, I had the advantage of having investigated a previous fire at the same location a few days earlier."

Anderson, apparently noticing the curious glances in Veranda's direction, clarified for the group. "That first fire was definitely unintentional. Over time, grease accumulates in the cooking vent that goes up through the attic. Some of the grease loosens and develops a void. Excessive heat builds up in the pocket and can ignite the grease. I verified this on the first fire because the scorch marks and other damage were confined to the inside of the cooking vent shaft."

He checked to be sure his audience followed his explanation. "There are two vents in the roof. A cooking vent and an attic vent. Yesterday's fire originated in the same area as the previous one, but the damage occurred outside of the cooking vent. The restaurant owner, Veranda's mother, assured me the ductwork over the range had been replaced after the first fire, and the inside surface was not discolored by flames. All of the charring radiated outward from the attic vent. I determined that someone poured fuel into the attic vent and ignited it. Our arson canine responded to the scene and detected an accelerant."

Anderson clicked the remote. A metal exhaust tube had been photographed from above. The vent was blackened on the outside, but not inside. "This is the cooking vent. Someone was trying to make it look like a grease fire, but notice that there's no scorching internal to that vent. The arsonist may have known that grease fires are a common cause for restaurants to burn and thought we might not look too closely."

"Or," Sam said, a dark expression crossing his face, "they may have known there was a recent grease fire at that restaurant."

Veranda threw him a look of agreement but said nothing.

"Once we establish the origin point, we look for the cause," Anderson said. "In this case, the cause of the fire was a cigarette with a bundle of matches wrapped around it using a rubber band." He pressed the remote again and an image of the charred residue of a cigarette filter with slender black strips stuck to it popped up on the whiteboard. "The perpetrator poured what I believe to be lighter fluid into the attic vent from the roof, then threw in the lit cigarette." He looked around the silent room. "There's no doubt this was arson."

Marci sat forward in her chair. "Matches!" She turned to Veranda. "Bartolo left a matchstick in your house with the photo of Pablo." She paused. "Or one of his cronies did."

"I agree. He left us a clue we couldn't figure out until the fire yesterday," Veranda said. "Bartolo also made a comment when Sam and I interviewed him about people who play with matches getting burned."

"It's in my report," Sam said, looking at Sergeant Jackson. "I put it on your desk."

Aldridge tapped his pen on the notepad in front of him. "There's not enough for a warrant to search his property," he said. "But Bartolo made sure we know he's behind it."

Anderson raised the remote. "I obtained footage from a security camera at a pawn shop across the street from the restaurant. This is a copy." He pressed the remote and everyone leaned forward to see.

Anderson pointed with his free hand. "The images are fairly grainy, but they show a man cross the roof and fumble with a cigarette like he's attaching something to it. Then he squats down and lights up his smoke. He takes a few drags until it glows, then tosses it into the attic vent." Anderson turned to the group, eyes wide with excitement.

Everyone looked at each other, nonplussed.

Marci voiced the unspoken question. "Okay, so you have arson with an unidentifiable suspect on a grainy video. Did you send it to our video forensics unit to see if they can clear up the image?"

Lieutenant Aldridge dropped his pen onto the table. "I didn't authorize that."

The excitement evaporated from Anderson's face. "I apologize for not making myself clear. The video forensics unit can wait until we go to trial."

"Trial?" Aldridge asked. "What are you talking about?"

"I'm used to dealing with fellow arson investigators. They would have offered to buy me a beer by now." Anderson grinned. "Allow me to explain."

Veranda read confusion on the faces around the table. *Anderson's enjoying this.* As a fireman, it must be nice for him to be one up on the PD Homicide squad.

Anderson closed the laptop and someone turned on the lights. His voice took on the animated tone of an instructor teaching his favorite subject. "People think a fire will destroy DNA evidence, but it often survives even a strong blaze. Several arsonists have been caught by residual DNA on a cigarette filter."

He pulled out the thumb drive and held it up. "This video shows that the suspect, who was careful to wear latex gloves, used his mouth to suck on the cigarette and get it going." He waited for the group to catch up. "We have his DNA."

Now his audience smiled with him.

Hope surged in Veranda's chest. "Bartolo's DNA is on file. He submitted to a buccal swab when he was arrested a few years back." The drug lord had been convicted only once in his lengthy career, and served a reduced sentence. Even though he had served his time, his photos, prints, scars, marks, tattoos, characteristics, and DNA remained in the database.

Sam stroked his mustache. "As we mentioned before, Bartolo could have ordered one of his men to set the fire."

"If the DNA matches one of his known henchmen, we'll at least have another lead to follow," Doc said.

Marci pursed her lips. "Because Pablo Moreno worked out so well for us."

"Let's not get ahead of ourselves," Aldridge said, and turned to Anderson. "Where is the evidence now?"

"The Phoenix Police Crime Scene Response Unit came out to process the scene. That's who we normally use to collect our forensic evidence. They took it to the police lab for processing."

Tony stretched in his chair. "The Fire Department is riding on our coattails as usual, I see."

Commander Webster glared at the detective, but Anderson didn't appear to be bothered by the dig. "Arson is one of a small number of criminal cases we work, why should we set up a lab and an evidence room?"

Veranda brought the discussion back to the main point. "How soon will you know something?"

"The fire chief contacted the lab to expedite," Anderson said. "They've agreed to run the test tomorrow. It's Saturday, but they called in a tech on overtime. If there's a match, I'll get a warrant. Arson is a class two felony."

Aldridge looked at Anderson. "Let us know if there's a match immediately. SAU will have to be involved in serving a felony warrant on someone high up in the cartel."

"Agreed," Anderson said. "We frequently use PPD assets to make apprehensions anyway. This is just higher risk than most."

Veranda and Sam exchanged covert glances. She was furious that Bartolo would find out about this development as soon as the mole could make a phone call. What would Bartolo do when he found out?

Jackson stood. "Does anyone else have a report?" No one responded. He turned to Veranda. "Detective Cruz, have you had any luck decoding that printout from the cell phone yet?"

She looked him straight in the eye and lied. "Not yet. Still trying."

He turned back to the group. "I want everyone working on their assignments and writing reports. Keep your cell phones handy. I'll send out a blast text the minute I hear anything from Captain Anderson tomorrow. Dismissed."

Sam whispered in Veranda's ear. "Hang back a minute."

They waited for the room to clear before Sam looked over his shoulder and glanced back at her. "Do you think the mole might try to get that evidence out of the lab tonight?"

"I'm not worried. Only the investigating officer or the lab techs can sign out evidence."

"True." Sam grunted. "But I don't like it. Bartolo has a history of making things disappear when he wants to tie up loose ends."

"If the mole tried to get those materials from the lab, he would completely blow his cover. We would know his identity if he even asked to *see* the evidence. The lab is covered in surveillance cameras."

"The mole has no direct access to the Fire Department investigation, so I have to admit I was irritated when Anderson briefed everyone this morning. We need to shut that conduit of information down. I don't normally like to share, but I think we need to loop him in on this."

"Loop me in on what?" Anderson asked as he walked through the war room's open door.

Sam's head snapped up. "You firemen make a habit of lurking around?"

Anderson shrugged. "No lurking. I came back to ask Veranda to lunch." He paused. "You too, of course. How could I pass up such charming company?"

"I've got a better idea," Sam turned to Veranda. "You go with Captain Anderson and bring him up to speed. I'll head to FIB."

Veranda nodded. She understood that Sam intended to advise Commander Murphy of the Family Investigations Bureau about the new developments from their morning briefing.

She turned to Anderson. "Sam needs the car to get to FIB. Can I hitch a ride?"

His cheeks dimpled. "If you don't mind being seen in a Fire Department pickup truck."

"Captain?" Sam addressed Anderson.

"Yes, Detective?"

Sam dropped his voice. "Things could get dangerous for you. Be careful."

Anderson adopted a thoughtful pose. "Hmmm, I wonder what it would be like to have a dangerous job."

Sam smirked. "Yeah, I forgot. You fire guys don't get scared. You don't even have the sense to run out of a burning building."

"And you police types," Anderson replied, "don't have the sense to run out of a building when people are shooting at you."

"Are we finished peeing in our respective corners?" Veranda asked. The men chuckled and she tugged Anderson's elbow. "Let's go. We have a lot to talk about."

———————

She filled him in about the mole and the secondary investigation as he drove her out of the downtown governmental district. He listened in silence, the only outward sign of concern a deepening of the creases above his thick, sandy brows.

"Damn," he said. "I wish I'd known about this when I gave that briefing."

"I couldn't have stopped you without making it obvious we're aware of a leak."

"I'll be careful about what I say from now on."

She realized they were driving over the bridge to enter South Phoenix. "Where are you taking me for lunch?"

He stared straight ahead. "I hear there's a place around here that has the best authentic Mexican food in Arizona." The corners of his mouth kicked up. "I got a call from a city license services supervisor early this morning. He wanted to approve the use of a previously permitted food truck in the *Casa Cruz Cocina* parking lot. He was checking to be sure it wouldn't compromise my investigation." Anderson's eyes found hers. "I said there would be no problem."

Her jaw dropped as they rounded a corner and she saw Felipe and Juan's food truck, the *Casa Cruz Camión*, parked in the lot next to the burned-out hull of the restaurant. After Anderson stopped, she threw open the passenger door, jumped out, and ran past the blackened remains of the once proud establishment. The smell of charred, wet ash still hung in the air.

She yanked open the shiny food truck door to discordant voices. Her mother, along with her Aunt Juana and Uncles Rico, Felipe, and Juan, were all crowded inside the cramped space. Arms flailed, voices rose, heads bobbed. Spanglish flew back and forth as they held a family discussion, Latino style.

"*Mamá*." She caught her mother by the elbow. "What's going on?"

Lorena pointed at tío Rico. "He wants to leave."

"Leave what, this corner? Open the restaurant in a new location instead of rebuilding?"

"No," tía Juana cut in. "He wants to leave Arizona!"

A flurry of Spanish erupted around her as Veranda took in their meaning. This was her fault. Some of them wanted to flee again as they had over thirty years ago. She sensed their fear and couldn't blame them.

Tío Juan's voice boomed above the others. "*Silencio!*" All eyes turned to him. "We are divided. Some want to rebuild here, others want to go north to get farther away from the Villalobos cartel." He turned to Veranda. "We know they burned the restaurant down." He held up a hand to forestall her. "Do not blame yourself."

How could she not? Her eyes glided from one anxious face to another. These were the people she loved, and they were wrestling with a dilemma she had caused. They had seen the news stories about her and knew she was at war with the cartel. It wasn't a giant leap for them to figure out the Villalobos family was responsible for the fire.

Her family had left everything behind to outrun their old enemy. And now Veranda had brought the wolves back to their door.

"We must decide now," tío Rico said. "The insurance man is coming today. We must tell him what we will do."

Tío Felipe glanced at his watch. "And we have customers coming in an hour. I posted our new location on every foodie fan page and social media site in Phoenix. We got to start cooking."

"This is our home now," Lorena said, picking up her argument. "We spent many years building our homes and our business here. We have done nothing wrong. Why should we run again?"

Tío Rico pointed in the direction of the rubble that had been the restaurant. "For the same reason we ran before. Because killers are after us." He waved a spatula with his other hand. "Better to leave all of this behind and protect our children."

Tía Juana stepped forward, eyes blazing. "Our children!" She dug a hand into her blouse and jerked out a metal chain. A set of military dog tags dangled from her whitened fingers. "My son gave his life to fight for this country. Did he die so we could run like rabbits?" She took another step, the chain swinging from her fist as her voice rose. "We are Americans now!" Her eyes misted. "We have worked hard." She pinned each of them with her eyes. "Built lives." Her voice dropped to a hoarse whisper. "Paid the highest price." She took a deep breath. "I will never run away again. This is my home. Who stays with me?"

Veranda swallowed hard as she watched her mother step forward to put her arms around tía Juana. Lorena's soft voice carried through her sister's hair. "I will stay."

One by one, the rest of the family walked quietly to Juana and Lorena to embrace them. Tío Rico's features formed grim lines of resignation as he finally joined the others. Veranda's heart swelled with pride for her family's fighting spirit as she looked on.

After a long moment, she turned and stepped outside the food truck to Anderson. Without a word, he put an arm around her shoulder.

"They're nowhere near ready for lunch," she said, glancing over her shoulder at the vehicle. "If you're hungry, we'll have to go somewhere else."

He kept his arm where it was and followed her gaze. "You know you can't make it to the rank of fire captain without learning how to cook."

"Ah yes, the fireman's motto." She looked up at him with a mischievous smile. "Eat till you're tired, then sleep till you're hungry."

He chuckled as he bent his head to return her gaze. "Hey, we work thirty-six-hour shifts. A man's got to eat and sleep sometime."

"Do I understand correctly that you're offering to help with lunch prep?"

"Sure. Chop, cook, clean, serve customers—I can multitask."

"Why are you doing this?"

He slid his hand up to her chin. "Your family has gotten a raw deal."

"So have a lot of other immigrants over the years."

"Those families don't have a feisty Latina with beautiful hazel eyes."

"Veranda!" Lorena called her from the doorway of the truck. "Can you stay long enough to serve a few customers?" Her mother eyed her as if she wondered what she might have interrupted. "Gabriela can't come until late this afternoon. She's at the mall helping Carmelita pick out a tiara for her *quinceañera*."

It was hard for Veranda to believe that tío Rico's daughter, Carmelita, would turn fifteen in two weeks. Hadn't she just been to Carmelita and Gabby's fourth-grade school play? Born only a month apart, the cousins were inseparable. In the past few weeks, Veranda had seen them giggling and whispering over the elaborate plans for Carmelita's coming out party.

Veranda turned to her mother. "I have to call my sergeant to ask for a couple hours leave. I'm in a holding pattern on my investigation until Sam gets back to me." She jerked a thumb at Anderson. "Then it's up to him. He's my ride."

"My shift ended this morning," Anderson said. "I've cooked for crowds. Happy to help. Tell me what you need."

Veranda was sure her mother would never have agreed to an outsider in the kitchen in any other situation. It was a measure of their current crisis when Lorena beckoned him inside the van.

————

Two hours later, Veranda bussed paper plates smeared with tomatillo sauce from card tables placed haphazardly in the parking lot next to the food truck. She had tossed her suit jacket onto a folding chair, and now wasn't sure if it would ever be free from the aroma of caramelized onions, roasted poblano peppers, and spicy chorizo. Her sleeveless top damp with perspiration, she mopped her forehead with a paper towel. Anderson had helped her uncles erect a canvas tarp above several of the tables. It blocked out the worst of the scorching sun, but she was still overheated.

Her cell phone buzzed and she pulled it from her pocket. "Go ahead, Sam."

As usual, he didn't waste time with small talk. "Been busy all morning. Commander Murphy had me give an update to Chief Tobias."

"And?"

"Murphy hasn't had any luck figuring out who the mole is."

"What about Captain Anderson's evidence?"

"They both agree with you. It's safe at the lab. The cartel really doesn't have a play. Looks like we'll wait for the lab techs to run it through DNA analysis tomorrow and see what happens."

"If Bartolo personally set that fire, the mole will just tell him to head to Mexico before we can get an arrest warrant."

"I don't like it any more than you do, but that's where we stand. At least we can flush him out. Didn't you say you wanted to disrupt the cartel's narcotics trafficking operation?"

"Yes, but I also want to destabilize the entire Villalobos organization. I'm hoping that if Bartolo ends up in jail, or is banished to Mexico, one of the other siblings will try to take his place. Infighting in the pack undermines leadership."

"I imagine *El Lobo* knows that. He didn't build the cartel just to watch the younger generation tear it down with squabbling. He'll take action."

"And I have no idea what he'll do. That's the only part that bothers me."

"Are you still with Anderson? Jackson told me to let you know we're off duty until we hear from him tomorrow."

"I'm still with him. Thanks to the mole, Bartolo will have the safe house flagged on his GPS by now, so there's no point in keeping it a secret. Anderson can drop me off there."

"You sure? You could spend the night with Sarah and me at our house."

"Thanks for the offer, but you were right when you said we should keep up pretenses. I'll stay at the safe house, but I plan to sleep with one eye open and my gun under the pillow."

She disconnected and looked for Anderson. She spotted his muscular arm handing an order of carne asada street tacos out of the food truck window. Blond hair on the bicep glistened against tanned skin. She sucked in some air. *Cálmate, chica.*

Her tía Juana appeared in the window next to Anderson. "This one"—she looked him up and down—"can stay as long as he wants." She winked at Veranda. "Knows his way around the stove too."

Heat rose up Veranda's neck and flushed through her cheeks. Her family had set her up with every eligible Latino north of Yuma without any luck. Apparently they had decided the handsome *gringo* would do in a pinch.

———

The safe house was a short drive from the restaurant parking lot. Veranda sat in the passenger seat, reveling in the delicious cool of the air-conditioned Fire Department pickup as they crossed the bridge into downtown Phoenix. The readout on the dash indicated the outside temperature was 116 degrees. The dog days of summer were in full force.

Anderson pulled up to the curb in front of the little bungalow. Her city car was parked in the driveway. "Going to invite me in for a shower?"

She smiled. "It's bad enough I let you see where the safe house is located, you probably shouldn't come inside."

"The mole knows where this place is by now." He turned off the engine. "I'm trying to figure out a way to keep an eye on you until Bartolo is arrested."

"Did you forget that I carry a gun?"

"Did you forget that I do too?"

She rolled her eyes. "Please don't tell me your gun is bigger than mine."

His smile dazzled her. "You'll have to find out how big my gun is for yourself."

"A fireman with a gun. Still think it's weird."

"And I have police training too."

"Also weird."

He became serious. "Veranda, I think you should go somewhere no one can find you. How about my place?"

"If I sleep somewhere else tonight, the mole might figure out we're onto him."

"Are you sure?"

His implication was clear. And tempting. She gave him a slow smile. "You can walk me inside if you're that worried."

He followed her to the front door and watched as Veranda turned the key to the reinforced front door and stepped over the threshold. She deactivated the alarm and waited for Anderson to enter, then latched the dead bolt. She switched on a ceiling fan to disperse the stuffy air and strolled to the kitchen. "I've got iced tea, beer, and water. You thirsty?"

He leaned his tall frame against the wall by the Saltillo tiled kitchen counter. "Parched."

She turned to see his eyes burn a path up and down her body. She licked her lips, ambled over to him, and tilted her head up to his. "What would … quench your thirst?"

He wound an arm around her waist and pulled her against him. "Right now, I have a taste for caramel latte." He brought his mouth down to hers.

Heat rushed from her head down to her belly. She slid her hands up his neck to bury her fingers in his thick blond hair. A moan escaped her as he caressed the curve of her bottom. She pushed her leg between his and felt his excitement.

His hands drew her tighter to him.

The doorbell chimed.

She wrenched away, bent to pull her gun out of its ankle holster, and pressed a finger to her lips. Anderson had already drawn his Glock.

She stood to the side of the door, wishing it had a peephole. "Who's there?"

A man's voice, slightly muffled, came from outside. "Sergeant Diaz."

"Shit." She shoved her gun back into its holster, unlocked the bolt on the front door, and flung it wide. "What do you want?"

Diaz stood on the stoop, hand resting on the gleaming gold sergeant's shield clipped to his belt. "I got off work and dropped by to check on you. Was just going to drive by when I noticed a city truck parked out front." His eyes narrowed as Anderson stepped behind Veranda. "What is *he* doing here?"

Aware she was already on shaky ground with the PSB sergeant, she tilted her chin up as if she had done nothing wrong. "He gave me a lift home."

"You could've called for a ride. He's not supposed to know the location of the safe house. This is completely unprofessional."

"I'm not sure how confidential the safe house really is."

"What's that supposed to mean?"

She had said too much and back-pedaled. "What I mean to say is, he's a sworn law enforcement officer like us. He's investigating the suspects in this case. He can be trusted."

"He may be sworn, but he's not like us." Diaz's voice dripped with contempt.

Anderson moved in front of her. "Do you have something to say to me, Sergeant?"

Diaz took a step forward and tilted his head back a fraction to glare into the fireman's eyes. "I don't like you interfering with a police investigation, or sniffing around Detective Cruz. I want you out of our safe house. Now."

"You can't order me around, Diaz."

It was Veranda who answered in a quiet voice. "He can order you out of a clandestine police facility."

Anderson turned to her. "Then come with me. We'll go someplace else."

Diaz interrupted. "I am ordering Detective Cruz to stay here."

Anderson's eyes implored Veranda. "Surely he can't—"

"He can," she said.

"We're both off duty. This is our personal time."

Diaz crossed his arms. "Something else you firemen don't understand. There is no 'off duty' for us." He inclined his head toward Veranda. "We are always accountable for our actions. Always subject to discipline. My orders have to do with maintaining this detective's safety and the integrity of the investigation she is conducting. Your presence does not facilitate either objective."

Anderson looked as if he wanted to throw a punch. "Fine. I'll be in touch tomorrow with the test results." He glowered at Diaz and strode down the front walkway to his truck.

Diaz turned to her. "You never should have brought him here."

"You know, I resent you checking up on me. We're all on the same side, trying to apprehend Bartolo." She narrowed her eyes. "Aren't we?"

He returned her stare, his dark brown eyes giving nothing away. "He's not a cop. He's trying to get in your pants. And he generally pisses me off."

"Get over it. We need to work together."

"Your pushing it, Cruz." He leaned in. "Especially for someone in your position."

She arched an eyebrow in question.

"Despite what I said, I didn't come here simply to check on you." His jaw muscle tightened. "I didn't want to discuss police business in front of that *pinche* fireman."

"What business couldn't wait until Monday?"

"I have an appointment scheduled first thing Monday morning in my commander's office to give him a progress report on my investigation. Unfortunately, I can't update him when I'm in the dark about key facts." He paused for a beat. "I came by to give you one last chance to come clean before I tell my commander you're being less than forthcoming."

She widened her eyes. "I have no idea what you're talking about."

"I read Detective Stark's report on your interview with Bartolo Villalobos this afternoon."

"Why?"

"I told you I wanted to be kept in the loop on all of your dealings with the cartel because it could have a bearing on my investigation. Sergeant Jackson agreed and gave me a thumb drive with the case file on it." He uncrossed his arms to jam his fists onto his hips. "There are things you're not telling me."

She knew better than to say anything more than necessary at this point. Let Diaz show his cards.

"What did Bartolo mean when he said he checked into your background and knew things about you?"

She gave a derisive snort. "You're going to take the rantings of a coked-out criminal seriously?"

He pointed a finger at her. "There's more, Detective Cruz. I can feel it. Either talk to me now, or I report that you are being evasive."

"Evasive!" She went on the offensive. "I never lied to you." *Left out pertinent facts, yes. Lied, no.* She knew the Department would consider it a lie of omission, so she was screwed either way if he caught her.

He took a step closer, invading her space. "Why don't we put that to the test, Detective? I can call out a polygraph examiner to meet us at PSB in twenty minutes."

Her pulse ticked up at the mere mention of the polygraph. No matter how well she masked her outward symptoms of stress, she couldn't fool the machine. Time to change tactics. Go for sympathy. Buy time.

"Look, I've got nothing left in my tank. My family's restaurant burned to the ground. I spent the past several hours trying to help them pick up the pieces of their lives." She let her shoulders sag. "I'm exhausted."

The tension in his features eased a fraction. "I know you've been through a lot." He hesitated. "I'll let you get some rest tonight, but I need answers tomorrow."

Her temper flared again. "Tomorrow is Saturday. Don't you have a family life?"

Diaz's face hardened into stone. "My personal life is none of your business. You will report to PSB at zero-nine-hundred hours."

She mentally kicked herself for her insensitive comment. It had pissed him off. "I don't have authorization for overtime."

He pursed his lips. "My OT budget is unlimited for this investigation. I'll make sure you're covered."

So much for softening him up. Damn if he didn't push her buttons. "Can't this wait until Monday?"

"I've extended you a great deal of credit, Detective Cruz." He leveled a dark gaze on her. "It's time to pay the bill."

24

BARTOLO SAT BEHIND THE wheel of a nondescript delivery van, hidden behind a nearby stand of mesquite trees. He lifted the night vision binoculars to his eyes a second time. All of the lights in the house had gone out over an hour ago. He checked his watch. Half past two in the morning. Everyone should be well asleep by now.

He'd seen her earlier that night. Long and lean with supple caramel-colored skin and thick dark hair cascading down her back. She had come into the house with the rest of the family. They hadn't noticed him hiding. Now his plans were about to pay off. Plans for her. Sweet, innocent, beautiful. He had learned her name from his research. "Gabriela," he murmured.

Bartolo crept forward to her bedroom window. He had watched her silhouetted figure as she changed into a short summer nightgown, her lithe body backlit from the glow of her bedroom light. He had become aroused and had to suppress his excitement so he could focus on his mission. He would take his time with the girl later.

When he reached the window, he pulled on heavy duty rubber gloves before silently sliding it open. He had checked it earlier. Unlocked. He slipped in and listened to the steady rhythm of her breathing. He reached into his pocket and pulled out a plastic baggie containing a damp cloth, withdrew the rag, then shoved the empty bag back into his pocket.

Delicious anticipation raced through him as he inched toward the bed and got into position. In one swift motion, he pounced on top of Veranda's younger sister, pinning her with his bulk. At the same time, he slapped the cloth over her nose and mouth, clamping down hard. The girl thrashed, but she was no match for his size and strength. He knew the more she struggled, the deeper she would have to breathe. Sure enough, he felt her suck air into her lungs. Within ten seconds, she went limp.

Well aware of the limitations of chloroform, he knew he had to act quickly. Gabriela would begin to recover as soon as she started to breathe fresh air. He lifted her from the mattress, draped her over his right shoulder, then climbed through the window. He paused to close it behind him before he checked her breathing. A few seconds later, she moaned. He carried her across the yard to his waiting van.

The handle to the rear cargo area gleamed in the moonlight. He wrenched the door open, thrust Gabriela inside, and scrambled in after her. She began to groan and writhe. Bartolo slapped her hard across the face. She whimpered and slumped onto the metal floor. He grasped both of her hands, placing one on top of the other. He twisted to jerk flex cuffs from his pocket. A staccato ratcheting sound broke the silence in the van as he cinched the black plastic strip until it bit into her delicate wrists. Finally, he fumbled in the dark recesses of the cargo area until his fingers found a roll of duct tape. He used his teeth to tear off a piece. A silver shaft of moonlight sliced into the darkness in the van, playing across her lovely features. He admired her full young lips, gently parted in repose. Then he pressed the tape over her mouth.

Bartolo drove away slowly, careful to obey all traffic laws. This was no time to get pulled over for a traffic infraction. He wanted to deal with only one person on the Phoenix Police Department.

25

VERANDA WOKE UP THE next morning disoriented in the unfamiliar bed, convinced she would never be comfortable in the safe house. She shuffled to the bathroom and took a hot shower. When she emerged, she went back into the bedroom and pulled out black bikini briefs and a matching bra from the bureau, then started for the closet. She stopped short at her nightstand. A missed call light pulsed on her cell phone. She picked up the phone and tapped the screen. Eight text messages and a voicemail from her mother. She cursed herself for switching the phone to silent mode before she fell asleep.

She touched the voicemail icon. Her mother sounded frantic. "*Mi'ja*, Gabriela is missing! We checked her room when she did not come to breakfast. She was gone. She has never run away. I am scared something terrible happened. Please call me."

Veranda's heart slammed against her ribs. Instinctively, she knew her mother was right. Something terrible had happened. Scenarios ran through her mind, each one more horrific than the last.

Just as she caught her breath, her phone vibrated in her hand and she looked at the screen. Her racing heart stuttered. A text message from Flaco's old cell phone. Her fingers trembled as she tapped the icon to open the message. The grainy, low-lit image of a crying young girl appeared. She was gagged and tied to a chair, with one eye swollen. Veranda clutched the nightstand to steady herself. "Gabby," she breathed, and hit the call button.

A masculine voice she recognized answered. "Good morning, Detective Cruz."

Her gut clenched. "Bartolo."

"Nice to speak to you again."

She wanted to tear him to shreds. "What have you done to Gabriela?"

A soft chuckle. "Nothing ... yet. But that won't last."

Veranda had to think strategically. Screaming at Bartolo would only feed his feeling of power. Giving in to her worst fears wouldn't help. She called up every ounce of resolve she possessed and forced calm into her voice.

"What do you want, Bartolo?"

"This is between us. Tell no one I have contacted you. I will exchange the cigarette butt the fireman found at the restaurant for Gabriela."

"What cigarette butt?"

"You don't want to play with me, *puta*. If I don't have that evidence in my hands by noon today, your sweet little sister will become the property of Carlos."

Veranda fought down a wave of nausea when Bartolo mentioned the brother in charge of the coyotes and their human trafficking operation. Her little sister could be sent into any of the underground brothels run by Carlos Villalobos in the States, or even smuggled into Mexico. Veranda might never find her.

Bartolo's voice broke into her thoughts. "That is, after I've had my fun with her."

He wants to provoke me. Get me to lose control. She took another steadying breath and focused her mind. "You seem to have a lot of inside information about the investigation."

"I've been watching you."

"Getting the cigarette butt isn't that simple. The evidence is secured at the forensics lab downtown. There are controls in place. The investigating officer has to sign it out. It's not even a police case. The Fire Department has jurisdiction."

"Then get the fireman to sign it out and give it to you. Fuck him if you need to. Just bring it to my warehouse by noon."

"Do you think that if the butt is missing you'll walk?"

"As I said before, I have a law degree. If you can't produce the physical evidence at trial, any tests from that evidence are inadmissible. If the investigating official loses the evidence after signing it out, his testimony has no credibility." He paused. "So, yes, Detective, I think I'll walk."

"How about I just put a bullet in your brain?"

"Then Gabriela would start her new … profession."

Veranda had to maintain her composure, to think like a cop. Her mind whirred as she struggled to come up with a plan. "I'll call you when I get the evidence so we can make the exchange."

His hollow laugh met her ear. "Detective, you must think I'm stupid. I know full well that if I leave this cell phone on you will use the signal to trace my location. I can't give you that information until I'm ready to receive you as my guest."

He'd guessed her plan. "How the hell am I supposed to meet with you then?"

"First, I destroy this phone. Then I'll use a new phone to contact you at noon. You will text me a photo of the evidence in your hands.

At that time, I will send you the location of the warehouse where I'm holding Gabriela. I have an alarm system and men on the perimeter. If you bring anyone with you, I will know. And your sister will die."

"How can I trust you not to kill us both?"

"Interesting question. I guess you'll have to figure that one out for yourself. And, speaking of trust, you had better not double-cross me. I have a way to verify that the cigarette butt has been signed out of the lab. I'll know if you try to substitute a fake."

Veranda realized he was referring to the mole, who could check to see if she had obtained the real evidence. She assumed Bartolo was still not aware she knew about the mole, so she played the game. "How would you know what's going on at the lab?"

"I know every move you make. If you dare try anything, my men will arrange for the rest of your family to die in very unpleasant ways." He disconnected.

"*Dios mio*," she whispered, and crossed herself.

This would take divine intervention. Bartolo was insane. How could she deal with a madman? She rushed to her closet, grabbed her go-bag, put on a fitted black Under Armour shirt, then stepped into black cargo pants. She finished the outfit with tactical boots and a nylon webbed belt before pulling her thick mane into an elastic band high on the back of her head.

While she dressed, she formulated the beginnings of a strategy. Still in her closet, she called Sam.

"Hello?" His calm baritone rumble reassured her.

"Something just happened. I'll brief you in person. Meet me at Encanto Park in twenty minutes. Same entrance as before."

"Veranda, what's going on?"

"Can't talk now." She paused. "You'd better call Commander Murphy and tell him to come too." She disconnected.

She dialed Anderson and repeated the conversation. He seemed equally baffled when she refused to explain the situation. She grabbed her ballistic vest and slung her gun belt over her shoulder as she reactivated the alarm and locked the door behind her.

Scanning the area, she strode to the Malibu parked in the driveway. All quiet. She unlocked the car door and slid into the driver's seat, tossing her vest and gun belt onto the passenger seat.

She paused and stared at the cell phone in her hand. What should she say to her mother? She recalled the panic in her mother's voice and didn't want her to contact the authorities. A standard police response to a missing juvenile would only complicate matters. Veranda drew in a deep breath and released it before she made the call.

"Veranda?" Lorena's plaintive voice sounded desperate.

"*Mamá*, I have difficult news for you." She steeled herself. Better to get it out right away. "Bartolo kidnapped Gabby. I'm on my way to get her." A gasp followed by a torrent of sobs from the other end wrenched Veranda's heart. "*Mamá*, he has not hurt her. I promise I will bring her back to you safe and sound." More anguished wails. "I have to go. Please tell the others to stay with you. Everyone needs to remain at home … and *Mamá* …" Veranda waited until her mother caught her breath. "Pray for us."

26

VERANDA WATCHED SAM'S PURPOSEFUL stride as he approached the Encanto Park bench where she waited. Her eyes slid to the parking lot when the *thunk* of a truck door slamming shut drew her attention to Anderson, who jogged toward her. She got to her feet.

Sam reached her first. "I came as fast as I could. What the hell is going on?"

"Things just got a lot more complicated."

During the time it took for the men to arrive, she had finalized her plan. After analyzing the situation from every angle, she could not see herself surviving a direct encounter with Bartolo and his men. Once she resigned herself to this fact, she had been able to devise a strategy that offered the best hope to save Gabby, and send Bartolo to prison.

Anderson joined them, forming a triangle. He scanned her face. "Veranda, what's wrong?"

She drew a deep breath. "Bartolo kidnapped my sister, Gabriela. She's only fourteen." She paused while Anderson swore. Sam betrayed no emotion. "Bartolo contacted me using Flaco's old cell phone thirty minutes ago. He's demanding the cigarette butt in exchange for her."

"How do you know he has her?" Sam asked.

"Remember how Bartolo texted me that picture of a wolf after the restaurant fire?"

Sam nodded.

Anderson put his palms up. "Who's Flaco?"

"He was my confidential informant. The one Bartolo tortured and killed after the botched interdiction. Bartolo kept Flaco's cell, and it had my phone number in the memory. He used it to send me this." She held out her phone with the image of Gabby on the display screen. Sam's jaw tightened as he looked at it.

Anderson's face suffused with color. "That asshole sergeant from last night. He's the mole."

Sam's eyes snapped to Anderson's. "What sergeant?"

Veranda responded. "Anderson came into the safe house after he drove me home yesterday." She put her hands up to stave off Sam's unspoken question. "Nothing happened. He was inside for less than five minutes before Diaz showed up and ejected him."

"It was him," Anderson said. "Diaz was at the briefing yesterday. He must have gone straight to Bartolo and told him about the cigarette butt."

Sam looked back and forth between Veranda and Anderson. He stroked his mustache but said nothing.

She threw her hands in the air. "Can we worry about how Bartolo found out about the evidence later? Right now, let's focus on the fact that this bastard has Gabby. I've come up with a way to get to her. It's not perfect, but it's our only chance. I'll need help from both of you."

"Shoot," Sam said.

She knew they wouldn't like certain aspects of her plan. Especially the last part. She squared her shoulders. "When Bartolo spoke to me, he said he had a way to verify that the cigarette butt had actually been signed out from the forensics lab. Threatened me not to give him fake evidence."

Sam raised an eyebrow. "He told you he had an inside guy?"

"Not exactly. Just hinted at it. I think he wanted to leave me wondering how he would know what was going on at the lab. He also made a comment about knowing every move we made."

"So where does that leave us?" Anderson asked.

"First, we should assume the mole will be aware of what's going on with the evidence in the arson case, even if he can't access it directly."

"You mean Diaz," Anderson said.

"We don't know that for sure." Sam raised a hand in a calming gesture. "Let's hear Veranda out."

She turned to Anderson. This part of the operation depended on his cooperation. "You need to go to the lab and sign out the cigarette butt."

"What?" He reared back, appalled. "If you think I'm going to turn my evidence over to that—"

"We're not going to give him the real evidence." She turned to Sam. "Is Murphy on his way?"

Sam nodded. "He lives in Mesa. It'll take him another ten minutes to get here."

"Good," Veranda said. "Anderson will turn the evidence over to Murphy, who will sign it into the lab under *his* name for *his* investigation. He can request processing and receive the results. That way, the chain of custody is maintained. When we get to trial, the prosecutor will add Commander Murphy to his list of witnesses to call to the stand."

Sam grimaced. "I'll withhold judgment on the feasibility of all this until I hear the rest of your plan."

"While Murphy submits the real evidence for testing, we mock up a fake to look exactly like it. We find the same brand of cigarette, smoke it down to a butt and burn it a bit to look like it was recovered from a fire scene. Then Anderson sticks it in an evidence bag, fills out the label, and dates it and initials it just like the original."

"Let me get this straight," Sam said. "You want to do precisely what he told you not to?"

"Yes. In fact, he gave me the idea. Bartolo's relying on the mole to tell him the evidence is signed out, and it will be. We'll have to get as many components as possible ready ahead of time, because we want a short time window between when we check out the evidence and when Bartolo calls. We don't want Bartolo to think we've been playing with it for hours."

Everyone was silent for a moment as they considered the plan.

Sam spoke first. "Okay, so you'll have fake evidence. How do you get it to Bartolo?"

Veranda tilted her chin up and looked directly into Sam's eyes. *Let the shit storm begin.* "I plan to follow his instructions. Take it to his warehouse and turn it over to him in exchange for Gabby."

Anderson clenched his hand into a tight fist. "Like hell!"

Sam glared at him before he turned to her. "Veranda, you'd be walking into a setup. Bartolo will kill you both. He has no reason to release your sister."

A lump caught in her throat. "Don't you think I know that?" She looked from one man to the other. "There's a slim possibility that I can rescue her somehow. The point is, if I do nothing, she'll die for sure. This way, at least she's got a chance."

Sam's forehead creased with lines of concern. "Veranda, I can't support this. There's a high probability that you *and* your sister will die. You're offering yourself in exchange for a hostage, and you know we never do that." He lowered his voice. "We don't do it because it usually ends badly."

"I agree," Anderson said. "There has to be a better way."

She played her final card. "You two are investigators. My specialty is operations, remember? Trust my judgment. I figured out a way to get backup from SAU."

A confused frown crossed Anderson's features. "What's SAU?"

Veranda spared him a glance. "Special Assignment Unit, it's what the PPD calls our SWAT team."

Sam narrowed his eyes. "How does SAU fit into this?"

"We can pre-alert the team about the situation. We know they can be trusted because our interdictions were never compromised." Sam nodded as she continued. "SAU has the capability for rapid response. We can have everything in place before the deadline if we work fast."

Sam's bushy brows drew together. "We call out SAU, do a quick and dirty ops plan, wire you up—"

"Whoa." She held up a hand. "We don't use wires anymore. We use micro transmitters. The problem is that Bartolo has the technology to detect them, and he'll scan me. I have a plan for that though."

Before she could elaborate, Anderson seemed to brighten with an idea. "What about the FBI? Don't they handle kidnapping cases?"

Two sets of eyes fixed him with a withering glare. He spread his arms. "What?"

She fought to keep her voice under control. If Anderson had been a cop, he would never have made the suggestion. The FBI had cultivated a mystique. People thought they could solve any problem. She had no such illusions. "We're under a tight deadline. There's no time for interference from the Feds."

She assumed his suggestion was an attempt to keep her out of harm's way. A well-intended but completely misplaced gesture.

"SAU deployment requires authorization from a supervisor," Sam said, moving the conversation forward.

Veranda turned back to her partner. "That's one of the reasons I needed you to call Murphy. As a commander, he has the juice to get things done. We'll fill him in when he gets here. He can explain to the SAU supervisor that they can't make any notifications until the last possible second. We don't want to run the risk of the mole getting wind of this ahead of time."

She hesitated a moment. It kept coming back to the mole. Every contingency she could think of was tainted because of his possible interference. Was it Diaz?

Sam interrupted her thoughts. "What's your plan to get around Bartolo's electronics scanner?"

"We use a micro transmitter with a kill switch. Some of our newer micro transmitters can be deactivated manually. I can tuck it into my hair band. When Bartolo finishes his scan, I pretend to adjust my ponytail and switch it on."

"Why not put it in one of your pockets?" Anderson asked.

She braced herself. This would probably push him over the edge. She tried for a nonchalant expression as she answered. "It doesn't always happen, but when Bartolo is feeling particularly paranoid, he's been known to strip search people for weapons or listening devices."

Anderson's face flushed to the roots of his hair. "Could this get any more fucked up? The whole operation depends on you being able to turn on the transmitter. What if you don't get the chance? What if he knocks you out?"

"This is what I do," she snapped. "Over the years I've been in hundreds of dangerous situations where I deal with bad guys, most of them paranoid tweakers on meth. It's what undercover work is all about. You start with a plan, but you can't account for every possibility. A good narc goes in, assesses the situation, and adapts. You learn to think on your feet, hide your emotions, and lie your ass off ... or you die."

Sam broke the awkward silence that followed her words. "Does SAU have the proper transmitters?"

She nodded, relieved they had moved past the last hurdle. "Long range too, so everyone should be able to stay out of sight."

"How does SAU back Veranda if she can't turn on the transmitter or if it doesn't work?" Anderson asked.

Sam rubbed the back of his neck. "That's a problem. We won't be able to see her, so we'll have to put her on a timer."

"A timer?" Anderson looked back and forth between them.

"SAU makes entry at a predetermined interval from my first contact," Veranda said. "No signal needed." She turned to Sam. "I don't like it though. They could come in at the wrong moment."

Sam shrugged. "I defer to your operational expertise. You have a better idea?"

She discarded one possibility after another. "I don't."

Sam narrowed his eyes at her. "If we don't hear you on the transmitter, SAU will go in after five minutes."

She set her jaw. "Ten."

Anderson crossed his arms. "How about two?"

She shot him an exasperated look. "Fine. We'll settle on five. But that's only if you can't monitor the conversation. If you can hear me talk, wait for my verbal signal for SAU to make entry."

"What's the code phrase?" Sam asked.

She thought a moment. It had to be something memorable, that she could easily work into the conversation, but wouldn't come up on its own by chance. "When I ask him how he likes orange jumpsuits."

Sam snorted. "Appropriate."

Anderson shook his head. "I hate this plan. You're still turning yourself over to Bartolo."

226

Veranda put her hands on her hips. "I'll have an entire tactical team backing me up. Our SAU trains for this. Extractions and hostage rescues are what they do."

Anderson looked at Sam. "I can't believe you're supporting this suicidal plan."

Veranda tapped Anderson's elbow to gain his full attention. "Sam is trying to make a burrito out of a turd sandwich. He knows I'm going in one way or another. He wants to improve my odds."

Anderson's lips tightened to a thin white line before he said, "What if I don't cooperate? What if I don't sign out the evidence?"

She gave him a wry smile. "Then my odds will truly suck." She straightened. "I'm doing this, with your help or without it. Sam understands that, even though he doesn't like it any more than you do. You need to get on board."

She could sense Anderson's resolve crumble. His bright blue eyes searched her face. "I can't stop you, can I?"

She shook her head.

His shoulders slumped as he heaved a sigh and looked at Sam. "Just explain to me how we can keep her alive."

Sam tapped his chin. "Actually, I've been thinking about that while we tweaked our plan."

Veranda was pleased to hear him call it "our" plan. He was with her.

"You mentioned Bartolo having Flaco's old cell phone. Why don't we ping his location?"

"Bartolo already thought of that. I'm sure he's been briefed on our tracking techniques by the mole. He said he would destroy the phone as soon as he disconnected."

"Back in the war room you described the technical capabilities of the cartel. They're very sophisticated." Sam rubbed his temple. "Shit,

I'm slipping. Should've thought of this before. He could have a trace on you. Maybe that's how he knows where you are all the time."

"You're not the only one who slipped," she said. "That also dawned on me after I spoke to Bartolo. I powered my phone off after I called my mother. I won't turn it on again until I get to the forensics lab. If he is tracking me, I want him to see me there when he calls."

Sam addressed both of them. "If this is going to work, we play it as tight to the deadline as possible. If word gets to the mole, we don't want him to have time to communicate with Bartolo."

Veranda nodded, but did not delude herself. She was certain the mole would tip off Bartolo before she set foot in the warehouse. She would have to rely on all of her skills to save Gabby, her first and most important objective. If Sam could put Bartolo behind bars, that would make her sacrifice even more worthwhile. Despite all of their plans and contingencies, Veranda, deep in her bones, did not expect to leave the warehouse alive.

27

Villalobos family compound, Mexico

ADOLFO'S HAND TIGHTENED AROUND the grip of the massive Desert Eagle pistol. His sister had gone all out when selecting the family firearms. Daria was obsessed with weapons of every sort, but she put special emphasis on the piece carried by members of the Villalobos family. He looked at the titanium gold nitride tiger stripe finish of the Mark XIX Action Express model. It was a cannon designed for two-handed shooting. To Adolfo, it was the definition of overkill.

El Lobo had summoned Adolfo, Carlos, and Daria early in the morning. As soon as they stepped off of the family jet at the Villalobos compound airstrip two hours later, they had been escorted to the armory. Adolfo was not sure what to make of this. Meetings usually took place in his father's office. He peered at his siblings to see if their body language revealed any knowledge of what was going on.

Daria strolled down the rows of rifles, her slender hand out, caressing each muzzle as she passed. She licked her lips as she languidly stroked an Uzi.

Carlos had positioned himself in front of a glass cabinet. He practiced his quick-draw technique, whipping his gun out of the holster on his right hip and pointing it at his reflection.

Adolfo sighed, realizing his younger siblings had no inkling about the significance of the meeting. He would have to wait for his father's arrival. In the meantime, he pulled out a box of fresh ammo and loaded fifty caliber rounds into his magazine.

His father pushed through the double doors to the armory. He had forgone his usual tailored suit in favor of range clothing. *El Lobo* looked every bit the alpha of his pack in black military-style dress, a tooled leather holster with the butt of a black pistol attached to the right side of his heavy belt.

A chill ran down Adolfo's spine as Hector Villalobos surveyed each of his children in turn. As usual, his father addressed them in Spanish. "As you all may have guessed because he is not with you, we are here to discuss Bartolo. After I learned he is taking drugs again, I sent one of my most loyal men, Umberto Camacho, to replace Pablo."

Perspiration prickled Adolfo's scalp. Pablo had been Bartolo's second-in-command. Adolfo had last seen him that night at the warehouse when his brother killed Flaco, the snitch. Pablo was executed when he became a loose end after dumping Flaco's body.

Adolfo was disconcerted to learn his father had sent an informant into Bartolo's camp. *El Lobo* wanted a direct source of intelligence. Had he sent a spy into Adolfo's operation as well? He pictured the men in his inner circle, replayed conversations in his mind, then snapped back to attention when he realized his father was speaking again.

"I originally called you all here after I learned that Bartolo had set fire to a family restaurant owned by Detective Cruz's mother."

Adolfo thought he detected a slight smile play at the corners of his father's mouth. A moment later, the fleeting expression disappeared, and Adolfo decided he was mistaken.

Hector sauntered over to the glass cabinet next to Carlos. "Our police mole told me the arson investigator found a cigarette butt at the scene of the fire." He leveled his gaze at his audience. "The butt was sent to a forensics lab where they will no doubt find Bartolo's DNA, which is already on file from his past narcotics arrest."

His father's voice had become dangerously soft and Adolfo could tell he was livid.

Hector opened the cabinet door and drew the gun from his holster. Adolfo froze.

Silently, Hector placed the black pistol on a lower shelf. "I had planned to discuss bringing Bartolo here to Mexico permanently. Unfortunately, I just received a rather disturbing phone call from Umberto Camacho, which forces me to change my strategy." With infinite care, he lifted his personalized gold-plated Desert Eagle from its display stand on the next shelf up.

Daria broke her silence. "What did Camacho tell you just now?"

Hector gripped the slide and racked it back, chambering a round. "That Bartolo abducted Detective Cruz's young half sister, and that he is trying to ransom her for the evidence against him. To make matters worse, he is holding her in one of our warehouses."

Adolfo stifled a grin. His brother had just sealed his fate with this desperate scheme. He arranged his face to show a mixture of bafflement and concern. "That will expose us all. They'll get search warrants for every property holding we own."

El Lobo turned his dark, fathomless eyes to Adolfo. "I discussed the legal implications with our mole. Our front companies should provide us some cover."

Adolfo quailed under his father's gaze. "I didn't mean to—"

"I can now see that Bartolo has become a liability."

El Lobo's words hung in the air. The three siblings exchanged nervous glances before looking back at their father.

"I have other business to discuss with all of you before we decide what to do about Bartolo," Hector said. "While my men set up the shooting range for our target practice, I will give you the history of Detective Veranda Cruz." He glanced at Adolfo. "I have told you part of this information, but I did not know all of the facts when we last spoke."

Hector took on a grave expression as he recounted the past. "As you all know, over forty years ago, I joined the Mexican Federal Judicial Police. I was assigned to headquarters in Mexico City on a team with another new agent, Ernesto Hidalgo. I have never spoken to you about him, but today, you will hear his story."

His voice took on a disdainful tone. "Hidalgo was born with a silver spoon in his mouth. His family paid for an elite law school, but he claimed to have high ideals, so he went into criminal justice instead of his family's law firm."

Adolfo straightened as his father continued. Bartolo had attended an elite law school as well. In fact, all of the Villalobos children had the finest education money could buy. He wondered if his father knew he was describing his own children's upbringing when he scoffed at Hidalgo.

"Soon, Hidalgo was the golden boy," Hector said. "We were on the same team and worked cases together, but he moved effortlessly up the ladder while I scratched and clawed for every advancement." His father's face twisted into a sneer. "Then came the final straw. We were both up for the same promotion. Hidalgo used his connections to get the position that I had earned."

Hector turned the gleaming weapon over in his hand. "After that, he immediately ran out and asked my woman to marry him. We both wanted her, but he stole her from me."

A muscle in Hector's jaw worked. "From that moment, I was finished being an underpaid police flunky with no future. I saw how crooked the upper echelon was." He slid the pistol into his empty holster. "I met with a local cartel leader and got on the payroll that very day. I kept my badge but sold information. Earned more in one month than I had the previous five years."

His father rarely discussed his time in law enforcement and had never mentioned Ernesto Hidalgo. Hector was not one to prattle for no reason. Adolfo had the sense their current situation had direct ties to something that had occurred decades earlier.

"Next, I arranged to meet the daughter of another cartel leader. I courted and married your mother within a few months." He glanced at Adolfo. "You were born the following year." He gazed up at the ceiling as if dredging pictures from a distant memory. "I worked my way into a position to consolidate both organizations under my rule. I still held onto my badge, but Hidalgo grew suspicious. I learned he was about to arrest me."

"What did you do?" Carlos asked.

"Hidalgo was working late. Alone. I shot him at his desk and burned the office building to the ground." Hector waved a hand as if the killing was of no consequence.

Adolfo struggled to place this story in their current dilemma.

"After I eliminated Hidalgo, I paid a visit to his wife at their home." A feral smile crept across Hector's visage. "I had ... unfinished business with her."

Adolfo noticed that Daria had crossed her arms tightly across her body as their father spoke these last words.

"After our ... encounter, his wife fled to the United States with her younger brothers and sisters. They filed for asylum because of Hidalgo's murder. I decided not to pursue them further. I had other business opportunities to develop at the time."

Hector rested a hand on the butt of his holstered pistol. "I did not realize it until recently, but Hidalgo's wife gave birth in Phoenix a few months after her arrival in the States."

Daria gasped. "Veranda Cruz."

Hector smiled. "You always were quick to grasp things, *mi'ja*."

Adolfo recalled his earlier meeting with his father. This must be the secret Hector had wanted to investigate further before he shared. "So Veranda Cruz is your daughter?" He looked at the others. "Our half sister?"

Hector flicked a glance at his son. "That is not what I said." He ran a finger along his goatee. "Do you remember that I asked you to bring me a package from our mole when you flew here to meet with me four days ago?"

"Yes." Adolfo had been uncomfortable about transporting the parcel. His father had assured him it didn't contain contraband but emphasized that he was not to open it. It had been the first thing his father asked for when Adolfo arrived.

"That package contained a DNA sample obtained from Detective Cruz without her knowledge. I provided a sample and had them both analyzed at our laboratory here."

Daria looked stricken. "What did the test reveal? Are you her father or not?"

Hector's smile was enigmatic. "I prefer to keep that information private for now."

"Do you think Veranda knows her father may not be Ernesto Hidalgo?" Carlos asked.

Hector gave a derisive snort. "Lorena would have told Veranda she was born of her poor martyred Ernesto."

Carlos looked perplexed. "I still don't understand how this makes Veranda dangerous."

Hector's lip curled. "Because Lorena would have filled her head with stories of how I killed her father and forced them to flee Mexico from the time she was old enough to understand."

Hector clasped his hands behind his back. "There's more." He paced across the armory as he spoke. "After I told Bartolo about the paternity question, he hired a private investigator to research her family's background." He reached into his breast pocket and pulled out a sheaf of papers. "I have a copy of the report."

"Hold on," Adolfo said. "You told Bartolo you might be Veranda's father? Why did you give Bartolo more information than you gave me?" Adolfo remembered he was trying to recruit his younger siblings and included them in a sweeping gesture. "Why couldn't all of us have been trusted with the same knowledge?"

Adolfo sensed he had gone too far when his father strode directly in front of him. *El Lobo's* eyes fastened onto him. Unable to withstand the intensity of the lupine gaze, Adolfo looked down in submission. Hector leaned in to whisper in his son's ear. "Never question me again."

It took all of Adolfo's self-control not to cringe. "Yes, sir."

Apparently satisfied, Hector turned back to the others and continued. "Before that rude interruption, I was about to share the information Bartolo's investigator uncovered." He patted his breast pocket containing the report. "He found out that Lorena married again and had two more children. In fact, that is how Bartolo knew about Veranda's half sister."

Hector resumed his steady pacing. "The other child was a boy, Roberto, who attended South Phoenix High School when he died of an overdose three years ago. Veranda's half brother bought the drugs that killed him from one of our dealers. It turns out the dealer we sent to replace him was none other than Flaco." He paused for emphasis. "Veranda's snitch. The one who began this entire sequence of events."

Carlos knitted his brows. "Let me be sure I'm clear on this. Veranda believes that our family murdered her father, forced her mother out of Mexico, caused the death of her kid brother, and has now kidnapped her little sister?"

Hector halted. "Now you see why she is dangerous to us. I am quite certain she recruited Flaco specifically to target our family after her brother died." He crossed his arms. "You all know how I feel about genetics. They rule our destiny. In this case, it does not matter who her father is. If she is Hidalgo's daughter, she will continue on a self-righteous suicide mission in a quixotic quest for justice. If she's mine, she will ruthlessly pursue all of us until she exacts her revenge. Either way, she will never stop." He lowered his voice. "Until she is dead."

Hector looked at Adolfo. "That is what I meant when I told you she could be more dangerous to us than even she knew."

———

They filed in to the cavernous indoor range and gathered in a circle at the twenty-five-meter mark. A range assistant handed each of them eye and ear protection.

Hector slid the clear plastic shooting glasses onto his nose. "You may wonder why I wanted us to meet at the range today. You will understand when we have finished shooting."

Adolfo turned down range to survey the targets. A line of five metal poles stood erect from the poured cement floor. A man with a black cloth sack over his head was lashed to each pole. Adolfo dreaded his father's idea of shooting practice, which always involved live targets.

El Lobo moved to the fifteen-meter line and swung an arm out to encompass the tableau in front of them. "All of these men are my employees. I've just had them brought up from the dungeon." He looked at each of his children to drive the point home before turning to face down range. "The first target is Digoberto Ruiz, one of my bill collectors. He took part of the payments for himself. He is a thief." Muffled sounds of protest from under the sack reached Adolfo as his father took aim with his pistol. Adolfo jammed the ear covers on just before Hector pulled the trigger.

Even with sound-dampening hearing protection, the blast from the fifty-caliber gun thundered through the vast indoor shooting range. Ruiz crumpled against the ropes that bound him to the metal pole. What was left of his head dangled against his chest in the tattered remains of the blood-soaked bag. Bits of scalp and brain had showered the man tied to the next pole.

Hector strolled to the second firing position. "This is Renaldo Perez. His shipment of heroin was intercepted at the border by *federales*." A stream of urine ran down Perez's pants to puddle on the floor at his quivering feet. Hector took aim and fired. This time, the prisoner's chest exploded in a spray of blood and chunks of flesh.

Adolfo swallowed the bile that had surged into his throat. He stole a glance at his siblings, who seemed to relish the show.

Hector lowered his pistol as he stood next to the third spot. "The next target is Manuel Garcia. He hired a worker to plant crops in one of our grow operations. The worker turned out to be an informant for the police." He faced his children. "The last three are for you. Who would like to go first?"

Daria raised a hand to get her father's attention. She spoke in a loud voice so everyone could hear her with their ear protection on. *"Papá*, may I?"

El Lobo beamed at her and stepped aside. Adolfo couldn't miss the gleam in her eye as Daria assumed a shooting stance at the line. She raised the enormous weapon and leveled it at her target. Even though her arms were locked, she struggled to maintain her footing as the recoil from the blast forced her to take a step backward.

The prisoner's legs gave out. He dangled from the pole, writhing. Adolfo narrowed his eyes to see that Manuel Garcia was still alive. He had been gut shot.

"You need more practice, *mi'ja*," Hector said to Daria.

She looked indignant. "I aimed for his belt buckle, *Papá*." Her eyes were bright with bloodlust. "The bastard deserved to suffer. He will be dead soon enough."

Adolfo averted his eyes to avoid puking. Part of the prisoner's intestines hung in bloody coils halfway down his legs.

His father pointed down range at the next prisoner. "This is Ignacio Lopez. He took it upon himself to attack a rival cartel without my authorization." Hector turned to Carlos, raising his eyebrows in unspoken invitation.

Carlos swaggered over to the firing line. He assumed a stance reminiscent of an Old West gunslinger. Adolfo looked on in horror as Carlos whipped the pistol from its holster in a quick draw and fired in less than a second. The echo of the missed shot reverberated through the range. The prisoner thrashed against his bindings.

"Quit playing, Carlos," Hector said, his face set in grim lines. "This is not a game."

Apparently chastened, Carlos took aim and effected a clean headshot on his next attempt.

There was one more prisoner left. Adolfo's hands grew damp. He had tried to conceal his distaste for violence over the years, but was sure he had fooled no one. He was an intellectual. In a war, he viewed himself more as a general than a foot soldier. Bartolo was the one who enjoyed bloodshed. Knowing Hector always acted with a specific purpose in mind, Adolfo felt certain his father had deliberately saved his firstborn's target practice for last.

El Lobo approached Adolfo. He stood next to his son, but his eyes were fixed on the whimpering figure strapped to the last pole. "That one is Eduardo Ochoa. He was careless when he executed a high-ranking police official. A witness identified him. He tried to cover his mistake by killing the witness. Instead, he compounded his error and left evidence at the scene. When Ochoa was arrested, a police official on my payroll faked his escape and turned him over to me."

Hands trembling, Adolfo drew his pistol and pointed it at the prisoner.

Hector laid a hand on his son's shoulder. "No, *mi'jo*."

Adolfo turned to his father. "I don't understand. Didn't you want me to shoot him?"

Hector pulled off his ear protection and slowly shook his head. Adolfo slid the gun back into its holster and prepared for another one of his father's lessons. Adolfo looked at the figure struggling against the ropes, then back at his father's pitiless dark eyes. Dread filled him as realization took hold. He pulled off his ear covers and tossed them to the ground.

Never taking his eyes from his father, Adolfo fumbled to unsnap the sheath that held the ornate dagger against his left hip. He inched the knife out and held up the glistening blade.

El Lobo nodded his approval. "I am aware that you wish to take your rightful place as my firstborn son," he said. "Leading an organization is not just about keeping the books. At times, you must get your hands bloody."

This was it. His father had issued a challenge. If Adolfo wanted to take Bartolo's place as heir apparent, he had to prove he, too, could spill the blood of his own men. He knew that any of his siblings would not have hesitated. His father knew it too.

Adolfo grasped the handle firmly and strode toward the row of targets, all of them slumped against their bindings except Eduardo Ochoa. When he finally stood in front of the condemned man, Adolfo knew what his father would expect. He reached behind Ochoa and tugged the black bag off of his head.

Ochoa blinked in the glare of the fluorescent range lights. Eyes wide with fear, his nostrils flared as air whistled into his nose above the duct tape that covered his mouth.

Adolfo inhaled the acidic stench of perspiration that coursed through the dark stubble on Ochoa's face. He raised his dagger to the man's throat. He replayed Bartolo's killing of Flaco in his mind's eye and tried to recall how his brother had done it. Unfortunately, Ochoa was in a different position. Adolfo had never killed with a knife and had no idea how to go about it.

He muttered a halfhearted apology, pulled his arm back, and plunged the dagger into Ochoa's throat with all of his strength. Ochoa thrashed wildly, jerking and gurgling as blood spewed from the gaping wound.

Crimson droplets spattered Adolfo's face. Spurts of red saturated his crisp white shirt. He yanked the blade back over his head and brought it down in a fierce arc, stabbing Ochoa in the center of his neck, ramming the knife in until he heard it hit the metal pole. Satisfied that he had delivered a fatal blow, he forced himself to stand in place and watch Ochoa die.

Still clutching the bloody knife, Adolfo pivoted and marched back to his family. He thought he glimpsed respect in their eyes for the first time.

Hector signaled his children to gather around. "I selected those five particular men to make a point. Each of their crimes was worthy of the death penalty in my organization." He drew a deep breath. "Bartolo has committed not one, but *all* of the same crimes as the people we just executed."

Hector held up a finger. "He embezzled money from his part of the business." He inclined his head toward Adolfo. "This was just recently brought to my attention."

Hector held up a second finger. "Then, he lost millions in product because Detective Cruz…" He paused and looked up as he searched for the right word. "Took an interest in him." He held up another finger. "He allowed a spy to infiltrate his organization." A fourth finger went up. "He broke into Detective Cruz's house without my authorization." He lifted the final finger on his hand. "He burned her family's restaurant against my specific orders to stand down. In doing so, he compromised himself and tried to correct the problem with this stupid kidnapping scheme."

Adolfo thought he should say something that appeared to defend his brother. He didn't want to look too mercenary. "*Papá*, perhaps Bartolo just needs to go into drug treatment. He's not using his best judgment right now."

"Bartolo has been warned about taking drugs. He has only made things worse with this last reckless action." Hector locked eyes with each of his children in turn. "I have been lenient because he is my son, but my patience is at an end. Now he must be held accountable." He waited a beat before he continued. "You all know the price to be paid, but I want to hear from each of you because we are family. What is to be Bartolo's fate?"

Knowing his father watched to see if he had what it took to lead the organization, Adolfo shoved the dripping dagger into its sheath and extended his bloody hand straight out, palm down. "Death." He deliberately chose his right hand, where he wore the gold signet ring with the Villalobos crest.

Apparently heedless of the gore, Daria laid her slender hand on top of his. Her matching ring glittered under the fluorescent lights. "Death."

Carlos took a long look at his brother before following suit. "Death."

Hector put his rough hand on the others. "So be it," he said in his quietest tone. "I have never ordered the killing of my own flesh and blood." He held their hands under his. "Let this be a lesson to you all that I will not tolerate dishonesty, disloyalty, and incompetence from anyone. Even my own children."

He released their hands. "I will contact our police mole and give him the order directly. He is to entrust this assignment to no one else. He must *personally* eliminate Bartolo at his first opportunity."

Adolfo put a closed fist over the bloodstained fabric of his shirt where the wolf's head tattoo covered his heart. "Tell me what you want, *Papá*, and I will do it."

Hector's mouth narrowed into a thin line. His voice chilled Adolfo to the bone. "Because of Veranda, I will have to bury one of my children." An understanding passed between father and firstborn son. "Lorena Cruz must bury one of hers as well."

28

THE MOLE'S SPECIAL PHONE vibrated in his pants pocket. He pulled out the mobile and checked the display. An incoming call from *El Lobo* himself. Tendrils of fear spread down the length of his spine. He had called Hector earlier, intending to give him the news. When he got no answer, he disconnected without leaving a message. He had spent the past hour in turmoil, unable to determine how to describe the situation to Hector. He knew *El Lobo* was perfectly capable of shooting the messenger. His hands shook as he tapped the screen.

Hector's heavily accented English abraded his ears. "I see that you called me."

"Yes sir. It went straight to voicemail, but I wanted to give you the information personally. I tried Adolfo too, but—"

"We were in a meeting. What did you want?"

"Bartolo asked me to check with the forensics lab before noon to see if the cigarette butt with his DNA had been signed out. He said he had figured out a way to get Cruz to turn the evidence over to him."

243

"What did you say?"

"I told him I couldn't do it without compromising myself. There are surveillance cameras all over the building, and the lab personnel would remember I requested information about the evidence if I tried to check by phone. I would have to identify myself before asking."

"You always have excuses. When I wanted you to stop the narcs from taking our deliveries. You say the same thing. You cannot do it."

"Sir, as I explained before, the Drug Enforcement Bureau has its own database. I can't access it. I can't even walk into their facility because my pass card isn't authorized. Their security is—"

"Excuses!" Hector released a stream of obscenities in Spanish before he continued. "Tell Bartolo the evidence was signed out. You do not need to check if it is true. It does not matter now."

"Why not, sir?"

"Because Bartolo will be dead."

Silence stretched as he struggled to find his voice. "Sir?"

"Your assignment is to kill Bartolo. I do not want him to suffer. You will shoot him in the head."

His heart palpitated with fear. *El Lobo* had just ordered him to execute his own son. Hector could have directed any number of his people to perform the task. *Why does he want me to do it?* He came to the only conclusion that made sense. *Because I'm an outsider.*

He thought back to his dealings with the cartel leader over the years. Hector used the occasions when he killed his men to set an example for the others. There was always a special emphasis placed on who pulled the trigger. Such decisions were not made at random or for the sake of expediency.

"Sir, surely there must be some other option—"

Hector lowered his voice. "If there was another way, do you think I would not take it?"

The mole knew the menace simmering under the soft tones. He appealed to Hector's status when he asked the most critical question. "Señor Villalobos, you are the leader of a vast army of men, many trained in combat. Why do you wish *me* to carry out this order? I've never killed anyone."

"With this act, you will finish your contract. After it is done, you may retire from my service."

A wave of nausea swept through him as he heard the words that meant a death sentence for Bartolo, and possibly for himself. His mind went back to the first day he came in contact with the cartel. He had lost a particularly high stakes poker match. The game had been set up, by invitation only, at a local hotel room in downtown Phoenix. In hindsight, he realized he had been targeted. Word had spread in the local casinos that he was a regular at the high-limit table, and a fellow player invited him to a special game. He didn't know that the organizer was Adolfo Villalobos, the cartel's CFO, who handled their gambling operations among his other duties.

The mole was a booter on the PPD at the time, and his ambition had been to become a K-9 officer. That night, his career path—and his entire life—changed. Adolfo had strolled over to him and demanded payment of eighty thousand dollars. It might as well have been a million.

As the interest on his debt compounded daily, he had been assured he could work it off and even make a hefty profit. All he had to do was get promoted into a key position on the police department and provide information. The cartel left him alone until after his promotion, when Adolfo called him to say he had been activated.

The trouble was that once you broke the rules to do a favor for a crime syndicate, they owned you forever. There was no going back. He was trapped in a nightmare that would not end until he left the force. And he could not do that without *El Lobo*'s permission.

He put the extra money the cartel paid him into an offshore account, and it had grown into a nice nest egg over the years. He would retire to Mexico, collect his pension, and live off the interest from his investments. The cartel would protect him.

Now his gut churned at the realization that his usefulness to the cartel had reached its end. Surely no one who had killed a Villalobos family member would ever be allowed to enjoy retirement. It made no difference that he had been ordered to do so.

All of his careful plans, his dreams, his very future … had just evaporated.

Even to his own ears, his voice sounded hollow and resigned as he spoke into the phone. "I will do it, sir."

29

VERANDA SAT NEXT TO Sam in an enormous conference room in the Tactical Support Bureau building in South Phoenix. The secure facility, several miles from headquarters, was ideal for a clandestine briefing. Veranda wanted to be sure no one other than Commander Murphy and the tactical personnel were aware of the meeting. She could not risk the mole learning of the operation before it began.

They had been there for half an hour fine-tuning the plan. Special Assignment Unit members stood with their backs pressed against the walls. Decked out in black tactical gear, they awaited final instructions for deployment. Their supervisor, Sergeant Grigg, wore his dark hair in a buzz cut and ate scrap metal for breakfast.

Grigg glowered at Veranda from across the Formica table. "Still don't like it. Too many variables."

Veranda had to force herself not to smack her forehead. The SAU Sergeant ran tactically sound operations, not the improvised plan she had foisted on him. He would follow the orders Commander Murphy had given his unit, but Veranda wanted to gain the team leader's support. "We only had a short time to throw a strategy together, and this was our best option," she said.

"Strategy?" Grigg's jaw muscles tightened. "This isn't a strategy. It's a monkey fucking a football."

Sam looked like he might grin. She pierced him with a hard stare before turning her attention back to Grigg. She decided to appeal to his professional pride. "Sergeant, your team is the best at what they do. This is like any other hostage situation."

Grigg waved a huge paw of a hand. "Sure, only it involves a heavily armed drug cartel at one of their strongholds. Total cake."

She felt her patience fray around the edges. "Sergeant, I have to leave now. Bartolo Villalobos will call me in twenty minutes. I need to be in front of the forensics lab to meet the arson investigator. I will go wherever Bartolo tells me, even inside one of his warehouses. I would love to have your team back me up, but I'm going in either way." She got to her feet.

Every eye in the room was on Grigg as he stood and looked down at her. After a long moment in which the pair silently faced off, Grigg blew out a sigh. "Let's run through the operation one more time, and we'll test the transmitter in your hair band again."

She knew it cost the sergeant to accede to her plan. His consent was a formality since SAU had been ordered to deploy, but Veranda understood team dynamics. The unit would feel more confident if their leader was on board. SAU had backed up her task force on dozens of takedowns over the past two years, and she was used to working with them. Even though she did not expect to survive, SAU was critical to her private plan to buy time for Gabby's rescue.

———

Veranda paced across the concrete courtyard in front of the forensics lab. She had switched her cell phone on when she drove across the bridge back into downtown Phoenix after leaving SAU. No sense taking chances in case Bartolo was tracking her location.

She glanced at her watch. Six minutes before noon. Where was Anderson? She turned to the main entrance of the Phoenix Crime Lab. A glint of light caught her eye, and she tilted her head up to take in the colossal art piece that dangled from the ceiling inside the glass-enclosed two-story foyer. The sculpture towered over fifteen feet high and featured laboratory analysis equipment, including Petri dishes and beakers, suspended in the air surrounding a DNA helix at its center. Even from her vantage point outside the building, sections of glass, copper, and scientific instruments could be seen hanging above the floor in a dazzling synthesis of art and science.

Anderson pushed through the door and strode to her. "Fortunately, I remembered the brand of cigarettes that asshole used, so I was able to buy a pack and smoke a couple of them down to the filter before I got here." He made a disgusted face.

She smelled peppermint candy on his breath when he spoke. Apparently he didn't like the taste of tobacco any more than she did.

"I signed the real evidence out, then went into the break room and copied everything on the bag exactly. Damn near set off the smoke alarm burning the cigarette butt to look like it was in a fire." He showed her a sealed evidence bag with several times and initials scrawled on it. "Murphy has the original. This one is the fake. In case anyone is watching, they can see me give it to you. The log will also confirm that I signed it out."

She held the bag up and used her cell phone to take a picture with her free hand, moving in for a close-up of the initials. "I need to be ready to send this photo to him when he calls."

Anderson hooked a thumb in his jeans pocket. "I still can't believe Bartolo wouldn't have thought of this."

"First, he's not completely rational. Second, he thinks he has an ace in the hole with his mole. He's confident his rat can verify that the stuff was signed out and he's probably watching us now. By the way, did you remember to tell the lab guys to call Sam if anyone asks about the evidence?"

"I did. The techs were suspicious, but agreed to make the call. Whoever requests the info will have to identify themselves. They can use another name and employee number if they do it by phone, but the lab guys agreed to make a digital recording of all calls today."

"It would be great to catch the mole," she said.

"You mean Diaz."

She sighed. "Yeah, probably Diaz. I just can't figure out how the cartel got their hooks into him."

Anderson rubbed the back of his neck. "Bartolo is my main concern now. You mentioned he's not rational. How can he really think he'll get away with this?"

"Look at it from his perspective. He has nothing to lose and everything to gain. If it works, he walks. If it doesn't, he escapes to Mexico where the cartel can hide him."

"But kidnapping?"

"He's convinced I wouldn't put Gabby in danger by reporting the abduction and attempting a rescue operation. He thinks I'll try to ransom her back by turning over the evidence. Then, I'm sure he plans to kill both of us and make our bodies disappear. There are hundreds of abandoned mines all over the desert. The cartel probably has several they use on a regular basis."

She had said too much. Anderson paled and gripped her arm. "Veranda, please reconsider . . . "

She removed his hand and gave it a squeeze. "We've already gone over this. That's *his* plan, not mine."

Her cell phone vibrated.

She whipped it out of her pocket and checked the display. Text message. Her pulse raced as she read the screen. SEND THE PHOTO.

She opened the picture file, selected the image she had just taken, and attached it to a return text with no message.

She switched on the micro transmitter attached to her hair band so SAU could monitor the communication, then exchanged a look with Anderson as seconds lapsed into a full minute.

Her phone vibrated again. Incoming call from an unknown number. She touched the speaker icon so everyone could hear.

"I see you have the evidence, Detective. I have also verified this through other channels." Bartolo's words tumbled over each other, his breathing rapid. Experience with narcotics users told her he was high. Probably cocaine or methamphetamines.

She answered in a measured tone. "Let me speak to my sister."

A soft chuckle. "Gabriela can't … come to the phone."

Veranda clenched the phone so hard her knuckles whitened. Her mind flicked back to her kickboxing lessons. Physical defeat comes on the heels of mental defeat. You will sustain damage, but you can prevail if you don't let your opponent get inside your head.

She paused to get a grip on her anger before she allowed herself to speak. "Where do I meet you?"

"Drive to the warehouse district in West Phoenix. I have surveillance set up at the intersection of Thirty-First and Fifty-Fourth Avenues. Be sure you come alone. I will call you with further instructions when you arrive. I'm turning off my cell phone now."

She stuffed the phone back in her pocket, deactivated the micro transmitter in her hair band, then looked at Anderson. "Thank you for helping me." She didn't mean for it to sound like a farewell.

He took a step toward her but stopped when she put her hand up. He wore a somber expression. "Sam is following SAU in his car. I'm riding with him."

"I know you carry a gun and you're trained in police procedure, but you're a fireman, not a cop. You'll have to stay in the car and let SAU handle things."

"How good is SAU?"

She reached into her ponytail to switch the transmitter back on before giving him her most confident look. "I've trusted them with my life more times than I can count." She turned and walked to her car, hoping her words convinced him.

———

The City of Phoenix sprawls over five hundred square miles, an oasis in the desolate desertscape that surrounds it. After the advent of the interstate highway system, an industrial corridor emerged in the western quadrant due to ease of access from the I-10. It did not surprise Veranda to learn that the Villalobos cartel used a warehouse in that sector for the same reason. The I-10 connected to the 19, a direct route in and out of the US from the Mexican border. All manner of illicit drugs and other contraband could be unloaded, cut, and repackaged for distribution from the industrial corridor. The cartel's warehouse was a malignant tumor spewing carcinogens into the bloodstream of her city.

As Veranda approached the freeway entrance, her phone buzzed in her pocket. Without taking her eyes off the road to check the screen, she tapped the Bluetooth in her ear.

Sam's voice was one part exasperated and nine parts pissed off. "Am I on speakerphone?"

"No, I have a Bluetooth in my ear."

"Good. I don't want the SAU transmitter to pick up my half of the conversation. Just listen and be careful how you respond."

This sounded serious. "Are you able to speak freely?"

"Yes. I'm in the piece of shit Malibu following SAU. Anderson's with me. We're alone."

She tightened her grip on the steering wheel as she sped down the highway. "Talk."

"Commander Murphy left to call Chief Tobias and brief him about our operation right after he gave the order to deploy SAU. After the chief heard what we were doing, he insisted on looping Assistant Chief Delcore in on the whole thing."

"You're shitting me."

"Wish I was. Tobias said the Assistant Chief needed to know because it involved his chain of command. Tobias doesn't keep secrets from his top brass."

She grimaced. "Who briefed Delcore?"

"Commander Murphy. He called Delcore at home to advise him that you were on your way to meet Bartolo and rescue your sister. Because Murphy didn't know where the information might go, he chose not to mention the fake evidence or the mole."

"*Gracias a Dios,*" she mumbled.

"Don't be too thankful yet. Murphy told Delcore the information was confidential, but apparently Delcore thought Commander Webster needed to know since you work for him."

"I don't like where this is going, Sam."

"You're going to like it a hell of a lot less in a minute." He drew a deep breath. "Webster briefed Lieutenant Aldridge and Sergeant Jackson, who filled in our squad mates."

"I don't believe this."

"I'm not done yet. Apparently, you missed a nine o'clock appointment with Sergeant Diaz at PSB this morning. Diaz tried to call you, but your phone was turned off."

She groaned. All other concerns had been shunted out of her consciousness when she found out Gabby was missing. "Don't tell me ..."

"Diaz got his boxers in a wad and called Jackson to see why you didn't show, and the good sergeant brought him up to speed."

"Could this get any more fucked up?"

"Since you asked, yes, it could. I just got off the phone with Jackson. He told me the entire gang piled into Aldridge's Tahoe, and they're breaking the sound barrier on their way to you. That includes Webster, Aldridge, Jackson, and our squad. Oh yeah, and Diaz hitched a ride too."

"I'm screwed."

"Pretty much. No way you'll be able to go in under the radar." There was a beat of silence before Sam said, "Veranda, I need to call the SAU command vehicle and brief Sergeant Grigg. The operation is compromised. Bartolo will know the tactical unit is coming behind you. We can't let them walk into an ambush."

"I would never let that happen. Of course you need to call them." Aware they were listening to her half of the conversation, she aimed her next words at Grigg. "When you get SAU on the phone, tell them I will not stand down. I don't care if I have backup or not. This is my operation, my call. I'm going in." She disconnected.

———————

Twelve minutes later, she parked in the dusty lot of a tire storage facility and waited only a moment before her phone vibrated.

On speaker again, Bartolo's voice sounded more controlled. "Drive another two miles west until you see an access road to your right. Turn onto it and go to the dead end. There's a main warehouse and three outbuildings on the property. Get out and walk around the side to the metal security door of the warehouse. It will be unlocked."

"I'm not driving one inch farther until I speak to Gabby."

"You need to remember you're not in charge, *puta*."

"Now, Bartolo. Or the deal is off." She waited through scuffling noises in the background.

After several seconds, her sister's terrified voice trembled in her ear. "Veranda?"

Veranda's heart stuttered in her chest. "Gabby, are you okay? Has he hurt you?"

"I'm scared."

"I know. It's going to be okay. I'm coming for you."

"Veranda, be careful, he—"

She heard a loud smack and Gabby's muffled scream. "Gabby!"

Bartolo's voice grated her ears. "She is finished talking."

"You motherfucker! What did you do?" Her tightly held control had slipped.

"Nothing … yet. You should get here soon, though. My patience wears thin."

"I'll be there in three minutes."

"Make it two. And, Detective … leave your Glock and any other toys in your car."

"Just make sure Gabby is unharmed or I won't need a weapon to kill you."

"Such bravado," he said. "Did you know this warehouse is where Flaco drew his last breath? In the end, he welcomed death."

The reminder of Flaco elicited its desired effect. Veranda's throat tightened. She had to satisfy herself with a small victory. With his last comment, Bartolo had implicated himself in Flaco's murder. Everything was being recorded through her micro transmitter. The CSI techs would finally have a crime scene to examine for evidence.

Bartolo lowered his voice to a whisper. "The branding iron is red hot now. How do you think your pretty sister would like a wolf seared on her silky skin?"

"Fuck you, Bartolo!"

His soft chuckle rumbled in her ear before he disconnected.

30

VERANDA SKIDDED TO A stop in the parking lot beside the largest of four industrial buildings. Three smaller structures squatted on cement slabs approximately fifty yards from the main warehouse.

The GPS tracking device SAU placed in her trunk would allow them to locate her vehicle. She took a few seconds to provide as much intel as possible to aid in their approach. She scanned the area from the driver's seat with the window up so she would not be overheard if Bartolo had listening devices on the perimeter of the warehouse.

Aware the tactical team was listening to her micro transmitter, she voiced her observations. "Structure is a large one-story corrugated steel and cinder block building. I can only assess the black and green sides. No entry on the black side. The metal door I'm supposed to go through is on the green side."

She leaned forward and squinted at the silhouette of a figure walking around the corner of the warehouse, a rifle slung over his shoulder. "I have a visual on a subject who just came from the red side of the building. Hispanic male, five feet six inches tall, one hundred sixty pounds, black hair, wearing sunglasses and a black, military-style uniform. Armed with a rifle and extended mag. Weapon might be modified to full auto. Subject just stopped at the corner in a lookout position." She craned her neck to glance up at the roof and swiveled in her seat to check the rest of the property. "He's the only subject visible on the perimeter."

She performed a breathing exercise she had learned years ago to control her respiration and heart rate. Fear kept you alive. Panic got you killed. After flipping the glove compartment open, she picked up her gunbelt from the passenger seat and slid her Glock from its holster. She shoved the weapon inside, along with her wallet containing her badge and credentials. Once she had locked the items in the glove box, she focused on the primary mission. Go in, establish contact with Gabby, get her out. Secondary mission, get Bartolo to implicate himself in as many other crimes as possible. While she worked on those objectives, she had to delay giving the code phrase as long as possible to allow SAU enough time to prepare for a dynamic entry.

She gave her final instructions as she turned off the engine. "Exiting my car now and turning off the transmitter. Once you hear my voice again, hold your positions until I mention an orange jumpsuit."

She drew a deep breath. "I'm going dark." She grasped her ponytail and switched off the micro transmitter clipped to the hair band. The timer was set. She would have five minutes to reestablish contact, or SAU would storm the building.

She jumped out of the car and jogged to the side door as the sentry, assault rifle trained on her, watched from the corner. She raised her open hands to show the guard she wasn't armed. He had obviously been told to expect her arrival and did not challenge her.

She found the metal security door on the side of the building and tried the handle. Unlocked. She pushed it open and peered into the gloom. All quiet. She stepped inside and let the door slam behind her.

As her eyes adjusted to the dim lighting, a tall, powerfully built man emerged from the corner. He strolled under the glow of the single bulb hanging from the ceiling. Bartolo. He approached her at an angle, a stalking predator.

She stood stock still. "I want to see Gabby."

He stepped closer. "There will be time enough for that. First, show me the package." His red-rimmed eyes watched her warily. Thick curly hair, damp with perspiration, clung to the sides of his face.

Not wanting to alarm him with a sudden move, she slowly reached into the side pocket of her cargo pants and grasped the top of the evidence bag. She withdrew it and held it out to him.

A raptor seizing prey, he snatched the bag, ripped it open, and examined the contents. He studied the writing on the front before sliding the package into his pocket. "Good. Now you will see your dear sister." He picked up a portable security scanner from a nearby folding table. "After you pass inspection, of course."

Veranda held her arms out at right angles from her body and widened her stance. Bartolo passed the instrument over her entire body. A high-pitched buzz sounded when he reached her pocket. He fished out her cell phone, powered it off, and tossed it on the floor. "That reminds me, I need to make a phone call." He put the sensor wand on the table.

Veranda's heart thudded as Bartolo pulled a smart phone from his pocket and tapped the screen. *He's checking in with the mole.* From the length of time Bartolo waited, and the frustration that crossed his features, she could tell there was no answer on the other end. *Of course the mole can't take a call if he's in the Tahoe with everyone else coming here.* She fought to keep herself from blowing out a sigh of relief.

"My visitor has arrived," he snarled into the phone, leaving a voicemail message. "Call me if anything comes up." He tapped the screen and stuffed the device back in his pants pocket. "You see, Detective Cruz, I have a contact who can tell me if you pull any stunts."

She drew her brows together to portray a perplexed look. "What do you mean?"

"If there is the slightest whiff of interference from your Department, I will get a call. Now," he licked his lips. "Strip."

Flaco had told her about Bartolo's growing paranoia. Even though she assumed this would happen, she dreaded it. She believed Bartolo used the searches not only to ensure his safety, but also to humiliate adversaries or underlings.

She steeled herself and focused on her mission. As she pulled her fitted Under Armour T-shirt over her head, she made sure to muss her hair. She paused a moment to adjust her ponytail and turn on the transmitter. Assuming it worked properly, the five-minute timer would stop and SAU would wait for her code phrase to make entry.

She spoke immediately so SAU could hear she was not in trouble and to provide tactical information. "Why a second reinforced door on the inside?" She waved an arm. "And where is your goon squad? I expected a bigger welcome." She wanted SAU to be aware she did not have a visual on any cartel members. They also needed to know there were two doors to breach when making entry.

Bartolo narrowed his eyes. "My men are no concern of yours. I have what I need here." Concerned that her comments might have made him suspicious, she slipped off her bra to distract him. His features transformed into a look of raw hunger. In that moment, she made a decision. She would not cringe, or even cower. She took off each remaining article of clothing and placed them in a neat pile beside her feet.

Completely nude, she squared her shoulders and made no attempt to cover herself. She raised her chin and met his eyes. "You've had your fun, now where is my sister?"

"My pleasure has barely started." He smiled and drew closer. "Gabriela is right behind that door, in the main warehouse." He circled behind her and bent his head down to whisper against her ear. "Do you offer yourself for her freedom?"

Bile rose in her throat. "I gave you the evidence in exchange for her freedom, remember?"

He slid his hand lightly down her back, then snaked his arm around her waist and pulled her tight to his body. His erection pressed against her bottom as his free hand cupped her breast. "You will take her place as my prisoner."

"As soon as she leaves this building, I will." She would agree to anything that meant Gabby's release.

He dropped his hands and strode to the interior door. His fingers touched a keypad and a loud metallic *click* echoed in the silence.

"What is that, a cipher lock?" she asked, intending SAU to have as much detail as possible.

Bartolo ignored her question and stood to one side. "Ladies first."

She walked inside. Her eyes had to readjust, this time to the glare. As she blinked and scanned the cavernous space inside the main warehouse, her gaze landed on Umberto Camacho. She recognized his pockmarked face and long dark hair tied at the nape of his neck from her visit to Bartolo's mansion. Dressed in the same tailored black suit as before, Camacho watched them enter. Gabby slumped nearby, chained to a bar bolted to the cement floor, a gag in her mouth.

Veranda ran to her side, then dropped to her knees to gather her sister in her arms. Gabby sobbed as Veranda pulled away the rag that had been twisted around her head. She fumbled to release the manacles

261

on Gabby's wrists and ankles. No luck. She smashed the heavy chains against the floor. Nothing.

Gabby's body trembled. "V-Veranda ... please get me out of here. He's insane."

Veranda turned molten eyes toward Bartolo. She clenched her jaw to keep from screaming at him and balled her hands into fists so she wouldn't tear his eyes out. Again, she mentally recited her objectives. First, rescue Gabby. Second, stall until SAU could position themselves. Third, put Bartolo away.

"Is this where you butchered Flaco?" She turned to Camacho. "Were you there to watch?"

Bartolo lifted the hem of his shirt and slid an ornate dagger from a sheath on his belt. Jewels glinted under the overhead lights as he held it up. "Perhaps you would like to see how I got him to talk?"

She drew on years of undercover experience to compartmentalize her emotions. She forced herself to think tactically, appear vulnerable, and evolve her strategy on the fly, all while keeping in mind the effects of any drugs Bartolo may have in his system. Her success depended on her ability to stay one step ahead of her adversary.

"Why do you need a knife and a bodyguard, Bartolo? Afraid of two females?" She continued her running commentary for the tactical team's benefit.

Bartolo's lip curled. "Don't let his appearance fool you. Camacho is much more than a mere bodyguard."

"I don't care what his job description is. Our business is finished. Unlock Gabby. Now."

"You are in no position to make demands, Detective. And I don't think Gabriela is ready to leave just yet."

"What have you done to her?"

"If you want to know whether your dear little sister is still a virgin, the answer is yes." He took a few steps closer to them. "Whether that remains the case is up to you."

"We had a deal, Bartolo. I honored our agreement, now let her go."

"Not until we settle some unfinished business between us."

"There is nothing between us."

Bartolo tilted the dagger so that the emeralds, rubies, and sapphires sparkled in the fluorescent light. "Do you remember that night when you and your partner visited my house?"

"Like I remember my last root canal."

He ignored her sarcasm. "I mentioned there were things I knew about you that even you don't know."

Aware that her transmission was being recorded, she downplayed the comment. "None of that matters now."

"It matters more than you think. Right after Flaco gave me your name, I shared it with my father, who hired a private investigator to check into your background." His eyes moved from the glittering jewels to lock with hers. "Your birth certificate says your mother is Lorena Cruz, who came from the same part of Mexico as my family." He lifted an eyebrow. "Your father is listed as ... unknown."

Her mother had said she reverted to her maiden name and didn't indicate Ernesto Hidalgo was her birth father to make it more difficult for Hector Villalobos to track the family down. Now Veranda realized there might have been another reason for the omission.

She stroked Gabby's hair and stared straight back at Bartolo. "A lot of people don't have a father listed on their birth certificate."

"When my father shared the results of the investigation with me, along with a few other pertinent details, I was intrigued."

"If there's a point to this, I'm not seeing it."

"My father informed me that your *puta* mother, who was married to someone else, fucked him before she left Mexico." He lowered the dagger to his side. "You were born a few months later, which begs the question." He gave her a considering look. "Who is your father?"

She shot to her feet. "Not another word!"

"I wanted answers." His smile grew wider. "So when I broke into your house, I did more than just leave you messages. I took hair from your brush." He tapped the tip of the knife against his thigh. "My father wasn't pleased about the burglary, but when I told him I had a DNA sample from you, he arranged to have it delivered to him so he could have it tested."

Every muscle in her body tensed. This level of violation was even worse than the burglary of her home. Her very essence had been stolen, sampled, analyzed. By her sworn enemies. Without her knowledge or consent.

"The Villalobos private lab sent me a copy of the results." He sheathed the dagger and tugged a folded business envelope from his back pocket. "I know who your father is."

Bartolo hadn't lied to her that night at his mansion. He did know more about her than she knew about herself. The very thought pierced her soul. He seemed to take great pleasure in dangling information she craved just out of reach.

"I sealed the document in this envelope for our meeting today. But nothing is free." He tucked the paperwork back away. "You'll have to earn it."

"What more do you want from me? You have the evidence." She tried to bring the discussion back to Gabby's release. Remind him that she had met his terms. End this nightmare.

"I want to offer you a choice." He flicked a glance at his bodyguard. "Camacho will unchain your sister, and you will personally bring her to me as an offering." His eyes wandered over to Gabby. "After I am finished with her, you may both leave." He patted the pocket containing the envelope. "With this in your possession."

She stalked over to him, too incensed to be afraid. "Listen to me, Bartolo." She jabbed a finger into his chest. "Nothing could ever make me put my sister into your filthy hands. You vile—"

He caught her hand and twisted it behind her back, forcing her body against him. "Your other option," he said, bending his head down to hers, "is to give yourself to me, willingly, and your sister will watch. Then, I burn the envelope, and you will never know who your father is." He inclined his head lower, his lips almost touched hers. "What is your answer?"

She spat in his face.

His features contorted with fury as he wiped away the saliva and wrenched her arm so hard she gasped. "You will pay for that, *puta.*"

Forced up on the balls of her bare feet, body rigid with pain, she thought he might dislocate her shoulder as he torqued her arm still further. Sweat beaded on her forehead and her breaths came in ragged gulps through gnashed teeth.

He jerked his chin at Camacho. "Bring it to me."

Camacho disappeared around a cinder block partition and returned moments later, a branding iron clutched in his hand. The wolf's head on the end glowed red.

Bartolo continued to press against her as he dipped his head to lick the side of her face. He groaned softly and closed his eyes as if to savor the taste of her sweat.

In that moment, Veranda knew her sister had been right. Bartolo was insane. His sadistic pleasure in her torment terrified her, but she had to control her emotions. Showing fear handed him whatever power she had left.

Bartolo's pupils dilated further as he spoke. "All of the Villalobos family, and those loyal to us, have the wolf emblem tattooed over their hearts." He accepted the metal rod from Camacho and held the glowing end so close that heat radiated onto Veranda's face. "Our prisoners and our property are not given that honor. Instead, they are branded."

"I am not your property, asshole!" The time had come to act. Certain she would be killed, her only objective was to buy enough time for SAU to get through the reinforced inner door and rescue Gabby.

Bartolo bared his teeth in a malevolent smile. "You will remain perfectly still while I sear the wolf onto your breast, over your heart." He glanced to her left and Veranda swallowed hard as she realized he was looking at Gabby. "If you don't, I will brand your little sister's pretty face." He turned back to Veranda. "Your choice."

Veranda's pulse pounded in her ears. "Before I give you my answer, I have a question for you, Bartolo."

"What is that?"

"How do you like orange jumpsuits?"

31

EVERY SINEW IN VERANDA'S body tensed, poised for action. The walls of the building shuddered with a thunderous crash as SAU breached the exterior entrance. Only the interior reinforced metal door kept the team from the main area of the warehouse now.

Bartolo's grip slackened and Veranda twisted out of his grasp. She darted to place her body in front of her sister and crouched in a fighting stance.

Bartolo turned his head to Camacho and barked a command in Spanish. Seizing the opportunity, Veranda launched herself, a tawny lioness pouncing on a huge wildebeest. She used the momentum of her body's forward motion to knock Bartolo off his feet. She bladed her hand and aimed for his throat, but he swung his arm to deflect her as he fell backward. When she connected with his bicep, the hot branding iron clattered to the floor.

The interior door groaned and its frame buckled as the SAU team pried it with a Halligan tool. It would not hold much longer.

As Bartolo sprawled on his back, she climbed onto him and pummeled his torso with her knees while smashing his face with one elbow, then the other. Subjected to continuous blows, he could not draw his knife or hit her. He tried to throw her off, but his hands slipped on Veranda's nude, sweat-slick body.

Camacho grabbed her ponytail from behind and yanked her head back. She stumbled as he dragged her off of Bartolo.

Camacho's fingers dug deeper into her hair. *"Qué es esto?"* he asked.

Head immobilized, she cut her eyes to the right and caught Camacho's outstretched hand in her peripheral vision. He held the micro transmitter.

Bartolo sprang to his feet, snatched the device, and narrowed his eyes. Her mouth went dry as he threw the transmitter on the floor and ground it with the heel of his shoe. Camacho released her hair to grab her elbows.

A cacophony of pops and cracks carried to her ears as the interior door frame began to splinter.

Bartolo lunged at her. "You bitch!"

As Camacho pinned her arms behind her, Bartolo opened his palm and slapped her across the face with such force that her head snapped to the side. Lights exploded in her head and her vision flickered.

Camacho let go of her and dropped to his knees. He scrabbled on the floor next to them. A round metal grate scraped against the cement as he heaved it to one side.

As she continued to reel from the blow, Bartolo snatched her wrist and jerked her over his shoulder in a fireman's carry. Before she could react, he used his arm to trap her legs against his body. Only her left hand was free.

She prepared to strike Bartolo's temple with the heel of her palm when the interior security door burst open, slamming back against the wall.

Veranda glanced down at the floor. Camacho had pulled the grate aside to expose an opening the size and shape of a manhole. Bartolo plunged into it, still holding her. They slid down the shoot of a fifteen-foot shaft that curved at the end and deposited them in a heap on a compacted dirt floor. Camacho thudded behind them a split second before two bone-jarring explosions shook the ceiling above.

SAU had deployed the Flash-Bangs, Veranda realized. Several feet below the warehouse, she had been spared the worst effects. She grimaced as she thought of poor Gabby, who would be terrified. The devices, which sounded like bombs, were used to stun and disorient anyone in the vicinity. Her little sister's rescue would traumatize her further, but at least she would be safe.

Veranda had enough experience with the tactical unit to know they would fan out and search the main level before exploring the hole in the floor. Help would not reach her quickly.

Bartolo's grip on her had loosened when they landed at the bottom of the shaft. She twisted, rolled away, and pushed up to her feet. "It's over, Bartolo. The tactical unit will be down here any minute."

He slid his gleaming dagger out of its sheath and pointed it at her. "We'll be long gone by then."

Veranda glanced at Camacho, who pulled a semi-automatic pistol from an ankle holster and trained it on her.

Bartolo flicked his knife toward the dark recess that stretched behind her. "Start walking. Now."

Veranda knew the cartel, famous for constructing lengthy and elaborate tunnels across the border, could have a warren of hidden passageways out of the warehouse. The deeper she went into the bowels of the underground corridors, the more likely she would come out in a body bag.

She tilted her head and drew a breath to yell to the tactical unit above her. Before she could get a sound out, Bartolo slammed his fist into her stomach. Caught off guard, she had not tensed her abdominal muscles. The sucker punch doubled her over, and once again Bartolo slung her across his broad back.

"You try anything, *puta*, and I will cut you." Bartolo loped down the dark passageway as she bounced painfully on his shoulders and fought the urge to retch.

She switched her brain into strategic mode. It dawned on her that she had accomplished all of her objectives and was still alive. Perhaps, if she played along and waited for the right moment, she could survive after all.

In Spanish, Bartolo ordered Camacho to trail them and shoot anyone who approached from behind.

Veranda recognized the tactic. *A tail-gunner to watch his six.* Bartolo had a plan, and it did not involve surrender. There must be an avenue of escape ahead. If she thrashed and fought to delay their progress at this point, SAU might catch up to them and get caught in an ambush. She decided not to resist until she formulated a new strategy.

Still carrying her, Bartolo trotted through the dim passageways. Bare bulbs dangled from support beams above them every few yards, casting ominous shadows. The scent of dank earth cloyed at her senses. The tunnel smelled of death to her.

Finally, Bartolo slowed at the end of a particularly narrow channel and wrenched open a steel door. His breathing grew labored as he started to climb a steep flight of metal stairs burdened by her added weight.

Good. He's tired. Her chest bumped against his sweating back as he halted midway up.

He released her legs, grabbed her hips, and shoved her feet down so that she stood on the step above him. A bulb fixed to the side of a heavy wooden beam illuminated a closed hatch above their heads. Bartolo jerked his chin upward. "After you."

Understanding that he was using her as a human shield or hostage if anyone was in the vicinity, she deliberately raised her voice. "You won't get away, Bartolo."

Bartolo's dagger flashed as he swung it in a short upward arc at her face. She managed to angle her head out of the way and bring up her forearm in time to deflect the blade.

"That was my last warning, *puta*." His eyes blazed. "Do you think I'm stupid? Keep quiet and open that hatch."

She turned and climbed three steps to reach the metal handle. She pushed the round portal door open with a grunt and it banged against the cement floor above. A stream of Spanish expletives carried up to her, but Bartolo didn't strike out at her for making noise again.

Veranda ascended from the stairwell and blinked in the fluorescent light as she performed a rapid scan of the outbuilding where the tunnel ended. Corrugated metal walls were riveted together under a tin roof covering a space approximately the size of a three-car garage, empty with the exception of a gleaming black Escalade. The vehicle was parked with its chrome grille facing a closed bay door. There were no windows, but she noticed a side access door on the opposite wall.

"Stay where you are." Bartolo's angry command carried up to her from the stairwell. He had remained in the shelter of the underground stairs while Veranda climbed out. Apparently satisfied no ambush awaited, he started up the final steps.

Veranda knew his attention would be divided as he emerged from the stairway. He would still be fatigued from the effort of carrying her fifty yards through the tunnel. This was her opportunity.

As his forehead surfaced from the edge of the stairwell, she squatted down to lower her center of gravity. When she saw his eyes flick to the parked vehicle, she lashed out with her foot and aimed a vicious kick at Bartolo's temple. The blow was potentially lethal, but he ducked in time to avoid the brunt of the impact.

A split second later, he leaped out. Eyes wild with fury, knife in hand, he flew at her. She rolled to one side. Bartolo thudded onto the floor where she had just been, then sprang to his feet and whirled to face her. He pointed the dagger directly at her face.

"In here!" Veranda yelled. She needed to draw attention to her location, but didn't want to waste breath screaming as she prepared for a fight to the death.

He stepped toward her. *He believes women are weak. Let him underestimate me.* She moved back a fraction slower than she could have.

A smile crept across his face. "Tired?"

She feigned a look of terror. "N-no."

The moment his muscles twitched in preparation for movement, she charged him. Using a standard disarming technique, she brought both arms up simultaneously. Her right palm struck the inside of his wrist as her left palm smacked the back of the hand that held the knife. The force and speed of both blows bent his hand inward and broke his grip. The dagger flew out of his grasp and skittered along the floor until it banged against the wall.

With a feral growl, Bartolo pounced. His muscular frame slammed her shoulder blades down onto the cool cement. He straddled her and wrapped his hands around her throat. Bright spots popped into her vision as he squeezed.

She brought her fists together in front of her chest and thrust them straight up in front of her face, breaking his hold on her neck. He grabbed her arms and began to force them down to her sides. She could tell he wanted to pin her arms with his knees and resume strangling her.

A phrase from her kickboxing coach came back to her. *Veranda, fight like a girl!* It was not an insult. Her coach reminded her that men and women are built differently. Her upper body strength was no match for a man's. A woman had a lower center of gravity and powerful hip flexors, thighs, and abs.

Lying on her back, she planted her feet and pushed her lower body up with her legs. Still straddling her, Bartolo was momentarily distracted as her hips lifted from the floor, pitching him forward. Before he could react, she dropped her buttocks down, throwing his weight backward. As the momentum of her movement forced his torso back, she brought her knees up hard, driving them against his spine. She used the distraction to slide her arms out from his grasp, then clenched her fist and slammed it into his Adam's apple.

He sputtered, gurgled, and rolled off of her. As he lay on the floor choking, the side door to the outbuilding burst open. Gun drawn, Sam was first inside. He trained his weapon on Bartolo as the other detectives and supervisors fanned out behind him.

Remembering Camacho, Veranda pointed at the open hatch. "Look out! There's another—"

Her words were interrupted by a deafening gun blast and the unmistakable sound of a bullet hitting flesh.

32

EARS RINGING, VERANDA COULD not hear the tinkle of the ejected casing as she watched it fall to the cement floor. Her eyes traveled upward, from the glint of the rolling brass cylinder, to the muzzle of Lieutenant Aldridge's gun.

Aldridge stood rooted to the spot, finger still on the trigger after the recoil, eyes fixed on Bartolo.

Veranda turned to Bartolo's lifeless body. Between the drug lord's glazed eyes, a dime-sized hole perforated his forehead. A crimson pool oozed on the floor from the back of his head.

Veranda jerked when a second shot whizzed by her. Aldridge crumpled before Diaz tackled her to the ground and covered her body with his.

Trapped beneath the sergeant, she watched the scene unfold.

Camacho was halfway out of the hatch opening, his semiauto still pointed at Aldridge. She had not warned her team in time. Bartolo's tail gunner had followed them up the stairwell and shot the lieutenant.

Camacho swiveled his head to lock eyes with Veranda. He swung his arm and leveled his gun at her. Diaz raised his Glock from his prone position on top of her, but Sam fired first. Two shots in rapid succession. Center mass.

Camacho groaned and slumped forward, then thudded on the ground. Marci darted over and kicked the gun out of his limp hand. She snatched cuffs from a loop on her ballistic vest and slapped them on Camacho's wrists. He lay still as blood soaked the back of his shirt. Doc knelt next to Aldridge to check his vitals.

Several men in black tactical gear swarmed in through the narrow side entrance. Weapons in ready position, SAU deployed and took command of the space in seconds.

Doc glanced up, shook his head and began chest compressions on Aldridge. "Get an ambulance. Tell them he's got no pulse."

The tallest SAU member pulled off his helmet and balaclava. It was Sergeant Grigg. He mashed the button on his transmitter. "Nine-nine-nine. Officer down. Request rescue for three gunshot victims. CPR in progress." He rattled off details about their location and the victims in response to the dispatcher's questions.

"You okay?" Diaz's breath brushed Veranda's cheek. She turned and her nose touched his. His dark brown eyes held a look of concern.

Before she could answer, his weight disappeared as he was yanked to his feet.

A wad of Diaz's shirt fabric still clutched in his fist, Anderson glowered at the sergeant. "Get the hell off of her, you asshole!" Anderson released his grip with more force than necessary.

Without Diaz for cover, Veranda felt the awkwardness of her naked state as all of her coworkers, supervisors, and the SAU team stared at her.

Diaz undid the fastenings on his ballistic vest, pulled it off and thrust it at Veranda. She slid into it and latched it over her torso. It barely covered her.

The gesture seemed to inflame Anderson even more. "Stay away from her!"

Diaz strode to Anderson and got in his face. "You lay another hand on me and I will drag your ass to jail."

Two inches taller, Anderson glared down at Diaz. "You're the one who should be in jail, you fucking traitor."

"What the hell are you talking about?"

"I'm talking about the cartel's mole on the Police Department." He jabbed a finger at Diaz. "You."

Veranda sucked in air. Anderson had blurted their secret. Compromised the investigation. Bartolo had taken the identity of the mole to his grave. Now they had no leads. She wasn't happy about the situation, but she would run with it. In the silence that followed Anderson's accusation, she watched Diaz for a reaction.

His brows drew together. "What is this bullshit about a cartel mole?"

Commander Webster took a step toward Anderson. "Are you saying Sergeant Diaz is a spy for the Villalobos cartel?"

Anderson jammed his hands on his hips. "That's exactly what I'm saying."

Diaz started for Anderson, fists clenched, eyes blazing.

Veranda darted in front of him and put her palm up. "Wait." His lungs heaved as he blew out air like an angry bull, but he stopped. *He's not defensive, he's furious.* She gave a silent signal to halt the three SAU members who had approached, apparently prepared to intervene. They stepped back in line with their comrades.

"You've made a very serious allegation about a respected police supervisor," Sergeant Jackson said, looking at Anderson. "You'd better have something to back it up."

Sam raised his hands in a calming gesture. "It's time to lay our cards on the table." He scowled at Anderson. "Unfortunately, our confidential investigation has just been compromised." He gestured to Veranda. "Detective Cruz found evidence indicating someone on the Department has been feeding information to the cartel. Chief Tobias assigned Commander Murphy to identify the mole."

All eyes turned to Veranda. "I couldn't admit it at the time, but I did decipher the messages from the printout, which turned out to be from Pablo Moreno's cell phone. In the last text, the mole told Pablo to run the night Sam and I did our unauthorized stakeout. That's how he knew when to leave."

Frank voiced the unspoken question. "So what makes you think it was Diaz?"

"He's been dogging Veranda constantly," Anderson said. "He keeps butting in, trying to get details about the case."

Diaz glared at Anderson over Veranda's head as he said, "Part of the agreement allowing her to do a temp in Homicide was that I have access to her for my investigation." He turned to the others. "In case you all didn't notice, I just protected Veranda from the shooter."

Veranda stood between the two men. She realized it was the second time Diaz had called her by her first name. He was right too. When they were under fire, he put her life before his. In fact, his previous behavior could be construed as overprotectiveness. As she considered his actions from a new perspective, doubt clouded her mind. Her eyes scanned the faces in the room. If Diaz wasn't the mole, then who was? And how could she figure it out?

Disjointed images coalesced in her thoughts. Finding the cipher. Poring over the printout. Decoding messages between phones. The mismatched pieces snapped into place. "Hold on!" She turned to Grigg. "Sergeant, I need an SAU member to cover every person in here who is not on your team."

Commander Webster's eyebrows shot up. "Detective Cruz, what's going on?" He motioned to encompass her entire team and chain of command. "Are you accusing one of us?"

The mere suggestion that one of them could be a traitor was a profound insult, but she had to go with her plan. "I am. And I'll root out the mole right now." She looked at Grigg. "With your help."

Grigg considered her for a long moment. She appreciated his predicament. If he did as she asked, he would give the order to detain several high-ranking officials based on pure trust. Such a decision could end his term as SAU leader.

Finally, Grigg signaled his team. "Do it."

Instantly, tactical officers spread throughout the room until two SAU members flanked every non-team member. The only sound in the outbuilding came from Doc, who continued giving chest compressions to Lieutenant Aldridge.

Webster's face reddened. "Cruz, you're way out of bounds." He glanced at Grigg. "Sergeant, if you value your position, you will stop this immediately."

Sam's baritone rumbled through the room. "Commander, a mole has jeopardized our detectives and compromised our investigation. If Detective Cruz has a way to identify that person, best we let her get on with it."

Webster's visage went from red to a muddy color, but he threw up his hands. "Fine."

Veranda strode to Bartolo. She crouched next to the body, plunged a hand into his pants pocket and fished out his cell phone. She got to her feet and showed the mobile specifically to Sam.

A knowing look crossed Sam's face. "I see where you're going."

The phone's screen illuminated at her touch. She tapped the call log icon, then held her breath and connected to the last number dialed.

A repetitive buzz pierced the silence.

All eyes scanned the room for the source of the noise.

"Doc," Sam said, "stop what you're doing."

Doc looked up, his arms continuing to piston up and down. "It's going to take a while for the ambulance to get here. I've got to keep giving compressions."

Sam lowered his voice. "Ten seconds won't make a difference. We need total quiet."

Doc paused.

Veranda tapped the screen to redial.

She scanned the group, stopping at Lieutenant Aldridge. A slight tremor vibrated the outer pocket of his ballistic vest.

33

FIVE HOURS LATER, VERANDA squinted and lowered her visor as the late-afternoon sun slanted into the Malibu's windshield. Despite her fatigue and aching head, she had been forced to relive the entire ordeal three times. As with any use of deadly force, the Department conducted both criminal and administrative investigations. Even though she had not pulled the trigger this time, her actions had brought about the entire confrontation.

First, a detective she didn't know from another Homicide squad interviewed her. Then, a PSB supervisor made her recount the entire story a second time. Finally, she was poked and prodded by various medical personnel at the hospital, who asked her to describe how she had sustained her injuries, which required her to explain most of what had occurred at the warehouse. Her shoulder was particularly tender where Bartolo had twisted her arm so far behind her back she thought she might pass out. The doctor told her it had not been dislocated, but was strained. The shoulder throbbed. She accepted the prescription for Vicodin, but knew she would never fill it.

While being treated, Veranda was reunited with Gabby, who had been transported to the emergency room by ambulance after her rescue. Her sister was badly shaken but sustained only cuts and bruises. Once Veranda found her, she refused to leave Gabby's side, insisting the medical staff put them next to each other.

Veranda's mother had become hysterical when she called to explain that she and Gabby were safe at the hospital. Veranda did everything in her power to dissuade her entire family from descending on the emergency room en masse. She knew her mother was capable of arranging a procession of vehicles worthy of a motorcade with Father Sanchez leading the convoy. She visualized fifty friends and relatives holding hands and praying in the waiting room and her mother counting the rosary until her fingers bled. It took Veranda a solid five minutes to assure Lorena that she and Gabby were both there as a precaution and that neither of them needed to be admitted.

When her mother pushed for details about the circumstances of the rescue, Veranda agreed to tell her everything once she got her sister home. She promised not to leave her sister's side and take her straight to Lorena as soon as they were released. Veranda insisted that the family wait at home for their return.

After concluding that Veranda's clothing had no forensic value, the CSI techs had allowed her to put on her black cargo pants, Under Armour T-shirt, and boots. She secured her nylon tactical belt in the trunk of her city car in the hospital parking lot—where Sam had left it for her—before easing Gabby into the vehicle.

As Veranda maneuvered through traffic, she cut her eyes to Gabby, huddled in the passenger seat. Her sister wore green medical scrubs given to her by a sympathetic orderly at the hospital before they checked out. The CSI techs had taken Gabby's clothes as evidence and Veranda doubted her sister would ever want them back. Gabby's cuts and bruises were cleaned and bandaged, filling the car with the pungent scent of antiseptic.

Veranda swallowed a lump in her throat as she reached out to squeeze her sister's hand. "You'll be home soon, Gabby."

Tears welled in her sister's lovely brown eyes. Veranda's heart lurched. She had promised her mother she would return Gabby safely. She had only partially succeeded. What kind of emotional scars would remain after the physical injuries healed? Gabby was only fourteen. She should be worrying about homework, boys, and her upcoming *quinceañera*. She should never have been subjected to someone like Bartolo Villalobos. It happened because Veranda had chosen to fight the cartel.

Veranda's cell phone vibrated in her pocket. She tapped her Bluetooth and Sam's voice transmitted directly into her ear. "Veranda, Commander Webster ordered everyone to the war room."

"He authorized me to drive my sister home."

"He said to come to VCB as soon as you're clear."

"I need time with my family."

"I can buy you an extra fifteen minutes, but you'll need to cut it short." He paused. "You can get back to them later."

"Fine. I'll be there as soon as I can." She pulled the earpiece from her ear as the car crunched onto the gravel driveway that connected the *casitas* on her family's property in South Phoenix.

All of her relatives stood behind Lorena, who waited in front of the main house. When the vehicle ground to a halt, Veranda jumped out and circled the car to open the passenger door. Gabby clambered from her seat and ran into her mother's waiting arms.

Aunts, uncles, and cousins gathered around Gabby as Veranda looked on in silence. She was an integral part of the family, yet separate.

Her mother broke loose and walked over to her. Veranda looked into the hazel eyes, so much like her own. "I'm sorry, *Mamá*."

"What are you saying, *mi'ja?*"

Veranda felt the bleakness of her words. "I brought this pain into our family."

Lorena reached out to take Veranda's face in her hands. She looked into her eldest daughter's eyes and spoke to her in Spanish. "Veranda, from the day you were born, you have brought only love into this family. I am grateful every day that you are my daughter." A tear coursed down her mother's cheek. "No one else could have brought Gabriela back to me."

"*Mamá*, I'm afraid the Villalobos family isn't finished with us." She paused before voicing her most agonizing thought. "Because of me."

Her mother shook her head. "This began in Mexico. Long before you were born. After Hector attacked me, I knew he would slaughter our whole family if we stayed. I could not fight *El Lobo* and his forces, so I fled with my little brothers and sisters."

"Of course, what else could you do?"

"I ran away that night, but I did not truly escape. Hector is not a man who forgets. Do not blame yourself, Veranda."

"But I'm the one who declared war on the Villalobos family." She lowered her head. "I admit I only thought of vengeance for our family, not about the danger. The Villalobos cartel has become rich and powerful. Now the next generation has joined the battle and there is nowhere to run where they can't reach us."

Lorena gently brought her daughter's face up to meet her eyes. "Our family has changed. You have taught us all courage. Even in the face of powerful evil."

Veranda's eyes widened. "You always had courage. Look how you brought up your younger siblings in a foreign country, where you didn't even speak the language."

"That was perseverance. Not courage. I had the strength to endure, but not the will to fight. You, *mi'ja*, have both. Your bravery inspires us." Still holding Veranda's face in her hands, Lorena eased her daughter's head down until their foreheads touched. "We will never run away again." When they straightened, her mother's eyes brimmed with unshed tears.

Veranda now fully understood her role in the family and why she always felt slightly apart from the others. She was a solitary sentinel who would lay down her life to defend her flock against the wolves. "Then I will protect you."

"Veranda, you cannot guarantee our safety. When our family voted to stay in Phoenix, we accepted the risk that went with our decision."

Veranda had to be honest. To be sure her mother understood the stakes. "Even though you know I'll keep going until I bring down the cartel?"

"I know who you are, Veranda. It is not in your nature to quit." Lorena tugged her into a tight embrace, then released her. "Go. I'm sure your police family is waiting for you."

Veranda nodded. Her mother had once been married to a law-enforcement officer. She understood the professional relationships that created a unique bond and the obligations of the job.

"I'll be back as soon as I can." Veranda waved at the rest of her relatives and turned to walk back to the Malibu.

Duty called.

34

Villalobos family compound, Mexico

ADOLFO SAT AT THE inlaid mahogany conference table in his father's office, eyes riveted to the massive flat screen on the wall. He struggled to wrap his mind around the spectacle unfolding on live television. His younger siblings, Carlos and Daria, flanked him as they watched a satellite feed of the Phoenix local news.

His father raised the volume on the remote in his hand as the anchorman's face filled the screen. "Police officials have released a preliminary statement in which they will only confirm three deaths at this time. Other sources, however, tell our onsite reporter this was the scene of a shootout between drug traffickers and police."

The news program cut to an overhead shot of a warehouse from a media helicopter. The mobile command vehicle squatted among a phalanx of police cars, vans, and technical equipment. Crime scene technicians in Tyvek suits carried materials to a white paneled van. Reporters and onlookers pressed against yellow crime scene tape surrounding the property.

In the background, the anchor's voice narrated. "This just in. An unnamed source close to the investigation has informed us that two of the deceased are a reputed drug lord and an enforcer from the notorious Villalobos cartel. The third victim is reportedly a Phoenix Police officer. We await official confirmation."

Hector raised the remote and clicked off the television. "We must act carefully," he said in the refined Spanish that belied his upbringing in the barrios of Mexico City. "The three of you are to stay here at the compound until the storm passes."

Adolfo was anxious to get back to Phoenix to take over his brother's position. "How long will that be?"

Hector tossed the remote on the table. "Not long. The reporters have a short attention span. Soon gas prices will go up, or there will be a terrorist bombing somewhere in the world and they will look elsewhere for news."

Carlos raked a hand through his thick, dark hair. "The police won't forget so quickly. They'll come after us like never before," he said, bouncing a knee under the table.

The faint rhythmic tapping of his brother's heel on the floor reached Adolfo's ears. He knew it was not a nervous gesture, but a sign that Carlos sought the release of taking action. His youngest brother reminded him of a shark, needing continuous motion for survival.

Hector leaned forward. "I am not afraid of police. What concerns me is competition. Every day we don't run our supply line is an opportunity for other cartels to gain a foothold in our market." His mouth twisted into a sneer. "All of this goes back to Detective Veranda Cruz. It was her interference that started Bartolo down the path that led us here.

I will not let the actions of one woman undermine my organization." His intense gaze landed on Adolfo. "What will you do about it?"

Adolfo sensed his father's challenge in the question, and straightened. "*Papá*, I promised you I would deal with Veranda Cruz, but I have to wait for the right time."

Hector snorted. "Do you recall Umberto Camacho?"

"He was the man you sent to watch Bartolo and report back to you." Adolfo resented his father sending a spy into Bartolo's camp. It meant Hector might have done the same thing to him.

"That was not his only assignment. I also gave him instructions to kill the mole."

Adolfo glanced at Carlos and Daria to see if they were as confused as he was. "I don't understand. You ordered the mole to shoot Bartolo. Why would you execute Aldridge for following directions?"

"No one who murders a member of our family can be allowed to survive. Even if it was done on my orders. If our men see that a Villalobos can be killed with impunity they will think us vulnerable. Plan a coup." He smoothed the lapel of his Armani suit. "Besides, the mole was a traitor to his own people. He had no honor."

Adolfo's brows drew together. "What does this have to do with my promise to avenge Bartolo?"

Hector gave him a penetrating stare. "Umberto Camacho's final order was to kill Veranda Cruz."

Understanding washed over him as Adolfo grasped the implicit insult his father had just dealt him. "She was *my* responsibility. I swore an oath."

"Which shows you how much faith I have in any vow you make, *mi'jo*. Bartolo had his faults, but he was strong." Hector clenched his fist. "Now, who will have the *cojones* to step up and lead our family business?" He looked at each of his children in turn.

"I might not have *cojones*," Daria said, "but I'm the smartest." She smoothed back a tendril of hair that had escaped the chignon at the back of her head. "I can put that bitch in the ground and no one will ever trace it back to us."

Hector smiled fondly at his only daughter. Adolfo sensed his opportunity slipping away and spoke quickly. "*Papá*, I am the one with knowledge of the entire operation. Because of my financial expertise, we have billions in assets. I plan to spread our organization throughout the Western Hemisphere. After we have consolidated our power, we'll make an incursion into the Asian markets. The name of Villalobos will be known throughout the world."

"Ambitious." Hector gave him an approving nod. "I was not aware you thought on such a large scale."

Adolfo leaned forward. Finally, his father might see his vision. "I have many plans, *Papá*. Let me take over Bartolo's operation in addition to mine and show you."

Hector pushed back his chair, clasped his hands behind his back, and strolled over to the mahogany-paneled wall. Adolfo observed his father's movements, hoping *El Lobo's* body language would give away private thoughts. Hector's head tilted back to study the massive family crest. Adolfo sensed the significance of the moment. Even though his father had never officially decreed it, everyone knew Bartolo was the heir apparent. Now that he was dead, Hector had to select a new successor to the family business.

Adolfo assessed his siblings. Carlos, the handsome playboy who ran the cartel's human trafficking and sex trade divisions. Adolfo had seen him ruthlessly execute people without hesitation. He was popular with his men, but Adolfo suspected this had more to do with regular offerings of women to his crew than any real leadership skills. A student of human nature who possessed a degree in psychology, Carlos could be highly manipulative.

Daria's personality combined elements from the rest of the family, which helped her deal in the dangerous underworld of illegal weaponry and explosives. She had her father's determination and Adolfo's head for business. Like Carlos, her smooth bronze skin and liquid brown eyes captivated unsuspecting prey. With a streak of cruelty that rivaled Bartolo's, she was a beautiful lethal weapon forged in the heat of her father's crucible.

After a full minute inspecting the intricately worked shield, Hector turned to his youngest son. "What do you think, Carlos?"

Adolfo held his breath as Carlos cast an appraising look in his direction. "I'm fine with Adolfo in charge." Daria scowled as Carlos continued. "It would make sense for him to handle the finances and the narcotics. I can help him with that too." A sense of relief flowed through Adolfo. Carlos would back him. In fact, it sounded as if his brother wished to form an alliance.

"I could run this organization better than both of you put together," Daria said. "In fact, I believe you two would like to join forces." She narrowed her eyes as she glanced at each of her brothers in turn. "I'll let you in on a secret." She dropped her voice. "There can only be one alpha in a pack."

Adolfo knew he needed to tread carefully. Daria would undermine him if it suited her goals. She often claimed she would become the most powerful cartel leader in the world, and he was certain she would do whatever it took to make that happen. He glanced at his father, who had smiled at Daria's acerbic remarks.

Carlos addressed his father. "Are we going to activate another police mole?"

Adolfo seized his opportunity to showcase a side project he had in development. "There's no need. I have a plan that will make moles obsolete." He focused on his father. "I was waiting to mention this until I had worked out the logistics, but I believe now is the time to let you all in on my research."

Hector traced his footsteps back to the head of the table and sat down at his traditional spot. "You have my attention."

Adolfo spread his arms expansively. "I've created a new counter-surveillance program in our technology division. We'll soon have the capability to hack into the Phoenix Police Department's computer system."

Daria's sharp intake of breath interrupted him. "Hacking attempts can be traced. Are you taking precautions?"

He deployed his most confident smile. "My second-in-command is a computer genius. He's covered his tracks in every conceivable way."

Carlos's expression darkened. "Why not let the rest of the family in on your little project? Trying to cut us out?"

Surprised by the unexpected attack, Adolfo mustered a defense. "Do you call a meeting for every idea you have to improve efficiency?" He waved a hand. "My plan is still in development. I haven't actually implemented it yet." He swiveled his eyes to his father. "And I wouldn't have until I received your blessing."

"Go on," Hector said.

Adolfo understood that he'd been granted a reprieve. His father would withhold judgment while he explained. Stomach in knots, Adolfo outlined his strategy. "We will no longer have to depend on human intelligence. The police record all of their operations and investigations in their system. Once we gain access, we'll be aware of every move they make." He allowed excitement into his voice. "That includes their drug busts. They file ops plans to intercept our transports well in advance. We never have to lose a shipment again."

He turned to Carlos and Daria. "Once I get the hacking program perfected, we can tweak the technology to use it on Federal systems. Imagine being able to access ICE, BATF, FBI, and DEA investigations at will. Each of you could run your part of our family business without interference." Adolfo narrowed his eyes. "For the first time, we'll be ahead of them."

Hector leaned back and steepled his fingers. "Impressive."

Adolfo pressed his advantage. "I am your firstborn, *Papá*. Let me take my rightful place and provide you with a comfortable retirement. Our family will be in good hands."

"I am not yet ready to leave. I will allow you to have more decision-making power and watch what you do. You have shown me that you are capable of strategic thinking."

"Thank you."

"I'm not finished yet." *El Lobo* drew a deep breath. "A vow made to me is binding. I understand that you must wait for the right opportunity to take revenge … but mark my words. You will never run this organization while Detective Cruz is alive."

After pausing a moment to reflect on his father's ominous declaration, Adolfo almost whispered his response. "Bartolo underestimated her. I won't make the same mistake. I know exactly what she is."

"And what is that?" *El Lobo* asked.

"Veranda Cruz is a threat to our family, our business, and our way of life." Adolfo put his fist on his chest. "And I will eliminate her."

35

VERANDA WALKED INSIDE THE front vestibule of the Phoenix Police Department headquarters building on Washington Street. She waved as she passed the desk sergeant and stopped short at the monitor featuring the rotating display of fallen officers. She wondered if she would see Lieutenant Aldridge's image on the screen in the future. Once his involvement with the cartel went public, he would be reviled as a traitor. She flinched at a tap on her shoulder.

When she spun around, Anderson swept her into a tight embrace. He held her for a moment, then grasped her arms and held her in front of him. His crystal blue eyes scanned her from head to toe. "You okay? I heard you were released from the hospital."

Aware that the desk sergeant was eyeing them, she placed her fingers in the crook of Anderson's elbow and led him around the corner. "I'm fine. Nothing's broken."

"How's Gabby?"

Her chest constricted. "Physically, she's all right, but she'll need counseling to deal with everything that happened."

"Fortunately, she has a loving family to help her get through it."

Her eyes misted as she looked up at him. He was right. All of her relatives would bond together to help Gabby recover from her ordeal. "My little sister is also stronger than she appears. She will overcome this."

He closed the distance between them and lowered his voice. "How about you?" He slid a finger under her chin. "When I got the call from Commander Webster about the meeting, I waited for you here in the lobby so we could have a moment alone." He gently tilted her head to peer into her eyes. "When I asked if you were okay, I wasn't just referring to your physical injuries."

She took stock of herself before answering. "I'm about the same inside as outside. I've sustained some damage, but it will heal with time." She sighed. "The worst part was seeing Gabby gagged and in shackles, scared out of her wits." Guilt wrapped itself around her heart and squeezed. "That image will never leave me."

When Anderson opened his mouth to speak, she touched her finger to his lips. "Please. No more. I don't have the luxury of coming unglued." She disengaged herself from the intimate contact and stepped back. "Right now, we have a meeting in the war room." She started toward the door to the stairwell that led to the second floor. "I need to be in cop mode."

He fell into step beside her. "Not sure why Commander Webster wants us here. Can't imagine what else there is to go over. We all gave statements in the mobile command vehicle at the scene."

She quirked an eyebrow at him as she started up the stairs. "That was just a warm-up. The investigation will go on for months. Get used to the PSB ferrets."

"Speaking of PSB," he rubbed his stubbled jaw. "I was so sure Diaz was the mole." He shook his head. "Can't decide if I should apologize or punch him in the face for acting like such a prick that I suspected him."

She pondered the PSB sergeant's behavior over the past week. "I think he tried to do the right thing."

"Well, I think he was jealous."

She halted as she opened the door to exit the stairwell. "What are you talking about?"

Anderson stopped behind her. "Looking back on how he acted, the only logical explanation is that he did everything he could to keep us apart." He looked down at her. "I thought he was interfering because he was the mole, but he also acted like an overprotective, possessive jackass."

She waved a dismissive hand. "You're off base. I've seen his type before. Consumed with policy and procedure. Can't see the difference between the letter of the law and the spirit of the law. I don't see him as a Latin lover overcome by his libido." She snorted. "His type would rather look at personnel regs than a skin magazine." She noticed the tension in Anderson's muscles ease and continued through the doorway. "Either way, he doesn't decide what I do with my social life."

He stepped out of the stairwell onto the second floor behind her. "Speaking of which, how about dinner tomorrow night?"

She turned to face him. "Maybe the night after. I need time with my family."

He gave her a slow smile. "I can wait." He tugged the door to the Violent Crimes Bureau conference room open and stood aside. "And I know where to get the best carne asada in Arizona."

Veranda paused before entering. The last time she had seen her entire team together had been in the outbuilding next to Bartolo's warehouse. She'd been standing over Lieutenant Aldridge's body as his cell phone vibrated, revealing him as the mole. In the chaos that ensued, the team had been separated for interviews.

She would face all of them again when she stepped through the doorway. If they hadn't been listening to her transmitter when Bartolo taunted her about her parentage, they would have been briefed by now. Everyone knew her secret. A thought rushed through her, leaving molten lead in its wake. Perhaps they had even seen what was in the envelope Bartolo had waved in front of her. *They might already know who my father is, even though I don't.* She was as naked before them now as she had been in the outbuilding.

She decided to handle her exposure as she did with Bartolo. No cowering or cringing. Raising her chin, she strode inside.

The buzz of conversation died out. She scanned the room. The Homicide squad was there, along with Sergeant Jackson, Commander Webster, and Sergeant Diaz. At the far end of the conference table, she spotted a slender man she didn't recognize with a salt-and-pepper afro and horn-rimmed glasses. He wore a business suit and a Phoenix Police ID dangled from a lanyard around his neck, but she couldn't make out the name beneath his photo. Sam indicated an empty chair to his right and she sat down. Anderson took a seat along the wall.

The conference table was cluttered with pizza boxes, soda cans, and water bottles. Scattered paper plates held half-eaten remnants of an ad hoc dinner. She wondered what she had missed by coming late. Had they discussed her possible blood ties to the cartel? Everyone looked as if they had just enjoyed a relaxed meal. She could detect no animosity from their body language.

Webster broke the silence. "How is your sister, Detective Cruz?"

"She'll be okay, Commander. Thank you for allowing me to drive her home to my family."

He dabbed his mouth with a napkin. "I have two daughters. Can't imagine what your family went through today. I'm glad she's safe now."

Uncomfortable discussing her family, Veranda pulled her police notebook from the side pocket on her cargo pants and plopped it on the table. She directed an intense gaze at her commander, ready for business. "What did I miss?"

Webster tilted his head in the direction of the stranger. "Commander Murphy briefed us on his investigation into the mole."

She surveyed the man with renewed interest. So this was Murphy. He looked unassuming, and his expression was inscrutable. He gave her a curt nod, which she returned.

Sergeant Jackson drummed his fingers on the table. "I'm still in shock the mole turned out to be Aldridge." He looked at Sam. "Do you remember when you requested overnight surveillance on Pablo?"

Sam's jaw hardened. "Yeah, and I recall Lieutenant Aldridge denying my request." He flicked a glance at Veranda before returning his gaze to Jackson. "We all thought he was pinching pennies, but now we know he was buying time for Bartolo to make arrangements for Pablo to escape." His eyes narrowed. "So he could kill him."

They still hadn't found Pablo's body, and probably never would. The photograph Bartolo left behind in her kitchen showing Pablo with a bullet hole in his forehead was the sole evidence of his fate.

Jackson stared down at his PPD mug. "Knowing it was Aldridge puts everything in a different light." His face clouded with remorse as he lifted his eyes to meet Sam's. "I apologize for coming down on you so hard about your unauthorized stakeout."

Sam stroked his mustache. "Nothing says you're sorry like a brand-new Impala."

Veranda grinned, watching a master at work. Jackson had assigned Sam the crappiest junker in the loaner fleet as punishment for defying Aldridge's orders. Sam would milk Jackson's guilt for all he could.

Tony addressed Sam in his heavy Brooklyn accent. "And give up that sweet ride you've got?"

Jackson raised a hand in defeat. "I'll see what I can do."

The brief moment of levity ended when Doc looked at Sam with a hurt expression. "What I don't understand is why you kept critical information about a spy from *us*." He waved an arm to encompass Tony,

Frank, and Marci. "You could've confided in your squad mates, you know."

Sam put his palms on the table and leaned forward. "Doc, we couldn't tell anyone in VCB or PSB. That's why Commander Murphy took over the investigation."

"Personally"—Marci cut her eyes to Diaz, who sat two chairs down from her—"I think PSB was way too involved in this case from the beginning."

Diaz bristled. "I have a duty to perform, just like you. We're all on the same side."

Frank opened his mouth to speak, but Jackson cut him off. "This case was unprecedented. We were behind the eight ball from the outset. None of the normal rules applied. If Sergeant Diaz was extra diligent, I'm certain he had the Department's best interests in mind." His tone indicated the discussion about PSB was closed.

"Speaking of policy and procedure." Webster cast his eyes to Veranda, then Sam. "You two should be suspended pending the outcome of an internal investigation, but Commander Murphy has also advised us that you were acting under the auspices of Chief Tobias during the entire enterprise."

Veranda caught a look that passed between Sam and Murphy. She knew the Chief had been briefed on her rescue attempt after it was already underway. He must have decided to back them up after the fact. Perhaps the Chief figured the scandal of having a high-ranking official revealed as an informant for a notorious cartel would damage the Department's reputation enough. Suspending two detectives would make matters worse. She shook her head. The vagaries of upper-management decisions baffled her. *Way above my pay grade.*

At the head of the table, Webster continued. "I ordered everyone to this briefing to go over a critical item that can't wait until Monday." He paused, eyes roving. "Namely, a missing piece of evidence."

Tension ricocheted around the room. Webster looked at Veranda. "We all heard Bartolo Villalobos over your micro transmitter indicating he had documentation as to the identity of your biological father when you were both in the warehouse."

Thoughts hurtled through Veranda's mind as every head swiveled in her direction. The moment she dreaded had arrived. Everyone knew she was either the legitimate daughter of a decorated Mexican *federale,* or the offspring of a notorious criminal.

Webster's gaze burned into her. "Did he show you some papers?"

She remembered that no video accompanied the voice transmission. Anyone listening would not have seen what Bartolo had done with the paternity document. "He held up a white, business-sized envelope. I never saw what was inside." She swallowed. "He put the envelope back in his pocket and never took it out again." She wanted to be sure he believed her. "I went over this in both of my interviews in the mobile command vehicle at the scene."

Webster's eyes remained locked on hers. "Well, it seems the envelope has disappeared."

She struggled to absorb his words. Where were the paternity documents? Someone had stolen information that should have been hers. Anger and resentment shot through her at the violation. She had to keep her emotions in check. A strong, visceral reaction might make the others suspicious. "Commander, I don't have it." She shrugged. "In fact, I literally had no place I could have stashed it. I didn't get my clothes back until an hour after the Crime Scene guys got there."

Webster looked around the table. "Does anyone know what happened to the envelope?"

Silence.

"That paperwork is evidence," he said. "The information it contains is critical to our understanding of Bartolo's mindset. Based on the result of that test, we might gain insight into what the cartel plans to do next." He leaned forward, scanned Veranda's team, then said in a low voice, "Did any of you ... accidentally pick it up?"

A few muttered "No, sirs" went around the room.

Veranda's mind raced. She was with Bartolo the entire time after he put the envelope in his pocket. He didn't have time to hide it someplace the forensics unit couldn't find it. She cut her eyes to Diaz and found him staring directly at her. He'd always wanted more information about her. *He told me he would keep digging into my past.* Then she remembered his obsession with regulations and shook off the thought. He would never take evidence from a crime scene.

Apparently not anxious to dwell on potential subterfuge, Webster's expression cleared and he raised his voice. "Now, for the final order of business." He gestured to Veranda. "Detective Cruz, you distinguished yourself today under extreme circumstances. You dealt with a situation no one on this Department has ever faced."

The whipsaw from implicit accusation to praise made Veranda squirm in her seat.

Webster exchanged a nod with Jackson before he continued. "I have filed an official request to make your temporary assignment to Homicide permanent."

Veranda's jaw slackened. Sam clapped a hand on her back. Jackson's face split into a wide grin. Her fellow squad mates beamed at her.

Webster stood. "On that note, we'll wrap up for the day. Everyone report back Monday morning for an official after-action debriefing." He and Murphy headed out, speaking to each other in an undertone.

Chairs dragged on the industrial-grade carpet as everyone pushed back from the table and shuffled toward the doorway.

As Veranda approached, Marci shook her hand. "Finally. Another woman on my team." She winked. "I mean, besides Doc."

"Hey," Doc said, looking at Anderson's retreating back. "Not every man has to look like Thor."

Veranda trailed the others as they left the war room, still bantering.

A finger tapped her shoulder. When she turned, Diaz faced her.

"Got a minute?" he asked.

"Sure." She caught Anderson's questioning gaze as she followed Diaz to an alcove along the wall of the VCB main area.

Diaz shifted his weight from one foot to the other and glanced at his shoes. "I wanted to let you know that I'm closing out all of the investigations into your actions." His dark eyes met hers. "That includes the death of your confidential informant, the shooting of the truck driver, and the unauthorized stakeout."

Veranda stilled. "What's the disposition on those cases?"

"Exonerated." The corners of his mouth tipped up. "You'll get an official memo through your chain of command in a few days."

She blew out a relieved sigh. Even though she would always feel responsible for Flaco's death, at least the Department would not reprimand her. It dawned on her that Diaz must have told Webster about his conclusions. The VCB Commander would never have asked for her permanent transfer if she had pending disciplinary action. She tilted her head and considered Diaz. He had actually paved the way for her new assignment.

In gratitude, she extended her hand. "Thank you."

He shook it. "I'm still concerned for your safety, Veranda."

Aware that he had used her first name again, and that he continued to clasp her hand, she arched a brow. "Why do you say that?"

"The Villalobos cartel is a dangerous enemy, and now the blood of one of their own has been spilled. They're not going away."

"I didn't shoot Bartolo. Aldridge did."

"Doesn't matter. *El Lobo* will blame you. None of it would have happened if you weren't—"

Anderson stalked up to them. "Get your paws off her, Diaz."

Diaz released his grip on her hand and turned a venomous gaze on Anderson. "I'm done with you getting in my face. It stops now."

Anderson's chest expanded as he drew himself up to his full height. Muscles tensed, he looked down his nose at Diaz. "Don't you have some papers to file?"

Diaz inched closer, tilting his head back a fraction to meet Anderson's eyes. "You think you can intimidate me? I was born and raised in south Phoenix, *pendejo*. We ate pretty boys like you for lunch."

Veranda pushed her way between them. "What's the matter with you two?"

"I'll tell you what's the matter," Sam said, walking up to the group. "Their brains are caught in their zippers." His tone dripped sarcasm as he addressed both men. "If you two want to snort and stamp, take it outside." He motioned to Veranda. "I have important business to discuss with Detective Cruz."

Intrigued, Veranda followed Sam down the empty corridor. She turned to see Anderson and Diaz staring after her as she walked away.

"I've seen more decorum at a cockfight," Sam muttered as he led her to Lieutenant Aldridge's office.

Veranda understood Sam's logic in choosing that location. The office would remain vacant until a replacement took Aldridge's position.

Sam closed the door behind them when they were both inside. As always, he came straight to the point. "Do you remember what happened in the outbuilding today after you found out Aldridge was the mole?"

"Sure," she said. "Doc continued CPR, but the rest of us tried to put the pieces together. We all compared notes about Aldridge." She shrugged, unsure what Sam wanted to know. "Rescue got there a few minutes later."

"You may not remember, but while everyone stood around discussing Aldridge's involvement with the cartel, I walked over to Bartolo, knelt beside his body, and checked for signs of life." He rested a hand on the butt of his holstered gun. "Frankly, I didn't care if the bastard was dead or alive." He reached into his back pocket. "I was looking for this."

Veranda's jaw dropped as Sam pulled out the sealed white business envelope that Bartolo had waved in front of her. A droplet of blood had stained the bottom corner. Her stomach twisted into a tight knot. "Sam, I don't want you to get in trouble. You heard Webster."

"If we're going to be on the same team there's something you need to understand." His expression was hard as stone. "I look after my own. And I expect the same in return."

"I'll watch your six, Sam." She meant it too.

Emotions warred as she dragged a hand through her hair. Part of her longed to snatch the envelope from his hand and read the contents right then and there. Another part wanted to burn it without opening it. "How did you smuggle that out of the crime scene?"

The corners of his mustache twitched. "Well, they don't frisk detectives, do they?"

"No, but Crime Scene's got to be scouring every inch of that place now. People seem very interested to see what those DNA results say."

"CSI's done everything short of a body cavity search on Bartolo to find this, but I decided you're the only one with a right to know what's inside."

Her hand trembled as she took the envelope from Sam. "I don't know how to thank you."

"There's no need. I won't ask you about it, but if you want to talk, you have my number." Sam turned to open the office door, stopped, and looked over his shoulder at her. "And Veranda ... "

"Yes?"

"Whatever that lab report says doesn't change the fact that you're one of the best cops I've ever worked with." He walked out and closed the door behind him, leaving her alone in the office.

She realized Sam had given her a choice. She could shred the envelope and its contents without opening it and no one would ever know. *Even me.* After all, what good would come from the information inside?

She weighed the pros and cons. If her father was Ernesto Hidalgo, she could tell mother and ease her mind. But was it really her mother's mind that needed to be eased, or her own?

If her father was Hector Villalobos, she would be the product of a brutal rape. Could she live with that? She cursed *El Lobo*. He had taken so much from her family. Now he could take her very identity.

She had always been proud of the man she thought of as her *papá*. His noble sacrifice as he tried to rid his country of ruthless crime syndicates had inspired her to follow in his footsteps. She'd made life choices based on information the documents in her hand could prove false. Would she be better off not knowing? *But I'll always wonder.*

She realized the Villalobos family already knew the answer. Bartolo said he had discussed it with his father. She could not have them continue to taunt her with knowledge of her hidden past. This was her chance to know the truth. And truth, no matter how painful, was better than ignorance.

She tore open the envelope, unfolded the papers, and scanned them. The world seemed to tilt as she read the conclusive analysis.

Hector Villalobos was her father.

She read the findings again, but the result refused to change. Her mind exploded in a torrent of discordant thoughts. She was *El Lobo's* daughter. Her pulse raced, making her think of the tainted blood that coursed through her veins. No wonder she was capable of such violence. She thought about her single-minded pursuit of the cartel. She had put her entire family at risk because of her desire for vengeance. Five men were dead in the aftermath of her vendetta.

Was she any better than her father?

Another thought gripped her. Ernesto Hidalgo was truly gone. No trace of him survived inside of her. *El Lobo* had snatched Ernesto's legacy from him and claimed total victory. She wanted to scream, but held herself firmly in check.

She had to decide what to do. There were those on the Department who would hold her blood ties to the cartel against her. They would secretly wonder if she could be compromised. Look at her differently. Judge her. She could not accept their scorn, nor tolerate their pity. She vowed not to reveal this information to anyone in the PPD.

Next, she thought about her family. She couldn't bear it if her mother ever looked at her with a shadow in her eyes. She would never tell her mother or the others about her biological father. Let them keep Ernesto's memory alive in their hearts.

She thought back to the day her mother explained why she had named her Veranda. Her mother had said it was a combination of *ver* and *andadura*, "watch" and "journey" or "path." Now it dawned on Veranda what her mother was trying to tell her. Lorena Cruz knew her daughter would choose her own path. She would love her little girl and withhold judgment. Leave it up to Veranda to decide how she would live her life. One potential father was an honorable man who sacrificed himself for his people; the other a traitor, a killer, and a criminal mastermind.

Her mother had accepted Veranda as her own person regardless of her paternity. In that moment, Veranda understood. Her biology did not define her. Instead, her journey would reveal her true nature.

She crumpled the papers in her hand, pushed open the office door, and strode out, head held high. She would drive to South Phoenix to visit her family—the only family she would ever acknowledge. On Monday, she would report for duty in the Homicide Unit.

She had chosen her path.

SkipStyle Photography

About the Author

Before her foray into the world of crime fiction, Isabella Maldonado wore a gun and badge in real life. She retired as a captain after over two decades on the Fairfax County Police Department and moved to the Phoenix area, where her uniform now consists of tank tops and yoga pants.

During her tenure on the department, she was a patrol officer, hostage negotiator, spokesperson, and recruit instructor at the police academy. After being promoted, she worked as a patrol sergeant and lieutenant before heading the Public Information Office. Finally, as a captain, she served as Gang Council Coordinator and oversaw a patrol district station before her final assignment as the Commander of the Special Investigations and Forensics Division (since renamed the Investigative Support Division).

She graduated from the FBI National Academy in Quantico in 2008 after eleven weeks of physically and mentally challenging study for 220 law enforcement executives from around the world. She is proud to have earned her "yellow brick" for completing the famous FBI obstacle course.

Now her activities involve chasing around her young son and enjoying her family when she's not handcuffed to her computer.

Ms. Maldonado is a member of the FBI National Academy Associates, Fairfax County Police Association, International Thriller Writers, Mystery Writers of America, and Sisters in Crime, where she served as president of the Desert Sleuths Chapter in Phoenix in 2015 and currently sits on the board.